ARENA TWO

(BOOK #2 OF THE SURVIVAL TRILOGY)

MORGAN RICE

ISBN: 978-1-939416-48-3

Books by Morgan Rice

THE SORCERER'S RING
A QUEST OF HEROES (BOOK #1)
A MARCH OF KINGS (BOOK #2)
A FEAST OF DRAGONS (BOOK #3)
A CLASH OF HONOR (BOOK #4)
A VOW OF GLORY (BOOK #5)
A CHARGE OF VALOR (BOOK #6)
A RITE OF SWORDS (BOOK #7)
A GRANT OF ARMS (BOOK #8)
A SKY OF SPELLS (BOOK #9)
A SEA OF SHIELDS (BOOK #10)
A REIGN OF STEEL (BOOK #11)

THE SURVIVAL TRILOGY
ARENA ONE (Book #1)
ARENA TWO (Book #2)

the Vampire Journals
turned (book #1)
loved (book #2)
betrayed (book #3)
destined (book #4)
desired (book #5)
betrothed (book #6)
vowed (book #7)
found (book #8)
resurrected (book #9)
craved (book #10)

"Cowards die many times before their deaths;
The valiant never taste of death but once.
Of all the wonders that I yet have heard,
It seems to me most strange that men should fear,
Seeing that death, a necessary end,
Will come when it will come."

--Shakespeare, *Julius Caesar*

ONE

There are some days in the world that just seem perfect. Some days when a certain stillness covers the world, when a calm blankets you so thoroughly that you feel as if you could just disappear, when you feel such a sense of peace, immune from all the worries of the world. Immune from fear. From tomorrow. I can count moments like these on a single hand.

And one of them is right now.

I am thirteen years old, Bree is six, and we stand on a beach of fine, soft sand. dad holds my hand, and mom holds Bree's, and the four of us step across the hot sand, on our way into the ocean. The cool spray of the waves feels so good on my face, tapering off the heat of this August day. Waves crash all around us, and dad and mom are laughing, carefree. I have never seen them so relaxed. I catch them looking at each other with such love, and I implant the image in my mind. It is one of the few times I've seen them so happy with each other, and I don't want to forget it. Bree yells in ecstasy, thrilled at the crash of the waves, which are at her chest, at the tug of the undertow, up to her thighs. Mom holds her tight and dad squeezes my hand, holding us back from the pull of the ocean.

"ONE! TWO! THREE!" dad yells.

I am lifted high into the air as dad pulls my hand and mom pulls Bree's. I go up high, over a wave, and scream as I clear it and it crashes behind me. I am amazed that dad can stand there like that, so strong, like a rock, seemingly oblivious to the force of nature.

As I sink down into the ocean I enter it with shock, the cold water at my chest. I squeeze dad's hand harder, as the undertow returns, and again he holds me firmly in place. I feel, in that moment, that he will protect me from everything, forever.

Wave after wave crashes down, and for the first time in as long as I can remember, mom and dad are in no rush. They hoist us again and again, Bree shouting with ever more delight. I don't know how much time passes on this magnificent summer day, on this peaceful beach, under a cloudless sky, the spray hitting my face. I never want the sun to set, never want any of this to change. I want to be here, like this, forever. And in this moment, I feel like I might be.

I open my eyes slowly, disoriented by what I see before me. I'm not at the ocean, but sitting in the passenger seat of a motor boat, racing its way up a river. It is not summer, but winter, and the banks are lined with snow. Occasional chunks of ice float past us. My face is sprayed with water, but it is not the cool mist of the ocean waves in summer but rather the freezing spray of the icy Hudson in winter. I blink several times until I realize it is not a cloudless summer morning, but a cloudy winter afternoon. I try to figure out what happened, how everything changed.

I sit up with a chill and look around, immediately on guard. I haven't fallen asleep in daylight in as long as I can remember, and it surprises me. I quickly get my bearings and see Logan, standing stoically behind the wheel, eyes fixed on the river, navigating the Hudson. I turn and see Ben, head in his hands, staring out at the river, lost in his own world. On the other side of the boat sit Bree, eyes closed, leaning back in her seat, and her new friend Rose cuddled up with her, asleep on her shoulder. Sitting in her lap is our new pet, the one-eyed Chihuahua, asleep.

I'm amazed I allowed myself to sleep, too, but as I look down and notice the half-drunk bottle of champagne in my hand, I realize the alcohol, which I haven't had in years, must have knocked me out—that, combined with so many sleepless nights, and so many days of adrenaline rush. My body is so banged up, so sore and bruised, it must've just fallen asleep by itself. I feel guilty: I never let Bree out of my sight before. But as I look over at Logan, his presence so strong, I realize I must've felt safe enough around him to do that. In some ways, it's like having my dad back. Is that why I dreamed of him?

"Nice to have you back," comes Logan's deep voice. He glances my way, a small smile playing at the corner of his lips.

I lean forward, surveying the river before us as we cut through it like butter. The roar of the engine is deafening, and the boat rides the current, moving up and down in subtle motions, rocking just a tiny bit. The freezing spray hits my face directly, and I look down and see I'm still dressed in the same clothes I've been wearing for days. The clothes practically cling to my skin, caked with sweat and blood and dirt—and now moist from the spray. I am damp, and cold, and hungry. I would do anything for a hot shower, a hot chocolate, a roaring fire, and a change of clothes.

I scan the horizon: the Hudson is like a vast and wide sea. We stick to the middle, far from either shore, Logan wisely keeping us away from any potential predators. Remembering, I immediately turn back, checking for any sign of slaverunners. I see none.

I turn back and look for any signs of any boats on the horizon before us. Nothing. I scan the shorelines, looking for any sign of activity. Nothing. It is as if we have the world to ourselves. It is comforting and desolate at the same time.

Slowly, I relax my guard. It feels like I've been asleep forever, but from the sun's position in the sky, it's only mid-afternoon. I couldn't have been asleep for more than an hour, at most. I look around for any familiar landmark. After all, we are nearly back near home. But I see none.

"How long was I out?" I ask Logan.

He shrugs. "Maybe an hour."

An hour, I think. It feels like an eternity.

I check the gas gauge, and it reads half empty. That doesn't bode well.

"Any sign of fuel anywhere?" I ask.

The moment I ask, I realize it is a stupid question.

Logan looks over at me, as if to say *really*? Of course, if he had seen a fuel depot, he would have hit it.

"Where are we?" I ask.

"These are your parts," he says. "I was going to ask you the same thing."

I scan the river again, but still can't recognize anything. That's the thing about the Hudson—it's so wide, and it stretches forever, and it's so easy to lose one's bearings.

"Why didn't you wake me?" I ask.

"Why should I? You needed the sleep."

I don't quite know what else to say to him. That's the thing about Logan: I like him, and I feel he likes me, but I don't know if we have all that much to say to each other. It doesn't help that he's guarded, and that I am, too.

We continue in silence, the white water churning beneath us, and I wonder how much longer we can go on. What will we do when our fuel runs out?

In the distance, I spot something on the horizon. It looks like some sort of structure, in the water. At first I wonder if I am seeing things, but then Logan cranes his neck, alert, and I realize he must see it, too.

"I think it's a bridge," he says. "A downed bridge."

I realize he's right. Growing ever closer is a towering hunk of twisted metal, sticking up out of the water like some sort of monument to hell. I remember this bridge: it once beautifully spanned the river; now, it's a huge heap of scrap metal, plunging at jagged angles down into the water.

Logan slows the boat, the engine quieting as we get closer. Our speed drops and the boat rocks wildly. The jagged metal protrudes from every direction, and Logan navigates, turning the boat left and right, creating his own little pathway. I look up as we go at the bridge's remains, looming over us. It looks like it rises hundreds of feet high, a testament to what humanity was once able to do before we started killing each other.

"The Tappan Zee," I remark. "We're about an hour north of the city. We've got a good jump on them, if they're coming after us."

"They *are* coming after us," he said. "You can bet on it."

I look at him. "How can you be so sure?"

"I know them. They never forget."

As we pass the last scrap of metal, Logan picks up speed and I lean back as we accelerate.

"How far behind us do you think they are?" I ask.

He looks at the horizon, stoic. Finally, he shrugs.

"Hard to say. Depends how long it takes to rally the troops. Snow's heavy, which is good for us. Maybe three hours? Maybe six, if we're lucky? Good thing is, this baby's fast. I think we can outrun them, as long as we have fuel."

"But we don't," I say, pointing out the obvious. "We left with a full tank—now we're half empty. We'll be empty in just a few hours. Canada's a long way away. How do you propose we find fuel?"

Logan stares at the water, thinking.

"We have no choice," he says. "We have to find it. There's no alternative. We can't stop."

"We're going to need to rest at some point," I say. "We're going to need food, and some sort of shelter. We can't stay out in this temperature all day and all night."

"Better to starve and freeze than be caught by slaverunners," he says.

I think of dad's house, farther upriver. We're going to pass right by it. I remember my vow to my old dog, Sasha, to bury her. I also think of all the food up there, in that stone cottage—we can salvage it, and it would sustain us for days. I think of all the tools in dad's garage, all the things we can make use of. Not to mention the extra clothes, blankets and matches.

"I want to make a stop."

Logan turns and looks at me as if I'm crazy. I can see that he doesn't like this.

"What are you talking about?"

"My dad's house. In Catskill. About an hour north of here. I want to stop there. There are a lot of things we can salvage. Things we'll need. Like food. And," I pause, "I want to bury my dog."

"Bury your dog?" he asks, his voice rising. "Are you crazy? You want to get us all killed for that?"

"I promised her," I say.

"Promised?" he shoots back. "Your dog? Your dead dog? You've got to be kidding."

I stare him down, and he realizes pretty quickly that I'm not.

"If I promise something, I deliver. I'd bury you if I promised."

He shakes his head.

"Listen," I say firmly. "You wanted Canada. We could have gone anywhere. That was *your* dream. Not mine. Who knows it this town even exists? I'm following you on a whim. And this boat's not just yours. All I want is to stop at my dad's place. Get some stuff, which we need, and put my dog to rest. It won't take long. We've got a big jump on the slaverunners. Not to mention, we have a small canister of fuel up there. It's not much, but it will help."

Logan slowly shakes his head.

"I'd rather not have that fuel and not take such a risk. You're talking about the mountains. You're talking about twenty miles inland, right? How do you propose we get there once we dock? Hike?"

"I know where there's an old truck. A beat-up pickup. It's just a rusted shell, but it runs, and it's got just enough fuel to get us there and back. It's hidden, by the river line. The river will take us right to it. The truck will take us up and back. It will be quick. And then we can continue on our long trip to Canada. And we'll be better for it."

Logan stares silently at the water for a long time, his fists clenched tight around the wheel.

Finally, he says, "Whatever. It's your life to risk. But I'm staying with the boat. You've got two hours. If you're not back in time, I'm taking off."

I turn away from him and look out at the water, fuming mad. I wanted him to come. I feel like he's looking out for himself, and it disappoints me. I thought he was better than that.

"So you only care about yourself, is that it?" I ask.

It also worries me that he doesn't want to accompany me to my dad's house; I hadn't thought of that. I know Ben won't want to come and I would've appreciated some backup. Whatever. I'm still resolved. I made a promise, and I will keep it. With or without him.

He doesn't respond, and I can tell he's annoyed.

I look out at the water, not wanting to see him. As the water churns amidst the constant whine of the engine, I realize I'm mad not only because I'm disappointed in him, but because I was actually starting to like him, to count on him. I haven't depended on anyone for a long time. It's a scary feeling, depending on someone again, and I feel betrayed.

"Brooke?"

My heart lifts at the sounds of the familiar voice, and I turn to see my little sister awake. Rose wakes, too. Those two are already like peas in a pod, like extensions of one person.

I still can hardly believe that Bree is here, back with me. It's like a dream. When she was taken, a part of me was sure I'd never see her alive again. Every moment I am with her, I feel like I've been given a second chance, and I feel more determined than ever to watch over her.

"I'm hungry," Bree says, rubbing her eyes with the back of her hands.

Penelope sits up, too, in Bree's lap. She won't stop trembling, and she raises her good eye and looks at me, as if she's hungry, too.

"I'm freezing," Rose echoes, rubbing her shoulders. She wears only a thin shirt, and I feel terrible for her.

I understand. I'm starving and freezing, too. My nose is red and I can barely feel it. Those goodies we found in the boat were amazing, but hardly filling—especially on an empty stomach. And that was hours ago. I think again of the food chest, of what little we have left, and wonder how long until it runs out. I know I should ration the food. But then again, we're all starving, and I can't stand to see Bree looking like that.

"There's not much food left," I tell her, "but I can give you guys a little bit of it now. We have some cookies, and some crackers."

"Cookies!" they both yell at once. Penelope barks.

"I wouldn't do that," comes Logan's voice beside me.

I look over, and see him glancing back disapprovingly.

"We need to ration it."

"Please!" Bree cries out. "I need something. I'm starving."

"I need to give them *something*," I say firmly back to Logan, understanding where his head is, but annoyed at his lack of compassion. "I'm doling out one cookie each. For all of us."

"What about Penelope?" Rose asks.

"The dog's not getting any of our food," Logan snaps. "She's on her own."

I feel another twinge of upset at Logan, though I know he's being rational. Still, as I see the crestfallen look on Rose and Bree's faces, and as I hear her bark again, I can't bear to let her starve. I quietly resign to give her some food from my own rations.

I open the chest, and survey once again our stash of food. I see two boxes of cookies, three boxes of crackers, several bags of gummy bears, and a half dozen chocolate bars. I wish there was some more substantial food, and I don't know how we're going to make this last, how this will suffice for three meals a day for five people.

I pull out the cookies and dole out one to each person. Ben finally snaps out of it at the site of the food, and accepts a cookie. His eyes have black circles under them, and he looks as if he hasn't slept. It is painful to see his expression, so devastated from the loss of his brother, and I look away as I hand him his cookie.

I come to the front of the boat, and hand Logan his. He takes it and silently puts into his pocket, of course, rationing it for later. I don't know where he gets his strength from. Myself, I go weak at the smell of the chocolate chip cookie. I know I should ration it, too, but I can't help it. I take a small bite, resolving to put it away—but it tastes so good, I can't help myself—I devour the entire thing, saving only the last bite, which I set aside for Penelope.

The food feels so good. The sugar rushes to my head, then through my body, and I wish I had a dozen more. I take a deep breath at the stomach pain, trying to control myself.

The river narrows, the shores becoming ever closer to each other, as it twists and turns. We're close to land and I'm on high alert, looking to the shorelines for any sign of danger. As we round a bend I look to my left and see, high up on a cliff, the ruins of an old fortification, now bombed out. I am shocked as I realize what it once was.

"West Point," Logan says. He must realize at the same time as I do.

It is shocking to see this bastion of American strength now just a pile of rubble, its twisted flagpole hanging limply over the Hudson. Hardly anything remains of what once was.

"What is that?" Bree asks, her teeth chattering. She and Rose have climbed to the front of the boat, beside me, and she looks out, following my gaze. I don't want to tell her.

"It's nothing sweetie," I say. "Just a ruin."

I put my arm around her and pull her close, and put my other arm around Rose and pull her close, too. I tried to warm them up, rubbing their shoulders as best I can.

"When are we going home?" Rose asks.

Logan and I exchange a look. I hardly know how to answer.

"We're not going home," I say to Rose, as gently as I can, "but we're on our way to find a new home."

"Are we going to pass by our old home?" Bree asks.

I hesitate. "Yes," I say.

"But we're not going back there, right?" she asks.

"Right," I say. "It's too dangerous to live there now."

"I don't want to live there again," she says. "I hated that place. But we can't just leave Sasha there. Are we going stop and bury her? You promised."

I think back to my argument with Logan.

"You're right," I say softly. "I did promise. And yes, we will stop."

Logan turns away, clearly miffed.

"And then what?" Rose asks. "And then where will we go?"

"We're going to keep going upriver," I explain. "As far as it will take us."

"Where does it end?" she asks.

It's a good question, and I take it as a much more profound question. Where does all of this end? With our deaths? With our survival? Will it ever end? Is there any end in sight?

I don't have the answer.

I turn, and kneel, and look into her eyes. I need to give her hope. Something to live for.

"It ends in a beautiful place," I say. "Where we're going, everything is good again. The streets are so clean that they shine, and everything is perfect and safe. There will be people there, friendly people, and they will take us in and protect us. There will be food, too, real food, all you can eat, all the time. It will be the most beautiful place you've ever seen."

Rose's eyes open wide.

"Is that true?" she asks.

I nod. Slowly, she breaks into a wide smile.

"How long until we make it there?"

I smile. "I don't know sweetheart."

Bree, though, is more cynical than Rose.

"Is that really true?" she asks, softly. "Is there really such a place?"

"It is," I say to her, trying my best to sound convincing. "Isn't that true, Logan?"

Logan looks over, nods at them briefly, then looks away. He is the one, after all, that believes in Canada, believes in a promised land. How can he deny it now?

The Hudson twists and turns, getting more narrow, then widening again. Finally, we enter familiar territory. We race past places I recognize, getting closer and closer to dad's house.

We turn another bank, and I see a small, uninhabited island, just a rocky outcropping. On it sits the remains of a lighthouse, its light long shattered, its structure hardly more than a façade.

We turn another bend in the river and in the distance I spot the bridge I'd been on just days before, when chasing after the slaverunners. There, in the middle of the bridge, I see the center blown out, the huge hole, as if a wrecking ball had been dropped through the middle. I flash back to when Ben and I raced across it in the motorcycle and nearly skidded into it. I can't believe it. We're almost there.

This makes me think of Ben, makes me remember how he saved my life that day. I turn and look at him. He stares into the water, morose.

"Ben?" I ask.

He turns and looks at me.

"Remember that bridge?"

He turns and looks, and I see fear in his eyes. He remembers.

Bree elbows me. "Is it okay if I give Penelope some of my cookie?" she asks.

"Me, too?" Rose echoes.

"Sure it is," I say loudly, so Logan can hear. He's not the only one in charge here, and we can do with our food as we wish.

The dog, in Rose's lap, perks up, as if she understands. It is incredible. I have never seen such a smart animal.

Bree leans in to feed her a piece of her cookie, but I stop her hand.

"Wait," I say. "If you're going to feed her, she should have a name, shouldn't she?"

"But she has no collar," Rose says. "Her name could be anything."

"She's your dog now," I say. "Give her a new one."

Rose and Bree exchange an excited glance.

"What should we call her?" Bree asks.

"How about Penelope?" Rose says.

"Penelope!" Bree screams. "I like that."

"I like it, too," I say.

"Penelope!" Rose cries out to the dog.

Amazingly, the dog actually turns to her when she says it, as if that were always her name.

Bree smiles as she reaches out and feeds her a piece of cookie. Penelope snatches it out of her hands and gobbles it up in one bite. Bree and Rose giggle hysterically, and Rose feeds her the rest of her cookie. She snatches that, too, and I reach out and feed her the last bite of my cookie. Penelope looks back at all three of us excitedly, trembling, and barks three times.

We all laugh. For a moment, I nearly forget our troubles.

But then, in the distance, over Bree's shoulder, I spot something.

"There," I say to Logan, stepping up and pointing to our left. "That's where we need to go. Turn there."

I spot the peninsula where Ben and I drove off on the motorcycle, onto the ice of the Hudson. It makes me flinch to think of it, to think of how crazy that chase was. It's amazing I'm still alive.

Logan checks over his shoulder to see if anyone is following; then, reluctantly, he eases up on the throttle and turns us off to the side, bringing us towards the inlet.

On edge, I look around warily as we reach the mouth of the peninsula. We glide beside it as it curves inland. We are so close to shore now, passing a dilapidated water tower. We continue on and soon glide alongside the ruins of a town, right into the heart of it. Catskill. There are burnt-out buildings on all sides and it looks like it's been hit by a bomb.

We are all on edge as we make our way slowly up the inlet, getting deeper inland, the shore now feet away as it narrows. We are exposed to ambush, and I find myself unconsciously reaching down and resting my hand on my hip, on my knife. I notice Logan do the same.

I check back over my shoulder for Ben; but he is still in a nearly catatonic state.

"Where's the truck?" Logan asks, an edge to his voice. "I'm not going too deep inland, I'll tell you right now. If anything happens, we need to be able to get out to the Hudson, and fast. This is a death trap," he says, warily eyeing the shore.

I eye it, too. But the shore is empty, desolate, frozen over with no humanity in sight as far as the eye can see.

"See there," I say, pointing. "That rusted shed? It's inside."

Logan drives us another thirty yards or so, then turns for the shed. There is an old crumbling dock, and he's able to pull the boat up, feet from shore. He kills the engine, grabs the anchor and throws it overboard. He then grabs the rope from the boat, makes a loose knot at one end, and throws it to a rusted metal post. It catches and he pulls us in all the way, tightening it, so we can walk onto the dock.

"Are we getting out?" Bree asks.

"I am," I say. "Wait for me here, with the boat. It's too dangerous for you to go. I'll be back soon. I'll bury Sasha. I promise."

"No!" she screams. "You promised we would never be apart again. You promised! You can't leave me here alone! You CAN'T!"

"I'm not leaving you alone," I answer, my heart breaking. "You'll be here with Logan, and Ben, and Rose. You'll be perfectly safe. I promise."

But Bree stands and to my surprise, she takes a running jump across the bow, and jumps onto the sandy shore, landing right in the snow.

She stands ashore, hands on her hips, glaring back at me defiantly.

"If you're going, I'm going too," she states.

I take a deep breath, seeing she's resigned. I know that when she gets like this, she means it.

It will be a liability, having her, but I have to admit, a part of me feels good having her in my sight at all times. And if I try to talk her out of it, I'll just waste more time.

"Fine," I say. "Just stay close the entire time. Promise?"

She nods. "I promise."

"I'm scared," Rose says, looking over at Bree, wide-eyed. "I don't want to leave the boat. I want to stay here, with Penelope. Is that okay?"

"I want you to," I say to her, silently refusing to take her, too.

I turn to Ben, and he turns and meets my eyes with his mournful ones. The look in them makes me want to look away, but I force myself not to.

"Are you coming?" I ask. I hope he says yes. I'm annoyed at Logan for staying here, for letting me down, and I could really use the backup.

But Ben, still clearly in shock, just stares back. He looks at me as if he doesn't comprehend. I wonder if he's fully registering all that's happening around him.

"Are you *coming*?" I ask more forcefully. I don't have the patience for this.

Slowly, he shakes his head, withdrawing. He's really out of it, and I try to forgive him—but it's hard.

I turn to leave the boat, and jump onto shore. It feels good to have my feet on dry land.

"Wait!"

I turn and see Logan get up from the driver seat.

"I knew some crap like this would happen," he says.

He walks across the boat, gathering his stuff.

"What are you doing?" I ask.

"What do you think?" he asks. "I'm not letting you two go alone."

My heart swells with relief. If it were just me I wouldn't care as much—but I am thrilled to have another set of eyes to watch Bree.

He jumps off the boat, and onto shore.

"I'm telling you right now, this is a stupid idea," he says, as he lands besides me. "We should keep moving. It will be night soon. The Hudson can freeze. We could get stuck here. Not to mention the slaverunners. You've got 90 minutes, understand? 30 minutes in, 30 there, and 30 back. No exceptions, for any reason. Otherwise, I'm leaving without you."

I look back at him, impressed and grateful.

"Deal," I say.

I think of the sacrifice he just made, and I am beginning to feel something else. Behind all his posturing, I am beginning to feel that Logan really likes me. And he's not as selfish as I thought.

As we turn to go, there's another shuffling on the boat.

"Wait!" Ben cries out.

I turn and look.

"You guys can't leave me here alone with Rose. What if someone comes? What am I supposed to do?

"Watch the boat," Logan says, turning again to leave.

"I don't know how to drive it!" Ben yells out. "I don't have any weapons!"

Logan turns again, annoyed, reaches down, takes one of the guns off a strap from his thigh, and chucks it to him. It hits him hard in the chest, and he fumbles with it.

"Maybe you'll learn how to use it," Logan sneers, as he turns away again.

I get a good look at Ben, who stands there, looking so helpless and afraid, holding a gun he barely seems to know how to use. He seems absolutely terrified.

I want to comfort him. To tell him everything will be OK, that we'll be back soon. But as I turn away and look up at the vast mountain range before us, for the first time, I am not so sure that we will.

TWO

We walk quickly through the snow and I look anxiously at the darkening sky, feeling the pressure of time. I glance back over my shoulder, see my footprints in the snow, and beyond them, standing there in the rocking boat, Ben and Rose, watching us wide-eyed. Rose clutches Penelope, equally afraid. Penelope barks. I feel bad leaving the three of them there, but I know our mission is necessary. I know we can salvage supplies and food that will help, and I feel we have a comfortable jump on the slaverunners.

I hurry to the rusted shed, covered in snow, and yank open its crooked door, praying that the truck I hid inside ages ago is still there. It was an old rusted pickup, on its last legs, more scrap than car, with only about an eighth tank of fuel left in it. I stumbled across it one day, in a ditch off Route 23, and hid it here, carefully down by the river, in case I ever needed it. I remember being amazed when it actually turned over.

The shed door opens with a creak, and there it is, as well hidden as it was on the day I stashed it, still covered with the hay. My heart swells with relief. I step forward and pull the hay back, my hands cold as I touch the freezing metal. I go to the back of the shed and pull open the double barn doors, and light comes flooding in.

"Nice wheels," Logan says, walking up behind me, surveying it. "You sure it runs?"

"No," I say. "But my dad's house is a good twenty miles away, and we can't exactly hike."

I can tell from his tone that he really doesn't want to be on this mission, that he wants to be back in the boat, moving upriver.

I jump into the driver seat and search the floor for the key. I finally feel it, hidden deep. I put it in the ignition, take a deep breath and close my eyes.

Please, god. Please.

At first nothing happens. My heart drops.

But I turn again and again, twist it farther to the right, and slowly, it begins to catch. At first it is a quiet sound, like a dying cat. But I hold it, twist again and again, and eventually, it turns over more.

Come on, come on.

It finally catches, rumbling and groaning to life. It clutters and gasps, clearly on its last legs. At least it's running.

I can't help smiling, flooding with relief. It works. It really works. We're going to be able to make it to my house, bury my dog, get food. I feel as if Sasha's looking down, helping us. Maybe my dad, too.

The passenger door opens and in jumps Bree, bristling with excitement, scooting over in the one vinyl seat, right next to me, as Logan jumps in beside her, slamming the door, looking straight ahead.

"What you waiting for?" he says. "Clock's ticking."

"You don't need to tell me twice," I say, equally short with him.

I put it into gear and floor it, reversing out of the shed and into the snow and afternoon sky. At first the wheels catch in the snow, but I give it more gas, and we sputter forward.

We drive, swerving on the bald tires, across a field, bumpy, getting jolted every which way. But we continue forward, and that's all I care about.

Soon, we are on a small country road. I am so thankful the snow was melting most of the day—otherwise, we'd never make it.

We start picking up good speed. The truck surprises me, calming down as it warms up. We hit almost 40 as we ride Route 23 heading west. I keep pushing it, until we hit a pothole, and I regret it. We all groan, as we slam our heads. I slow down. The potholes are nearly impossible to see in the snow, and I forgot how bad these roads have become.

It's eerie being back on this road, heading back to what was once home. I am retracing the road I took when chasing the slaverunners, and memories come flooding back. I remember racing down here on a motorcycle, thinking I was going to die, and I try to put it out of my mind.

As we go, we come across the huge tree felled in the road, now covered in snow. I recognize it as the tree that had been felled on my way out, the one downed to block the path of the slaverunners, by some unknown survivalist out there who was looking after us. I can't help but wonder if there are other people out there now, surviving, maybe even watching us. I look from side to side, combing the woods. But I see no signs.

We are making good time and to my relief, nothing is going wrong. I don't trust it. It is almost as if it is too easy. I glance at the gas gage and see we haven't used much. But I don't know how accurate it is, and for a moment I wonder if there'll be enough gas to get us there and back. I wonder if it was a stupid idea to try this.

We finally turn off the main road, onto the narrow, winding country road that will bring us up the mountain, to dad's house. I'm more on edge now, as we twist and turn of the mountain, the cliffs dropping off steeply to my right. I look out and can't help noticing the view is incredible, spanning the entire Catskill mountain range. But the drop-off is steep and the snow is thicker up here, and I know that with one wrong turn, one wrong skid, this old heap of rust will go right over the edge.

To my surprise, the truck hangs in there. It is like a bulldog. Soon we are past the worst of it, and as we turn a bend, I suddenly spot our former house.

"Hey! Dad's house!" Bree yells out, sitting up in excitement.

I'm relieved to see it, too. We're here, and we made good time.

"See," I say to Logan, "that wasn't so bad."

Logan doesn't seem relieved, though; his face is set in a grimace, on edge as he watches the trees.

"We made it here," he grumbles. "We didn't make it back."

Typical. Refusing to admit he was wrong.

I pull up in front of our house and see the old slaverunner tracks. It brings flashing back all the memories, all the dread I'd felt when they'd taken Bree. I reach over and drape an arm around her shoulder, clutch her tight, resolve to never let her out of my sight again.

I cut the ignition and we all jump out and head quickly towards the house.

"Sorry if it's a mess," I say to Logan as I step past him, up to the front door. "I wasn't expecting guests."

Despite himself, he suppresses a smile.

"Ha ha," he says, flatly. "Should I take off my shoes?"

A sense of humor. That surprises me.

As I open the door and step inside, any sense of humor I had suddenly falls away. When I see the site before me, my heart drops. There is Sasha, lying there, her blood dried, her body stiff and frozen. Just a few feet away is the corpse of the slaverunner Sasha had killed, his corpse frozen, too, stuck to the floor.

I look down at the jacket I'm wearing—his jacket—the clothes I'm wearing—his clothes—my boots—his boots—and it gives me a funny feeling. Almost as if I'm his walking double.

Logan looks over at me and must realize it too.

"You didn't take his pants?" he asks.

I look down and remember I did not. It was too much.

I shake my head.

"Stupid," he says.

Now that he mentions it, I realize he is right. My old jeans are wet and cold, and sticking to me. And even if I don't want them, Ben might. It's a shame to waste them: after all, it is perfectly good clothing.

I hear muffled cries and look over to see Bree standing there, looking down at Sasha. It breaks my heart to see her face like that, crumpled up, staring down at her former dog.

I walk over to her and put an arm around her.

"It's okay, Bree," I say. "Look away."

I kiss her on the forehead and try to turn her away, but she throws me off with surprising strength.

"No," she says.

She steps forward, kneels down and hugs Sasha on the ground. She wraps her arms around her neck, and leans over and kisses her head.

Logan I exchange a glance. Neither of us know what to do.

"We haven't time," Logan says. "You need to bury her, and move on."

I kneel down beside her, lean over and stroke Sasha's head.

"It's going to be okay, Bree. Sasha's in a better place now. She's happy now. Do you hear me?"

Tears drop from her eyes, and she reaches up, takes a deep breath, and wipes them away with the back of her hand.

"We can't leave her here like this," she says. "We have to bury her."

"We will," I say.

"We can't," Logan says. "The ground is frozen solid."

I stand and look at Logan, more annoyed than ever. Especially because I realize he is right. I should have thought of that.

"Then what do you suggest?" I ask.

"It's not my problem. I'll stand guard outside."

Logan turns and marches outside, slamming the front door behind him.

I turn back to Bree, trying to think quick.

"He's right," I say. "We don't have time to bury her."

"NO!" she wails. "You promised. You *promised*!"

She's right. I did promise. But I hadn't thought it all through carefully. The thought of leaving Sasha here like this kills me. But I can't risk our own lives either. Sasha wouldn't want that.

I have an idea.

"What about the river, Bree?"

She turns and looks at me.

"What if we give her a water burial? You know, like they do for soldiers who die in honor?"

"What soldiers?" she asks.

"When soldiers die at sea, sometimes they bury them at sea. It's a burial of honor. Sasha loved the river. I'm sure she'd be happy there. We can bring her down and bury her there. Would that be okay?"

My heart is pounding as I wait for a response. We are running out of time, and I know how intransigent Bree can be if something means a lot to her.

To my relief, she nods.

"Okay," she says. "But I get to carry her."

"I think she's too heavy for you."

"I'm not going unless I get to carry her," she says, her eyes flashing with determination as she stands, faces me, hands on her hips. I can see from her eyes that she will never give in otherwise.

"Okay," I say. "You can carry her."

We both pry Sasha off the floor, and then I quickly scan the house for anything we can salvage. I hurry to the slaverunner's corpse, strip his pants off, and as I do, feel something in his back pocket. I'm happily surprised to discover something bulky and metal inside. I pull out a small switch blade. I'm thrilled to have it, and cram it in my pocket.

I do a quick run-through of the rest of the house, hurrying from room to room, looking for anything that might be useful. I find a few old, empty burlap sacks and take them all. I open one and throw in

Bree's favorite book, *The Giving Tree*, and my copy of *Lord of the Flies*. I run to a closet, grab the remaining candles and matches and throw them in.

I run through the kitchen and out to the garage, the doors already busted open from when the slaverunners raided it. I hope desperately they didn't take time to search in the back, deeper in the garage, for his tool chest. I hid it well, in a recess in the wall, and I hurry back and am relieved to see it's still there. It's too heavy to carry the entire toolbox, so I rifle through it and cherry pick whatever might be useful. I take a small hammer, screwdriver, a small box of nails. I find a flashlight, with the battery inside. I test it, and it works. I grab a small set of pliers and a wrench and close it and get ready to leave.

As I'm about to run out, something catches my eye, high on the wall. It's a large zip line, all bunched up, tied up neatly and hanging on a hook. I forgot all about it. Years ago, dad bought this zip line and tied it between the trees, thinking we could all have fun. We did it once, and never again, and then he hung it in the garage. Looking at it now, I feel that it might be valuable. I jump up on the tool bench, reach up and take it down, slinging it over one shoulder and my burlap sack over the other.

I hurry out the garage and back into the house and Bree is standing there, holding Sasha in both her arms, looking down at her.

"I'm ready," she says.

We hurry out the front door, and Logan turns and sees Sasha. He shakes his head.

"Where are you taking her?" he asks.

"The river," I say.

He shakes head in disapproval.

"Clock's ticking," he says. "You got 15 more minutes, before we head back. Where's the food?"

"Not here," I say. "We have to head up higher, to a cottage I found. We can do it in 15."

I walk with Bree towards the truck and throw in the zip line and sack over the back of the pickup. I keep the empty sacks, though, knowing I'll need it to carry the food.

"What's that line for?" Logan asks, stepping up behind us. "We have no use for it."

"You never know," I say.

I turn, put an arm around Bree, who still stares at Sasha, and turn her away, looking up the mountain.

"Let's move," I say to Logan.

Reluctantly, he turns and hikes with us.

The three of us hike steadily up the mountain, the wind getting stronger, colder up here. I worriedly look up at the sky: it is getting darker much quicker than I thought. I know that Logan is right: we need to be back in the water by nightfall. And with sunset basically here, I'm feeling increasingly worried. But I also I know in my heart that we have to get the food.

The three of us trudge our way up the mountain face, and finally we reach the top clearing, as a strong gust hits me in the face. It's getting colder and darker by the minute.

I retrace my steps to the cottage, the snow thick up here; I feel it piercing through my boots as I go. I spot it, still hidden, covered in snow, still as well hidden and anonymous as ever. I hurry to it and pry open it small door. Logan and Bree stand behind me.

"Good find," he says, and for the first time I hear admiration in his voice. "Well hidden. I like it. Almost enough to make me want to stay here—if the slaverunners weren't chasing us, and if we had a food supply."

"I know," I say, as I step into the small house.

"It's beautiful," Bree says. "Is this the house we were going to move to?"

I turn back and look at her, feeling bad. I nod.

"Another time, okay?"

She understands. She's not anxious to wait around for the slaverunners either.

I hurry inside and pull open the trap door, and descend down the steep ladder. It's dark down here, and I feel my way. I reach out and feel a row of glass, clinking as I touch it. The jars. I waste no time. I take out my sacks and fill them as fast as I can with jars. I can barely make them out as my bag grows heavy, but I remember there being raspberry jam, blackberry jam, pickles, cucumbers…. I fill as much as the sack can carry then reach up and hand it up the ladder to Logan. He takes it and I fill three more.

I clean out the entire wall.

"No more," Logan says. "Can't haul it. And it's getting dark. We have to go."

Now there's a little bit more respect his voice. Clearly, he's impressed with the stash I found, and finally, he recognizes how much we needed to come here.

He reaches down and offers me a hand, but I scramble up the ladder myself, not needing his help and still miffed by his earlier attitude.

On my feet back in the cottage, I grab two of the heavy sacks myself, as Logan grabs the others. The three of us hurry out the cottage, and soon retrace our steps back down the steep trail. In minutes, we're back at the truck, and I'm relieved to see everything is still there. I check the horizon, and see no signs of any activity at all anywhere on the mountain, or in the distant valley.

We jump back in the truck, I turn the ignition, happy that it starts, and we take off back down the road. We've got food, supplies, our dog, and I was able to say goodbye to dad's house. I feel satisfied. I feel that Bree, beside me, is content, too. Logan looks out the window, lost in his own world, but I can't help feeling as if he thinks we made the right decision.

*

The trip back down the mountain is uneventful, the brakes in this old pickup holding pretty well, to my surprise. In some places, where it is really steep, it is more of a controlled slide than a break, but within minutes we are off the worst of it, back onto the stable Route 23, heading east. We pick up speed, and for the first time in a while, I'm feeling optimistic. We've got some precious tools, and enough food to last us for days. I'm feeling good, vindicated, as we cruise down 23, just minutes away from getting back to the boat.

And then, everything changes.

I slam on the brakes as a person jumps out of nowhere, right into the middle of the road, waving his arms hysterically, blocking our path. He's barely fifty yards out and I have to hit the brakes hard, sending our truck into a slide.

"DON'T STOP!" Logan commands. "Keep driving!" He's using his toughest military voice.

But I can't listen. There is a man there, standing out there, helpless, wearing just tattered jeans and a sleeveless vest in the freezing cold. He has a long black beard, wild hair, and large, black crazed eyes. He's so thin, he looks like he hasn't eaten in days. He has a bow and arrow strapped to his chest. He's a human, a survivor, just like us, that much is obvious.

He waves his arms frantically, and I can't run him over. I can't bear leaving him, either.

We come to an abrupt stop, just feet away from the man. He stands there, wide-eyed, as if he didn't expect us to really stop.

Logan wastes no time jumping out, both hands on his pistol, aiming it at the man's head.

"STEP BACK!" he screams.

I jump out, too.

The man slowly raises his arms, looking dazed as he takes several steps back.

"Don't shoot!" the man pleads. "Please! I'm just like you! I need help. Please. You can't leave me here to die. I'm starving. I haven't eaten in days. Let me come with you. Please. *Please*!"

His voice is cracking, and I see the anguish on his face. I know how he feels. Not long ago, I was just like him, scrounging to get by with every meal here in the mountains. I am hardly much better now.

"Here, take this!" the man says, taking off his bow and quiver of arrows. "It's yours! I mean no harm!"

"Move slowly," Logan cautions, still suspicious.

The man reaches out gingerly and hands out the weapon.

"Brooke, you get it," Logan says.

I step forward, grab the bow and arrows, and throw them in the back of the truck.

"See," the man says, breaking into a smile. "I'm no threat. I just want to join you. Please. You can't leave me here to die."

Slowly, Logan relaxes his guard and lowers his gun just a bit. But he still keeps an eye trained on the man.

"Sorry," Logan says. "We can't have another mouth to feed."

"Wait!" I yell at Logan. "You're not the only one here. You don't make all the decisions." I turn to the man. "What's your name?" I ask. "Where are you from?"

He looks at me desperately.

"My name is Rupert," he says. "I've survived up here for two years. I've seen you and your sister before. When the slaverunners took her, I tried to help. I'm the one that chopped down that tree!"

My heart breaks as he says this. He's the one that tried to help us. I can't just leave him here. It's not right.

"We have to take him," I say to Logan. "We can find room for one more."

"You don't know him," Logan replies. "Besides, we don't have the food."

"I can hunt," the man says. "I've got the bow and arrow."

"Much good it's doing you up here," Logan says.

"Please," Rupert says. "I can help. Please. I don't want any of your food."

"We're taking him," I say to Logan.

"No we're not," he says back. "You don't know this man. You don't know anything about him."

"I barely know anything about *you*," I say to Logan, my anger hardening. I hate how he can be so cynical, so guarded. "You're not the only one who has the right to live."

"If you take him, you jeopardize all of us," he says. "Not just you. Your sister, too."

"There are three of us here last I checked," comes Bree's voice.

I turn and see she's jumped out of the truck and stands behind us.

"And that means we're a democracy. And my vote counts. And I vote we take him. We can't just leave him here to die."

Logan shakes his head, looking disgusted. Without another word, his jaw hardening, he turns and jumps back into the truck.

The man looks at me with a huge smile, his face crumpling in a thousand wrinkles.

"Thank you," he whispers. "I don't know how to thank you."

"Just move, before he changes his mind," I say as we turn back to the truck.

As Rupert approaches the door, Logan says, "You're not sitting upfront. Get in the back of the pickup."

Before I can argue, Rupert happily jumps into the back of pickup. Bree jumps in, as do I, and we take off.

It is a nerve-racking remainder of the ride back to the river. As we go, the skies darkening, I constantly watching the sunset, bleeding red through the clouds. It's getting colder out by the second, and the snow is hardening even as we drive, turning to ice in some places, and making driving more precarious. The gas gauge is dropping, flashing red, and though we only have a mile or so to go, I feel as if we're fighting for every inch. I also feel how on-edge Logan is about our new passenger. It is just one more unknown. One more mouth to feed.

I silently will the truck to keep going, the sky to stay light, the snow not to harden as I step on the gas. Just when I think we'll never get there, we round the bend, and I see our turnoff. I turn hard onto the narrow country lane, sloping down towards the river, willing the truck to make it. The boat, I know, is only a couple hundred yards away.

We round another bend, and as we do, my heart floods with relief as I see the boat. It is still there, bobbing in the water, and I see Ben standing there, looking nervous, watching the horizon for our approach.

"Our boat!" Bree yells excitedly.

This road is even more bumpy as we accelerate downhill. But we're going to make it. My heart floods with relief.

Yet as I'm watching the horizon, in the distance I spot something that makes my heart drop. I can't believe it. Logan must see it at the same time.

"Goddamit," he whispers.

In the distance, on the Hudson, is a slaverunner boat—a large, sleek, black motorboat, racing towards us. It is twice the size of ours, and I'm sure, much better equipped. Making matters worse, I spot another boat behind that, even farther back.

Logan was right. They were much closer than I'd thought.

I slam on the brakes and we skid to a stop about ten yards from the shoreline. I throw it into park, open the door, and jump out, getting ready to race for the boat.

Suddenly, something is very wrong. I feel my breathing cut off as I feel an arm wrap tight around my throat; then I feel myself being dragged backwards. I am losing air, seeing stars, and I don't understand what's happening. Have the slaverunners ambushed us?

"Don't move," hisses a voice in my ear.

I feel something sharp and cold against my throat, and realize it's a knife.

It is then that I realize what has happened: Rupert. The stranger. He has ambushed me.

THREE

"LOWER YOUR WEAPON!" Rupert screams. "NOW!"

Logan stands a few feet away, pistol raised, aiming it right past my head. He holds it in place, and I can see him deliberating whether to take a head shot on this man. I see he wants to, but he's worried about hitting me.

I realize now how stupid I was to pick up this person. Logan had been right all along. I should have listened. Rupert was just using us all along, wanting to take our boat and food and supplies and have it all to himself. He is completely desperate. I realize in a flash that he will surely kill me. I have no doubt about it.

"Take the shot!" I scream out to Logan. "Do it!"

I trust Logan—I know he is a great shot. But Rupert holds me tight, and I see Logan wavering, unsure. It is in that moment that I see in Logan's eyes how scared he is of losing me. He does care, after all. He really does.

Slowly, Logan holds out his gun with an open palm, then gently places it down in the snow. My heart sinks.

"Let her go!" he commands.

"The food!" Rupert yells back, his breath hot in my ears. "Those sacks! Bring them to me! Now!"

Logan slowly walks to the back of the truck, reaches in, takes out the four heavy sacks, and walks towards the man.

"Place them on the ground!" Rupert yells. "Slowly!"

Slowly, Logan places them down the ground.

In the distance, I hear the whine of the slaverunners' engines, getting closer. I can't believe it, how stupid I was. Everything is falling apart, right before my eyes.

Bree gets out of the truck.

"Let my sister go!" she screams at him.

That is when I see the future unraveling before my eyes. I see what will happen. Rupert will slice my throat, then take Logan's gun and kill him and Bree. Then Ben and Rose. He will take our food and our boat and be gone.

His killing me is one thing. But his harming Bree is another matter. That is something I cannot allow.

Suddenly, I snap. Images of my dad flash through my mind, of his toughness, of the hand-to-hand combat moves he drilled into me. Pressure points. Strikes. Locks. How to get out of almost anything. How to bring a man to his knees with a single finger. And how to get a knife off your throat.

I summon some ancient reflex, and let my body take over. I raise my inner elbow up six inches, and bring it straight back, aiming for his solar plexus.

I make sharp impact, right where I wanted to. His knife digs into my throat a bit more, scratching it, and it hurts.

But the same time, I hear him gasp, and realize my strike worked.

I take a step forward, pull his arm away from my throat, and do a back kick, hitting him hard between the legs.

He stumbles back a few feet, and collapses in the snow.

I breathe deep, gasping, my throat killing me. Logan dives for his gun.

I turn and see Rupert hit the ground running, racing for our boat. He takes three big steps and leaps right to the center of it. In the same motion, he reaches over and cuts the line holding the boat to shore. It all happens in the blink of an eye; I can't believe how quickly he moves.

Ben stands there, dazed and confused, not knowing how to react. Rupert, on the other hand, doesn't hesitate: he leaps towards Ben and punches him hard across the face with his free hand.

Ben stumbles and is knocked over, and before he can get up, Rupert grabs him from behind in a chokehold, and holds the knife to his throat.

He turns and faces us, using Ben as a human shield. Inside the boat, Rose is cowering and screaming, and Penelope barks like crazy.

"You shoot me and you take him out, too!" Rupert screams.

Logan has his gun back, and he stands there, taking aim. But it is not an easy shot. The boat drifts farther from shore, a good fifteen yards away, bobbing wildly in the rough tide. Logan has about a two inch radius to take him out without killing Ben. Logan hesitates, and I can see he doesn't want to risk killing Ben, not even for our own survival. It is a redeeming quality.

"The keys!" Rupert yells at Ben.

Ben, to his credit, has at least done something right: he must have hid the keys somewhere when he saw Rupert coming. Smart move.

In the distance, I suddenly see the slaverunners come into view, as the whine of their engines grows louder. I feel a deepening sense of dread, of helplessness. I don't know what to do. Our boat is too far from shore to get to it now—and even if we could, Rupert might kill Ben in the process.

Penelope barks and jumps out of Rose's hands, race across the boat, and dig her teeth into Rupert's calf.

He screams and momentarily lets go of Ben.

A gunshot rings out. Logan found his chance, and wasted no time.

It is a clean shot, right between the eyes. Rupert stares back at us for a moment as the bullet enters his brain, wide-eyed. Then he slumps back, on the edge of the boat, as if sitting down, and falls over backwards, landing in the water with a splash.

It is over.

"Get our boat back to shore!" Logan screams to Ben. "NOW!"

Ben, still dazed, jumps into action. He fishes the keys out of his pocket, starts the boat, and steers it back toward shore. I grab two sacks of food and Logan grabs the others, and we throw them in the boat as it touches shore. I grab Bree and hoist her into the boat, then run back to the truck. Logan grabs my sacks of salvaged supplies, and I grab Sasha. Then, remembering, I run back to the truck and grab Rupert's bow and arrows. The last one in, I jump from the shore into the boat, as it starts to drift away. Logan takes over the wheel, hits the throttle and guns it, steering us out of the small channel.

We race towards the entrance to the Hudson, a few hundred yards ahead of us. On the horizon, the slaverunners' boat—sleek, black, menacing—races towards us, maybe half a mile away. It's going to be tight. It looks like we'll barely get out of the channel in time, and barely have a chance to make a run for it. They'll be right behind us.

We burst out into the Hudson just as it's getting dark and as we do, the slaverunners come into full view. They are barely a hundred yards behind us, and closing in fast. Behind them, on the horizon, I also spot the other boat, though that is still a good mile away.

I'm sure that if we had more time, Logan would say *I told you so.* And he would be right.

Just as I'm thinking these thoughts, suddenly, gunshots ring out. Bullets whiz by us, one impacting the side of our boat, shattering wood. Rose and Bree scream out.

"Get down!" I scream.

I lunge to Bree and Rose, grab them and throw them down to the ground. Logan, to his credit, doesn't flinch, and continues to drive the boat. He swerves a little but doesn't lose control. He crouches down low as he steers, trying to avoid bullets as he also tries to avoid the large chunks of ice beginning to form.

I take a knee in the back of the boat, raising my head only as high as I need to, and take aim, military style, with my handgun. I aim for the driver, and fire several shots.

They all miss, but I do manage to get their boat to swerve.

"Take the wheel!" Logan yells to Ben.

Ben, to his credit, doesn't hesitate. He hurries forward and takes the wheel; the boat swerves as he does.

Logan then hurries to my side, taking a knee beside me.

He fires and his bullets just miss, grazing off their boat. They return fire, and a bullet misses my head by inches. They're closing in fast.

Another bullet shatters a large chunk of wood off the back of our boat.

"They're going for our gas tank!" Logan screams out. "Go for theirs!"

"Where is it?" I scream out over the roar of the engine and flying bullets.

"In the back of their boat, on the left side!" he yells.

"I can't get a clean shot at it," I say. "Not while they're facing us."

Suddenly, I have an idea.

"Ben!" I scream out. "You need to make them turn. We need a clean shot at the gas tank!"

Ben doesn't hesitate; I've barely finished speaking the words when he turns hard on the wheel, the force of it throwing me sideways in the boat.

The slaverunners turn, too, trying to follow us. And that exposes the side of their boat.

I take a knee, as does Logan, and we fire several times.

At first, our barrage of fire misses.

Come on. Come on!

I think of my dad. I steady my wrist, breathe deep, and take one more shot.

To my surprise, I land a direct hit.

The slaverunners' boat suddenly explodes. The half dozen slaverunners on it burst into flames, shrieking as the boat speeds out of control. Seconds later, it smashes head on into the shoreline.

Another huge explosion. Their boat sinks quickly, and if anyone survived, they are surely drowning in the Hudson.

Ben turns us back upriver, keeping us going straight; slowly, I rise and take a deep breath. I can hardly believe it. We killed them.

"Nice shot," Logan says.

But it's not time to rest on our laurels. On the horizon, closing in, is another boat. I doubt we'll be so lucky a second time.

"I'm out of ammo," I say.

"I'm almost out, too," Logan says.

"We can't confront the next boat," I say. "And we're not fast enough to outrun them."

"What do you suggest?" he asks.

"We have to hide."

I turn to Ben.

"Find us shelter. Do it now. We have to hide this boat. NOW!"

Ben guns it and I run up to the front, standing beside him, scanning the river for any possible hiding spot. Maybe, if we're lucky, they'll zoom right past us.

Then again, maybe not.

FOUR

We all scan the horizon desperately, and finally, on the right, we spot a narrow inlet. It leads into the rusted shell of an old boat terminal.

"There, on the right!" I say to Ben.

"What if they see us?" he asks. "There's no way out. We'll be stuck. They'll kill us."

"That's a chance we have to take," I say.

Ben picks up speed, making a sharp turn into the narrow inlet. We race past the rusted gates, the narrow entryway of an old, rusted warehouse. As we pass through he cuts the engine, then turns to the left, hiding us behind the shoreline, as we bob in the water. I watch the wake we left in the moonlight, and pray it calms enough for the slaverunners to miss our trail.

We all sit anxiously in the silence, bobbing in the water, watching, waiting. The roar of the slaverunners' engine grows louder, and I hold my breath.

Please, God. Let them pass us by.

The seconds seem to last hours.

Finally, their boat whizzes past us, not slowing for a second.

I hold my breath for ten more seconds as their engine noise grows faint, praying that they don't come back our way.

They don't. It worked.

*

Nearly an hour has passed since we pulled in here, all of us huddled together, shell-shocked, in our boat. We barely move for fear of being detected. But I haven't heard a sound since, and haven't detected any activity since their boat passed us. I wonder where they went. Are they still racing up the Hudson, heading north in the blackness, still thinking we're just around the bend? Or have they wised up and are they circling back, combing the shores, looking for us? I can't help but feel that it will only be a matter of time until they come back our way.

But as I stretch out on the boat, I think we are all starting to feel a little bit more relaxed, a little bit less cautious. We are well hidden here, inside this rusted structure, and even if they circle back, I don't see how the slaverunners could possibly spot us.

My legs and feet are cramped from sitting, it's gotten much colder out, and I'm freezing. I can see by Bree and Rose's chattering teeth that they're freezing, too. I wish I had blankets or clothes to give them, or warmth of some sort. I wish we could build a fire—not just for warmth, but also to be able to see each other, to take comfort in each other's faces. But I know that's out of the question. It would be far too risky.

I see Ben sitting there, huddle over, shaking, and remember the pants I salvaged. I stand, the boat rocking as I do, and take a few steps over to my sack and reach in and pull them out. I toss them to Ben.

They land on his chest and he looks over at me, confused.

"They should fit," I say. "Try them on."

He's wearing tattered jeans, covered in holes, way too thin, and dampened with water. Slowly, he bends over and pries off his boots, then slides the leather pants on over his jeans. They look funny on him, the military pants of the slaverunner—but as I suspected, they are a perfect fit. He zips them up wordlessly as he leans back, and I can see the gratitude in his eyes.

I feel Logan looking over at me, and I feel as if he's jealous of my friendship with Ben. He's been like that ever since he saw Ben kiss me back at Penn Station. It's awkward, but there's nothing I can do about it. I like them both, in different ways. I've never met two more opposite people—yet somehow, they remind me of each other.

I go over to Bree, still shivering, huddled together with Rose, Penelope in her lap, and I sit beside her, drape an arm over her and kiss her forehead. She leans her head into my shoulder.

"It's okay Bree," I say.

"I'm hungry," she says in a soft voice.

"Me too," Rose echoes.

Penelope whimpers softly, and I can tell she is hungry, too. She is smarter than any dog I've ever met. And brave, despite her quivering. I can't believe she bit Rupert when she did; if it weren't for her, maybe we all wouldn't be here. I lean over and stroke her head, and she licks my hand back.

Now that they mention food, I realize it's a good idea. I've been trying to avoid my hunger pangs for way too long.

"You're right," I say. "Let's eat."

They both look at me with eyes wide open in hope and expectation. I stand, cross the boat, and reach into one of the sacks. I take out two large mason jars of raspberry jam and hand one to Bree, unscrewing it for her.

"You guys share this jar," I say to them. "The three of us will share the other."

I open the other jar and pass it to Logan, and he reaches in with his finger, takes a large amount, and puts it in his mouth. He breathes deeply with satisfaction—he must have been starving.

I hand it out to Ben, who takes one, too, then I reach in and scoop a fingerful and place it on my tongue. I get a sugar rush as the raspberry fills my senses, and it is quite possibly the best thing I've ever tasted. I know this is not a meal, but it feels like one.

I seem to be the keeper of food, so I head back to the bags and take out what's left of our cookies and hand one to each person, including myself. I look over and see Bree and Rose happily eating the jam; with every other fingerful, they give Penelope one. She licks their fingers like crazy, whining as she does. The poor thing must be as hungry as we are.

"They'll be back, you know," comes the ominous voice beside me.

I turn and see Logan sitting back, cleaning out his gun, looking at me.

"You know that, right?" he presses. "We're sitting ducks here."

"What do you propose?" I ask.

He shrugs and looks away, disappointed.

"We never should've stopped. We should've kept going, like I said."

"Well, it's too late now," I shoot back, irritated. "Stop complaining."

I'm getting tired of his gloom and doom at every turn, getting tired of our power struggle. I resent having him around, as much as I appreciate him at the same time.

"None of our options are good," he says. "If we head upriver tonight, we might run into them. Might ruin the boat. Maybe hit floating ice, maybe something else. Worse, they'd probably catch us. If we leave in the morning, they can see us in the light. We'd be able to navigate, but they might be waiting."

"So let's leave in the morning," I say. "At the crack of dawn. We'll head north and hope they circled back and went south."

"And what if they didn't?" he asks.

"You got any better ideas? We have to head away from the city, not towards it. Besides, Canada's North, isn't it?"

He turns and looks away, and sighs.

"We could stay put," he says. "Wait it out a few days. Make sure they pass us first."

"In this weather? If we don't get shelter, we'll freeze to death. And we'll be out of food by then. We can't stay here. We have to keep moving."

"Oh, now you want to keep moving," he says.

I glare back at him—he is really beginning to get on my nerves.

"Fine," he says. "Let's leave at dawn. In the meantime, if we're going to stay the night here, we need to stand guard. In shifts. I'll go first, then you, then Ben. You guys sleep now. None of us have slept, and we all need to. Deal?" he asks, looking back and forth from me to Ben.

"Deal," I say. He's right.

Ben doesn't respond, still looking out into space, lost in his own world.

"Hey," Logan says roughly, leaning back and kicking his foot, "I'm talking to you. *Deal?*"

Ben slowly turns and looks at him, still looking out of it, then nods. But I can't tell if he's really heard him. I feel so bad for Ben; it's like he's not really here. Clearly, he's consumed by grief and guilt for his brother. I can't even imagine what he's going through.

"Good," Logan says. He checks his ammo, cocks his gun, then jumps off the boat, onto the dock beside us. The boat rocks, but doesn't drift away. Logan stands on the dry dock, surveying our surroundings. He takes a seat on a wooden post and stares into the blackness, his gun rested on his lap.

I settle in beside Bree, wrapping my arm around her. Rose leans in, too, and I wrap my arm around them both.

"You guys get some rest. We'll have a long day ahead of us tomorrow," I say, secretly wondering if this will be our last night on earth. Wondering if there will even be a tomorrow.

"Not until I take care of Sasha," Bree says.

Sasha. I almost forgot.

I look over and see the frozen corpse of our dog at the far side of the boat. I can hardly believe that we brought her here. Bree is one loyal master.

Bree gets up, silently crosses the boat, and stands over Sasha. She kneels down and strokes her head. Her eyes well up in the moonlight.

I walk over and kneel down beside her. I stroke Sasha, too, forever grateful to her for protecting us.

"Can I help you bury her?" I ask.

Bree nods, still looking down, a tear falling.

Together, we reach down, pick up Sasha, and lean forward with her over the side of the boat. We both hold her there, neither of us wanting to let her go. I look down into the freezing, dark water of the Hudson below, waves bobbing.

"Do you want to say anything?" I ask, "before we let her go?"

Bree looks down, blinking away tears, her face lit up by the moonlight. She looks angelic.

"She was a good dog. She saved my life. I hope she's in a better place now. And I hope I see her again," she says, her voice breaking.

We reach all the way over, and gently place Sasha in. With a light splash, her body hits the water. If floats there for a second or two, then begins to sink. The tides of the Hudson are strong, and they quickly pull it out, towards the open water. We watch as she bobs, half-submerged, in the moonlight, drifting father and farther away. I feel my heart breaking. It reminds me how close I came to having Bree taken from me for good, to being washed away down the Hudson, just like Sasha.

*

I don't know how many hours have passed. It is now late in the night, and I lay there in the boat, curled up around Bree and Rose, thinking, unable to sleep. None of us have said a word since we set Sasha into to the water. We all just sit there in the grim silence, the boat rocking softly. A few feet from us sits Ben, also lost in his own world. He seems more dead than alive; sometimes when I look at him, I feel as if I'm looking at a walking ghost. It's odd: we're all sitting here together, yet we're all worlds apart.

Logan is about ten yards away, dutifully on guard on the pier, gun in hand as he looks around. I can imagine him as a soldier. I'm glad to have him protecting us, working the first shift. I'm tired, my bones are weary, and I'm not looking forward to taking over the next shift. I know I should be sleeping, but I can't. Lying there, with Bree in my arms, my mind races.

I think of what a crazy, crazy world it is out there now. I can hardly believe this is all real. It's like one long nightmare that won't end. Every time I think I'm safe, something happens. Thinking back, I can hardly believe how close I just came to getting killed by Rupert. It was so stupid of me to take pity on him, to let him ride with us. I still can't quite understand why he freaked out. What had he hoped to gain? Was he that desperate that he would kill all of us, take our boat and disappear—just to have more food for himself? And where would he have taken it? Was he just evil? Psychotic? Or was he a good man, and had all those years of being alone and starving and freezing just made him snap?

I want to believe it's the latter, that he was, deep down, a good man just made crazy by circumstance. I hope so. But I'll never know.

I close my eyes and think of how close I came to getting killed, feel the cold metal of his knife against my throat. Next time, I will trust no one. Stop for no one. Believe no one. I will do whatever I can to make sure that Bree and Rose and myself and the others survive. No more chances. No more risks. If that means becoming callous, then so be it.

Thinking back, I feel like every hour on the Hudson has been a life or death battle. I don't fathom how we will ever possibly make it all the way to Canada. I'd be amazed if we even survive the next few days, even the next few miles on the water. I know our chances aren't good. I hold Bree tight, knowing this may be our last night together. At least we'll go down fighting, on our own two feet, and not as slaves and prisoners.

"It was so scary," Brooks says.

Her voice startles me in the darkness. It is so soft, I wonder at first if she even spoke. She hasn't said a word for hours, and I thought she was asleep.

I turn and see her eyes are open, staring out with fear.

"What was scary, Bree?"

She shakes her head and waits several seconds before speaking. I realize she is remembering.

"They took me. I was all alone. Then they put me on a bus, and took me on a boat. We were all chained together. It was so cold, we were all so scared. They took me inside that house, and you wouldn't believe the things I saw. What they did to those other girls. I can still hear their screams. I can't get them out of my head."

Her face crumples as she starts to cry.

My heart breaks into a million pieces. I can't even imagine what she's been through. I don't want her to think about it. I feel as if she's scarred forever, and it's my fault.

I hug her tightly, and kiss her on the forehead.

"Shhh," I whisper. "It's all right. That's all behind us now. Don't think about that anymore."

But still, she continues to cry.

Bree buries her face my chest. I rock her as she cries and cries.

"I'm so sorry honey," I say. "I am so so sorry."

I wish I could take it all away from her. But I can't. It is now a part of her. I always wanted to shelter her, to shelter her from everything. And now her heart is filled with horrors.

As I rock her, I wish we could be anywhere but here. I wish things could be how they once were. Back in time. Back when the world was good. Back with our parents. But we can't. We're here.

And I have a sinking feeling things will only get worse.

*

I wake and realize it is daytime. I don't know how it got so late in the day, or how I slept so long. I look around me on the boat, and am completely disoriented. I don't understand what's happening. Our boat is now floating, adrift in the Hudson, in the middle of the huge river. Bree and I are the only ones in the boat. I don't know where everyone else is, and I can't understand how we got here.

We both stand at the edge of the boat, looking out at the horizon, and I see three slaverunner boats speed right for us.

I try to burst into action, but feel my arms bound from behind. I turn to see several slaverunners on the boat, see that they have cuffed me from behind, hold me back. I struggle for all I can, but am helpless.

A slaverunner boat stops and one of them gets out, his mask covering his face, steps onto our boat, reaches down and grabs Bree. She squirms, but is no match for him. He picks her up in one arm and begins to carry her away.

"BREE! NO!" I scream.

I struggle with everything in the world, but it is useless. I'm forced to stand there and watch as they drag Bree off, kicking and screaming into their boat. Their boat drifts away on the current, towards Manhattan. Soon, it is barely visible.

As I watch my little sister get farther and farther away from me, I know that this time I lost her for good.

I shriek, an unearthly shriek, begging, crying, for my sister to come back to me.

I wake up sweating. I sit bolt upright, breathing hard, looking all around, trying to figure out what happened.

It was a dream. I look over and see Bree lying beside me, everyone else asleep in the boat. It was all a dream. No one has come. No one has taken Bree.

I try to slow my breathing, my heart still pounding. I sit up and look out at the horizon and see dawn beginning to break, a faint sliver on the horizon. I look over at the dock, and see Ben sitting guard. I think back and remember Logan waking me, remember standing guard myself. Then I woke Ben, gave him the gun, and he took my position. I must have fallen asleep after that.

As I look over at Ben, I realize he is slumped over. I can see from here, in the faint light of dawn, that he is asleep, too. He is supposed to be standing guard. We are defenseless.

Suddenly, I spot movement, shadows in the darkness. It looks like a group of people, or creatures, heading closer to us. I wonder if my eyes are playing tricks on me.

But then, my heart starts pounding furiously in my chest, and my mouth goes dry, as I realize this is not a trick of the light.

We are unprepared. And people are ambushing us.

FIVE

"BEN!" I scream, sitting up.

But it's too late. A second later, they charge us.

One has overtaken Ben, tackling him, while the other two take a running jump right into our boat.

The boat rocks violently as they man our craft.

Logan wakes, but not in time. One of the men goes right for him, knife drawn, and is about to plunge it into his chest.

My reflexes kick in. I reach back, grab the knife from my waist, lean forward and throw it. The knife goes flying end over end.

It is a perfect strike. It lodges right into the man's throat, a second before he stabs Logan. He collapses, lifeless, on top of him.

Logan sits up and throws the corpse off, and it lands in the water with a splash. Luckily, he has the presence of mind to remove my knife before he does.

Two more come charging my way. With the light picking up, I can see that they are not men: they are mutants. Half men, half I don't know what. Radiated from the war. Crazies. This terrifies me: these types, unlike Rupert, are super strong, super vicious, and have nothing to lose.

One of them heads for Bree and Rose, and I can't let him. I dive for him, tackling him to the ground.

We both go down hard, the boat rocking wildly. I see Logan out of the corner of my eye diving on top of the other, bumping him hard and splashing him overboard.

We have stopped two of them. But a third one races past us.

The one I tackle spins me around and pins me down. He is on top of me, and he is strong. He reaches back and punches me hard in the face, and I feel the sting on my cheek.

I think quick: I raise a knee hard and slam it right between his legs.

It is a perfect strike. He groans and slumps, and as he does, I reach back and elbow him hard across the face. There's a cracking noise as I break cheekbone, and he collapses in the boat.

I hurl him overboard, into the water. It was a stupid move. I should've stripped him of his weapons first. The boat swings wildly as his body leaves.

I now turn to the last one, at the same time Logan does.

But neither of us are quick enough. He races past us, and for some reason, charges right for Bree.

Penelope leaps into the air and, snarling, digs her teeth into his wrist.

He shakes her like a ragdoll, trying to get her off. Penelope hangs on, but finally he gives her a violent shake and sends her flying across the boat.

Before I can reach him, he is about to descend on Bree. My heart stops as I realize I won't make it in time.

Rose jumps up to save Bree and gets in the way of the man's attack. He picks Rose up, leans over and sinks his teeth into her arm.

Rose lets out an unearthly shriek as he tears her flesh with his teeth. It is a sickening, awful site, one that will lodge in my mind forever.

The man leans back, about to bite her again—but now I catch him in time. I pull the spare knife from my pocket, reach back and prepare to throw it.

But before I do, Logan steps up, takes steady aim with his pistol, and fires.

Blood splatters everywhere as he shoots the man in the back of the head. He collapses down to the boat and Logan steps forward and hurls his corpse overboard.

I rush forward to Rose, hysterically shrieking, hardly knowing how to comfort her. I tear off a strip of my shirt and quickly wrap it around her profusely bleeding arm, trying to staunch the blood as best I can.

I detect motion out of the corner of my eye, and realize a crazy has Ben pinned down on the pier. He leans back, about to take a bite out of Ben's throat. I turn and throw my knife. It flies end over end and lodges in the back of the man's neck. His body goes still, as he slumps over to the ground.

Ben sits up, dazed.

"Back in the boat!" Logan yells. "NOW!"

I hear the anger in Logan's voice, and I feel it, too. Ben was on guard and he fell asleep. He left us all open to attack.

Ben stumbles back into the boat and as he does, Logan reaches over with his knife and cuts the rope. As I take care of Rose, shrieking in my arms, Logan takes the wheel, starting up the boat and hitting the throttle.

We gun it out of the channel in the breaking dawn. He's right to take off. Those gunshots might have alerted someone; who knows how much time we have now.

We tear out of the channel into the purple light of day, leaving several bodies floating behind us. Our place of shelter has quickly transformed into a place of horrors, and I hope I never see it again.

We race again down the center of the Hudson, the boat bobbing as Logan guns it. I am on guard, looking in every direction for any sign of slaverunners. If they are anywhere near us, there is nowhere left to hide: the sounds of the gunshots, of Rose's shrieking, and of a roaring engine hardly make us inconspicuous.

I just pray that at some point during the night they circled back looking for us and are farther south than we are; if so, they are somewhere behind us. If not, we will run right into them.

If we are really lucky, they gave up and turned all the way back and headed back to Manhattan. But somehow I doubt that. We've never been that lucky.

Like those crazies. That was just a stroke of bad luck to park there. I've heard rumors of predatory gangs of crazies turned cannibals, who survive by eating others, but I never believed it. I still can hardly believe it's true.

I hold Rose tight, blood seeping through her wound, onto my hand, rocking her, trying to console her. Her impromptu bandage is already red, so I tear a new piece off my shirt, my stomach exposed to the freezing cold, and replace her bandage. It is hardly hygienic, but is better than nothing, and I have to staunch the blood somehow. I wish I had medicine, antibiotics, or at least painkillers—anything I could give her. As I pull off the soaking bandage, I see the chunk of missing flesh on her arm, and I look away, trying not to think of the pain she must be going through. It is horrific.

Penelope sits on her lap, whining, looking up at her, clearly wanting to help, too. Bree looks traumatized once again, holding Rose's hand, trying to quiet her cries. But she is inconsolable.

I wish desperately I had a tranquilizer—*anything*. And then, suddenly, I remember. That bottle of champagne, half drunk. I hurry to the front of the boat, grab it, and race back to her.

"Drink this," I say.

Rose is hysterically crying, screaming in agony, and doesn't even acknowledge me.

I hold it to her lips and make her drink. She nearly chokes on it, spilling some out, but drinks a little.

"Please, Rose, drink. It will help."

I hold it again to her mouth, and in between her wails she takes a few more sips. I feel bad giving alcohol to a young child, but I'm hoping it will help numb her pain, and I don't know what else to do.

"I found pills," comes a voice.

I turn and see Ben, standing there, looking alert for the first time. The attack, what happened to Rose, must have snapped him out of it, maybe because he feels guilty for falling asleep on guard. He stands there, holding out a small container of pills.

I take it and examine it.

"I found it inside the cubby," he says. "I don't know what it is."

I read the label: Ambien. Sleeping pills. The slaverunners must have stashed this to help them sleep. The irony of it: there they are, keeping others awake all night, and stashing sleeping pills for themselves. But for Rose, this is perfect, exactly what we need.

I don't know how many to give her, but I need to calm her down. I hand her the champagne again, make sure she swallows it down, then give her two of them. I stash the rest in my pocket, so they won't get lost, then keep a close watch on Rose.

Within minutes, the booze and pills begin to take effect. Slowly, her wails become cries, then these become muffled. After about twenty minutes, her eyes begin to slump, and she falls asleep in my arms.

I give it another ten minutes, to make sure she's asleep, then look over at Bree.

"Can you hold her?" I ask.

Bree hurries over to my side, and slowly I get up and place Rose in her arms instead.

I stand, my legs cramped, and walk to the front of the boat, beside Logan. We continue to race upriver, the sky breaking, and as I look out at the water, I don't like what I see.

Small chunks of ice are beginning to form in the Hudson in this freezing morning. I can hear them pinging off the boat. This is the last thing we need.

But it gives me an idea. I lean over the boat, water spraying me in the face, and put my hands in the freezing water. It is painful to the touch, but I force my hand all the way, trying to grab a small chunk of ice as we go. We are going too fast, though, and it's hard to grab one. I keep missing by a few inches.

Finally, after a minute agony, I catch one. I lift my hand, shaking from the cold, rush over, and hand the ice to Bree.

She takes it, wide-eyed.

"Hold this," I say.

I go back and take the other bandage, the bloody one, and wrap the ice in it. I hand it to Bree.

"Hold this against her wound."

I am hoping it will help numb her pain, maybe stop the swelling.

I turn my attention back to the river and look around, on all sides, as the morning becomes increasingly bright. We are racing farther and farther north, and I'm relieved to see no signs of the slaverunners anywhere. I hear no engines and detect no movement on either side of the river. The silence is, in fact, ominous. Are they waiting for us?

I come up to the passenger seat, beside Logan, and glance down at the gas tank. Less than a quarter tank. It doesn't bode well.

"Maybe they're gone," I venture. "Maybe they turned back, gave up the search."

"Don't count on it," he says.

As if on cue, suddenly, I hear the roar of an engine. My heart stops. It is a sound I'd recognize anywhere in the world: their engine.

I turn to the back of the boat and look out at the horizon: sure enough, there, about a mile away, are the slaverunners. They are racing towards us. I watch them come, feeling helpless. We are nearly out of ammo, and they are well-equipped and well manned, with tons of weapons and ammunition. We don't stand a chance if we fight them, and we don't stand a chance of outrunning them: they are already closing in. We can't try to hide again, either.

We have no choice but to confront them. And that would be a losing battle. It is like a death sentence racing towards us on the horizon.

"Maybe we should surrender!" Ben yells out, looking back, terrified.

"Never," I say.

I can't imagine becoming their prisoner again.

"If I go down, it's as a dead man," Logan echoes.

I try to think, pressing my mind for any solution.

"Can't you go any faster!?" I press Logan, as I watch them close the gap.

"I'm going as fast as I can!" he shouts back, over the roar of the engine.

I don't know what else to do. I feel so helpless. Rose is awake now, wailing again, and Penelope barks. I feel as if the whole world is closing in on me. If I don't think quick, come up with some solution, we will all be dead in minutes.

I scan the boat, looking for any weapons, anything at all, that I can use.

Come on. Come on.

Suddenly, I spot something, and I get a crazy idea. It is so crazy, I realize, that it might just work.

Without hesitating, I jump into action. I run across the boat, going right for the huge ball of zip line I salvaged from my dad's house. I immediately start to untangle it.

"Help me!" I yell sharply to Ben.

He hurries over and together, we begin to loosen and untangle the hundreds of yards of zip line.

"Hold that end," I say. "I'll hold this end. Loop by loop, straighten it out as much as you can."

"What are you doing?" Logan screams, looking back.

"I have an idea," I say. I look straight ahead, and see the river narrowing. It's perfect. From one shore to the next is barely a hundred yards. I looked down at the huge ball of line, and guesstimate it must be at least twice that.

"If I can tie the line shore to shore before they reach us, we can snag them in it. Like a tripwire. It's risky, but I think it just might work."

"It's not like we have any options," he says. "Let's do it."

Finally, I feel like he's stopped arguing and is on my team.

"I need you to turn the boat, all the way over to one shore," I yell as I finish unraveling.

I scour the horizon, examining the shorelines, looking for something to secure the line to. I see a rusted metal post, dug into the shoreline where a pier used to be.

"There!" I scream to Logan. "That metal post!"

Logan makes a hard turn, doing as I ask, rushing right for the metal post. At least now, finally, he trusts my judgment.

I hurry to the front of the boat as Logan pulls up deftly beside the post. I grab one end of the line, reach over, and wrap it around the metal post, several times, forming a tight knot. I yank on it hard, testing it. It's secure.

"Now the other side!" I yell.

Logan hits the throttle, and we race straight across, to the other side of the river. As we do, I push Bree out of the way of the quickly unraveling line; I don't want her to get hurt.

I grab the very end of the line as it unravels like crazy, not wanting it to go overboard. We reach the other shore, and luckily, the line is long enough and there's plenty of room to spare.

As Logan pulls up, I grab the end of the line and jump out onto the sand, searching frantically for something to secure it to. I spot a tree, close to the water's edge. I hurry to it and loop the line around, pulling tight. I turn and see it rise up, out of the water. Perfect. Then I loosen it, so that the line drops down, and is resting on the surface of the water. I don't want the slaverunners to see it.

I jump back into the boat, keeping the line slack. There's is probably about fifty yards to spare on it.

I check over my shoulder and see the slaverunners are closing in fast. They're probably only a quarter-mile off. I hope they don't realize what I'm doing. It looks like they're just far enough away not to.

"Drive forward!" I yell to Logan. "But slowly, and not too far. Only about fifty yards. Then kill the engine. Let the boat stop, right out in the open."

"Kill it?" Logan asks.

"Trust me," I say.

He listens. He moves us forward slowly, out back into the middle of the Hudson. As he goes, the remainder of the line continues to unravel on the boat. When it's near done, I scream out, "STOP!"

Logan kills it, and there is an eerie silence. We all sit there, bobbing, turning and looking at the oncoming slaverunners. They are only a few hundred yards away.

"Take off your pants!" I yell at Ben.

He looks at me, confused.

"Now! Hurry!"

He quickly slides his leather pants off his jeans, the ones I gave him the other night, then hands them to me. I wrap them tightly around my hands, using them as a glove, so that the line won't tear off my skin.

Finally, Logan realizes what I'm doing. He hurries over, takes off his own jacket, wraps it around his hands, too, and together, the two of us hold the slack line, waiting.

I tremble as we watch the horizon. They are getting closer and closer, racing for us at full speed. I see them raise their guns. I hope they don't realize something is up.

"Ben, hold up your hands, as if you're surrendering!"

Ben steps forward and holds his hands high above his head. It works. The slaverunners lower their guns, conferring with each other.

But they don't cut back speed. They still come racing right for us. They don't see the line, sitting slack in the water. They have no idea.

As they get closer and closer to my line, I am sweating. I hold the slack line, trembling, Logan beside me. Waiting. They are twenty yards away from where the line sits in the water.

Please don't figure it out. Please don't stop. Please.

They are ten yards off. Five.

We only get one shot at this, and it needs to work perfectly. The line needs to raise to just the right height.

"NOW!" I scream to Logan.

At the same time, we both hoist the line.

The zip line jumps up, rising up out of the water and into the air, about eight feet. It is the perfect height.

The line rises right to the chest level of the slaverunners standing in the boat. It makes impact, cutting right into them, and as it does, I feel a tremendous tug on the force of the line. We hold it with all we have as it cuts right through them.

All five of them go flying off the boat, right into the water.

The boat continues speeding forward on its own without them for another fifty yards before it spins out-of-control and smashes right into a large outcropping of rock. With a horrific crash, it smashes into pieces, then bursts into flames.

Meanwhile, all the slaverunners bob in the freezing water, flailing.

I can't believe it. It worked. It actually worked.

Logan and I look at each other, amazed. We slowly drop the line.

Logan hurries back to the wheel, hits the throttle, and we're off.

I hear the screams of the slaverunners behind us, flailing in the water, crying for help, as we take off. A part of me feels bad. But I have learned my lesson—one too many times.

As we go, the sun rises, and for the first time in a while, I begin to relax again. There are no more boats behind us. For the first time in as long as I can remember, I'm beginning to think that we can really make it.

SIX

We continue up the Hudson, never slowing as morning morphs into late afternoon. Logan guns it hard, the roar of the engine ever-present, determined to get as far away from the slaverunners, from Manhattan, as possible. The entire morning I am on edge, looking and listening for any signs of anything.

But after more time passes, I begin to relax. Logan finally slows us just a bit, to cruising mode, and the engine quiets. I look over and see Rose, now fast asleep in Bree's arms. Bree leans back herself, eyes closed, Penelope in her lap. Ben sits slumped over, head in his hands. And Logan just stares, eyes fixed on the water, expressionless as always. The entire energy on our boat is more relaxed.

Logan slows the boat even more, and I wonder why, when I look out at the water and see huge chunks of ice. They become larger and more frequent as we go. Logan is slowing to avoid them, and he swerves us left and right constantly, weaving in and out. All of this ice concerns me, especially as I feel a bitter wind cut into my bones, feel it grow colder with every minute. The sky, bright just hours ago, is now thick and grey. In fact, a fog is even beginning to settle on the water. I feel a storm coming.

Suddenly, flakes of snow began to fall from the sky. They are large, soft flakes, and they feel reassuring as they land on my cheek, as if something is still pure in the world, still working as it should. They make me think of childhood, of happier times, when I loved the snow. When it meant no school, playing with my friends. Now, though, it just means being colder, wetter. Now, it is just an inconvenience.

Within minutes, the snow becomes blinding, whipping into our faces, whiting out the sky. It becomes hard to even see.

Logan slows even more, and I wonder if we are out of gas. I hurry over and stand beside him and glance at the gauge: less than an eighth of a tank, but not redlining yet. I don't understand why he's slowing, until I look up ahead and see it for myself: there, before us, sits an island in the middle of the Hudson. It's not huge but it's not tiny either: maybe a half mile long and half as wide. It's long and narrow, ringed by a sandy shore, and covered in thick trees, many of which are pine, covered in snow. I see Logan staring and I know what he's thinking. He turns and looks at me.

"We're nearly out of gas," he says. "And riding in this storm is asking for trouble. The ice is getting thicker and the river is hardening. We continue like this, we might sink her. And it will be dark soon. We can push it, or we can park on this island, wait it out here until the river thaws and the storm passes." He studies the skies. "If we push it, we might find ourselves out of gas and with no shelter. We know what happened last time we parked on the shoreline. Being on an island might be safer."

"I agree," I say. "It's safer."

He sighs.

"Not that I want to park," he continues. "I don't. We need to keep moving. We need to put as much distance between us and them as we can. We need to head north, and find fuel. But we have to ride out this storm. And I think an island is a safer place to do it. Maybe we stay a few hours. Maybe even overnight. Let it pass, then keep going. Who knows: maybe we'll even find something on it, maybe some hunting, or something to salvage."

"For once, I think we agree," I say, and can't help smiling.

Logan tries to suppress a smile, but I see it.

"Let's circle it," I say. "Make sure there's nothing hostile and find the best spot to dock."

"Agreed," he says.

Logan turns the boat, taking us around the perimeter of the island. It has a shallow shore, maybe ten feet deep, waves lapping lightly against it. Bordering the sand are thick trees, providing a nice shelter in every direction. As we come around the other side, I watch the trees closely, looking for any signs of movement. I see none. But then again, this island is deceptively big, and the trees are thick: there could be anything in there. I doubt, though, that there are any people. I don't see any evidence of it: no boats, no footprints. Maybe there could be animals in there. Maybe deer, or fox, or something else. My mouth waters at the thought.

We circle around the other side, nearly finishing our loop, when I spot a perfect place to dock the boat: an outcropping of rock juts out into the water, along which we could tie the boat and have it protected from the elements on two sides. Even better, the rock continues onto the land, morphing into a small mountain, inside of which is a large opening for a cave. It couldn't be more perfect: we can take shelter in that cave to wait out the wind and the storm—all while keeping an eye on our boat.

I reach out and point at it.

"I'm on it," Logan says. "One step ahead of you."

He cuts the engine as we get closer and we drift for the rock, out boat turned sideways. I grab the rope, head to the bow and jump off as we reach the shore. I land up to my ankles in the icy water, and it stings as it cuts through my leather boots. But I'm happy to be back on land, and I waste no time in grabbing the boat and yanking it up on the sand. Logan jumps out and helps, and together, we manage to yank it up a good five feet onto the sand. I tie the rope securely around the anchor hole in the front of the boat, then hand it to Logan, who finds a notch in the rock around which to wrap it. He tries it several times: it's secure. Our boat's not going anywhere.

The lack of movement finally snaps Ben out of it, and he lifts up his head and looks around for the first time. He looks at me, bleary-eyed.

"Where are we?" he asks.

"Our new home," Logan says.

"Until the storm passes," I add.

For a moment I wonder if Ben is going to argue, to voice a different opinion, maybe be mad at us for deciding without him. But he just gets up meekly out of the boat. His spirit is broken, and he barely seems to know where he is.

I jump back in the boat, hurry over to Bree and Rose. They are fast asleep and I gently wake Bree. As her eyes open, she immediately looks not at me, but at Rose, fear and worry etched into her face.

I examine Rose myself, and am equally afraid. She does not look good. She's paler than I've seen her, and while I know she's asleep, I can't help feeling that her face looks like that of a dying person. I look down at her arm, at her bandage, and already see large blotches of red forming on either side of the bite. It is infected—and spreading fast.

I swallow hard, my mouth dry, knowing this is not good. I feel so helpless. I wish there was something I could do, somewhere I could take her. But there's nothing. Champagne and sleeping pills are, pathetically, all I have to offer her.

I reach down and pick Rose up in my arms. Penelope refuses to leave her lap, so I hold the two of them, carry them like a baby. Rose is limp and asleep. Thank God for that. I hope she's not feeling any pain right now.

Bree gets up and walks beside me. I hand Rose to Logan, then jump down and grab Bree, carrying her off the boat. The snow falls harder all around us. I watch Logan carry Rose into the cave and take Bree's hand and follow.

"Grab the other sacks, will you?" I say to Ben. I don't want him to be completely useless, if nothing else than for his own sake.

Ben does as he's told, reaching into the boat and grabbing the packs of food and supplies. I turn with Bree and walk across the soft sand, towards the cave.

"Will Rose be okay?" Bree asks. "Where are we?"

"We're on a small island," I say. "We're going to stay here until the storm passes."

"Until Rose gets better?" she asks.

I swallow hard, not knowing how to answer. I wish I knew myself.

"I'm going to do everything I can for her," I say. "I promise."

We reach the mouth of the cave and I am relieved to see it will be the perfect shelter for us. About 15 feet high and 30 feet deep, with a 10 foot ceiling, it is not so deep where I can't see where it ends. I can see there are no animals—or people—hiding inside. And as I walk in, it already feels several degrees warmer in here—maybe because of the shelter from the wind. I look down and see the dirt floors are dry, too, the snow stopping a few feet from the entrance.

I feel we can build a fire here. We are protected from the wind, and protected from the eyes of anyone who might be watching. It's the perfect place for us all to rest and recover and get our bearings.

Logan places Rose down gently on the earthen floor; he takes off his jacket and delicately rests it beneath her head. Watching him, it surprises me. I had no idea he could be so gentle.

Penelope stands on Rose's chest, on all fours, shaking. She curls up in a ball, lying down and pressing her chin on Rose's chest, looking up at her with sad eyes, refusing to leave her side.

"The infection is bad," Logan says softly as he hurries over to me. "She needs medicine."

"I know," I say. "What do you propose we do?"

He shakes his head grimly. "I don't know," he finally answers.

Ben enters with all the bags of food and supplies, and sets them down inside the cave. Logan turns away from him with a look of disgust, still pissed at him for falling asleep on guard.

At least here, in this cave, we will be safer. There won't be as much of a need to stand guard. There is practically no way anyone could ambush us here without approaching by boat. And that would make noise. The way I see it, if this island is truly deserted, then we have no worries. I turn to Logan.

"Before we settle in," I say, "we need to know that there's no one else on the island, waiting to surprise us. We should also scavenge this place, before the storm gets worse, to see if there are any remnants, any supplies we can find, maybe even some kind of medicine. Maybe there are even some animals here we could hunt—maybe we can find dinner."

"Good idea," he says. "But you shouldn't go alone." He turns and looks at Ben. "I'd go with you, but I can't. I need to stand guard. I'm not about to leave all of our stuff—and our boat—under Ben's watch."

He says it loud enough for Ben to here, but Ben, still out of it, doesn't react.

"You go," Logan adds, "and take Ben with you."

I turn to Ben, expecting him to argue, or be upset. But to my surprise, he doesn't. He looks like a broken man. He lowers his head.

"I'm sorry," he says softly. "I'm really sorry I fell asleep."

I can hear in his voice that he means it. He is so burdened by guilt—guilt for his brother, and now, for what's happened to Rose. It's painful to even look at him, and I'd rather go myself. But Logan's right: I should have company. And having him watch my back is better, I suppose, than nothing.

I turn to Logan.

"This place is not that big. We'll be back within the hour."

"If you're not, I can't go looking for you," he says, "without endangering the others."

"Don't come looking for me," I say. "If I'm not back, you know I'm dead. And in that case, take the girls and the boat and move on."

Logan nods back at me solemnly, and I can see respect in his eyes.

"You'll be back," he says.

*

Ben and I trudge across the barren island, the bow and arrow slung over my shoulder. I've never shot a bow and arrow before, and I'll probably be terrible at it, but I figure if I run across any kind of animal, I'll figure it out. Having it makes me not feel so bad for stopping for Rupert, if for no other reason than to have this weapon.

As we walk in silence, the snow pouring down all around us, the world is incredibly still. I hear only the sound of the snow crunching beneath our feet, and the distant lapping of the waves. The late afternoon sky is a solid gray. We've only been gone for ten minutes, and in that time, the fresh snow has reached my ankles.

I am on guard as we go, one hand on the knife on my belt. We've crossed half the length of the island, and still no sign of anything. This island is like a miniature forest, covered in thick trees, no signs of any structures or any people, or even of any recent activity. I'm feeling increasingly safe, increasingly at ease.

In the distance I spot the far tip of the island, and continue to work my way towards it, weaving in and out of clumps of trees. Once we reach it I'll be much relieved, knowing for sure that there's no one else here and that we can rest easy tonight. Yet at the same time, if I don't find any supplies, anything I can salvage, I'll be disappointed, knowing I'm returning empty-handed to Rose, who is laying there dying.

I scour the trees again, looking for any sign of food, of anything. I stop in my tracks, and Ben stops beside me. I stand there, listening, for several seconds. But all I hear is the deep sound of silence. I close my eyes and listen, and can hear the sound of the snowflakes falling, touching my skin, and beyond that, the very light lapping of the river against the shore. I wait sixty seconds. Still nothing. It is as if we are completely alone in a prehistoric universe.

"Why are we stopped?" Ben asks.

I open my eyes and continue walking. We walk in silence for several more minutes, heading towards the tip of the island.

The more we walk, the more I begin to wonder about Ben. I can't help wondering what exactly happened to him back there, in Manhattan. What happened to his brother. I wonder if I can get him to open up. It sure seems as if he needs to.

"Don't beat yourself up so much," I say to him, breaking the silence. "I mean, your falling asleep back there: it could happen to any of us."

"But it didn't. It happened to me," he shoots back. "It was my fault. It's my fault that Rose is hurt."

"Guilt and blame isn't going to help any of us now," I say. "Nobody's blaming you. I'm not."

He shrugs, looking forlorn, as we continue to walk in silence.

"Do you want to talk about it?" I finally ask, wanting to get it out in the open. "What happened to you in the city? Your brother? It might make you feel better to talk about it."

I watch him as we walk. He looks down, as if thinking, then finally shakes his head no.

I tried. And I respect his privacy. I'm not sure I'd want to talk about it either, if I were in his shoes.

We reach the far end of the island, the trees opening to an open shore, covered in snow. I walk out to the tip and from here I have a sweeping view of the Hudson, in every direction. It is like a vast sea on all sides of us, huge chunks of ice hardening all around, snow falling down on it. It looks surreal, primordial. As the wind whips me in the face, I feel for a moment as if we're the only ones left, castaways in a vast sea.

I scan the shores in every direction, looking for any signs of structures, of motion, movement. But I see none. It is as if the wilderness, without man left to impose upon it, has returned back upon itself.

As I stand there, on the shore, I notice something on the sand, sticking up through the snow. I take a few steps forward, reach down, and pick it up. It is green and glowing, and as I pick it up, I realize it's a bottle—a large, glass bottle that must've washed up on shore.

I scour the rest of the shoreline, and see something else, glistening, bobbing in the water, brushing up against the shore. I hurry over and pick it up. It is an old, aluminum can.

I don't know what to make of these things—it is hardly the treasure chest I hoped to find. But still, I'm sure we can make some use of them, and it's at least something to bring them back.

I take a deep breath and turn around, preparing to head back. This time, I lead us back along the other side of the island, through a different grove of trees, in the hopes of finding something, anything.

We trudge silently back through the woods, and I feel disappointed that I didn't find anything of use, yet also relieved that we have the island to ourselves. I begin to let down my guard as I realize that soon I will be back in the warmth of the cave. My hands and feet are becoming more frozen as we walk, and I bunch them and release, trying to circulate the blood. My legs are weary, and I'll be happy to sit in the cave, and relax by a fire.

This makes me realize that we'll need supplies to start a fire. I happily remember the matches and candles I salvaged from dad's. But I realize we'll also need kindling—dry branches, pine needles, whatever I can find. I also realize we should bring back pine branches to make the ground more comfortable for everyone.

"Look for branches," I say to Ben. "Dry branches. Small ones. Higher off the ground, not covered in snow. We need kindling. Also look for large branches with soft pine needles, to use on the floor."

Ben walks a few feet behind me and doesn't respond, but I know he's heard me because he steps up to a tree, and I hear the cracking of a branch.

I spot a tree myself with a dry branch sticking out from it, and I reach up and snap it off. It's perfect. With an armful of these, we can have a fire going all night.

Just as I'm walking to another tree, suddenly, I hear a twig snap. Ben stands right beside me, so I know he didn't do it. My heart stops. We are being watched.

SEVEN

I spin around, in the direction of the snap, and I see motion. I freeze, my throat dry, as I realize what it is.

I can't believe it. There, in plain sight, not even twenty yards away, are two deer. They stop and lift their heads and stare right at me.

My heart is pounding with excitement. This would be enough food to feed us all for days. I can't believe our luck.

Without thinking, I grab my knife, step forward and hurl it, remembering the last time this worked.

But this time, my hands are too cold, and I miss. They take off, sprinting away.

I quickly pull the bow off my back, place an arrow between my fingers, and fire at the fleeing deer. But I'm even more clumsy with the bow, and the arrow lodges into a tree, nowhere near the deer.

"Dammit!" I yell out. This is a small island, but they're too fast. Without a gun, which I would never fire for fear of drawing attention, and without professional traps, I don't see how we could ever catch them.

Suddenly, Ben steps forward, takes the bow from my hand, and one arrow. He takes three steps forward in front of me, holds the bow expertly, strings the arrow, holds out his chest, and then bides his time, following the deer, which now must be a good fifty yards away and bounding off. They are also zigzagging in and out between trees. It's an impossible shot.

Ben releases, and the arrow goes flying through the air.

And then, to my amazement, there is the distant sound of arrow piercing flesh. I'm completely shocked, as I watch one deer fall.

I turn and look at Ben, my mouth hanging open. He stands there, not moving, and slowly lowers the bow. He looks sad, as if he regrets what he's done.

"You didn't tell me," I say in a hushed tone, "that you're an expert shot."

He turns and shrugs, as he hands back the bow.

"You didn't ask," he says nonchalantly.

Ben turns and walks off, in the direction of the deer. I stand there, too frozen in surprise to know what to say.

I follow him, still trying to comprehend what just happened. I had no idea that Ben had any skills—much less, hunting skills. That was an unbelievable, one-of-a-kind shot. I had written him off, but now I realize how valuable Ben is. And as I watch him walk with a new bounce to his step, I realize that this episode did something to him. It seems like maybe it helped snap him out of it, give him a sense of pride, of purpose. For the first time, I feel as if he's back with us, finally present, as a member of the team.

We both reach the deer, and stand over it. It lies on its side, blood oozing out into the snow, its legs still quivering. It was a perfect shot, right to its neck.

After several seconds, it stops quivering, dead.

Ben reaches down, slings the animal over his shoulder. He turns, and together we walk back to the cave. As we go, I grab kindling, dry branches everywhere, filling my arms. Then I grab wide pine branches, gathering what will be a huge blanket and pillow for Rose.

My heart fills with optimism. The skies grow darker and the snow stronger and the wind whips at full force, but I don't care. We have shelter—real shelter—with fresh food for all, and wood for fire. For once, I feel things are going our way.

*

Finally, a sense of peace has settled over us. We all sit huddled together, deep inside the cave, spread out around a roaring fire. It turned out that the matches I salvaged from dad's house were invaluable, as was the kindling I brought in from outside. It all helped to get the fire going, and once it started, we all took turns going outside, finding small logs that were as dry as possible, and throwing them on the ever-growing fire. dad's tools even came in handy, as I used the hammer and screwdriver to chip off the wet bark, get rid of all the wet layers and get the wood as dry as possible. Now the fire is roaring, giving us all the desperately needed warmth we've been craving for days.

As I sit there, holding my hands out before it, rubbing my palms, I slowly feel my limbs begin to relax. I didn't realize how tense they were, how frozen up I was. I feel like I'm de-thawing, getting back to myself again. It's amazing how warm it's becoming in here. With the roaring fire and the shelter from the wind and snow, it's almost like being inside.

As I glance outside, at the mouth of the cave, I see that it is dark. The storm has gotten worse, much worse, and continues to fall heavily, silently, ominously piling up outside the cave, now nearly a foot high. The wind whistles, and occasionally, a particularly strong gust sends a few flakes into the cave. But mostly, we are well sheltered. This place is a godsend. I don't know how we would have survived otherwise.

Logan sits by himself, at the mouth of the cave, looking out at the storm, watching the darkening sky, and mostly keeping his eyes fixed on the boat. I went over and checked on it myself a few times. Always it was the same: bobbing wildly in the stormy water, but tied securely, as sheltered as it could be from the storm. The boat's not going anywhere. There's no one in sight as far as the eye could see. And with the wind and snow raging, and the boat hidden on two sides, I don't see who would even see it. I think Logan's being paranoid. But if it makes him feel better to sit there and watch it, so be it. Eventually he'll have to come back to the fire and warm himself up.

Beside me, leaning over the fire, is Ben. He's impressed me with his skills: to my surprise, he took my hunting knife and went to work on the deer, and in minutes, he had it expertly skinned. Then he cut it into perfect chunks, knowing exactly which parts to dispose of. Then he cut the meat into five big portions, impaled each on a sharpened stick, and propped them over the roaring flames. He turns the meat every so often, and the smell of it has been filling my senses for an hour, making my stomach growl. It smells delicious and I'm salivating at the thought of eating a real meal.

I look over again at Rose. I brought her close to the fire, beneath a thick bed of pine needles, and I can see she's still sleeping an uneasy sleep, her brow furrowed. I changed her bandage again a few hours ago, and as I did, I recoiled at its color. Worse, her wound was badly inflamed, spreading up her arm in both directions, and was starting to smell. It has turned gangrene. I don't like how quickly her bandages are still soaking up blood.

Rose looks delirious. I give her a sleeping pill every few hours, but I don't know how much longer that's going to work. I don't know what else to do for her. I feel so helpless.

What she really needs is medicine. Specialized medicine. And I have no idea where to even begin to look. Even if somehow I could brave this weather and take the boat out into the blizzard with whatever fuel we have left, even if I could somehow find a town somewhere, it's not like we'd find a working pharmacy. I know it would be a lost cause—and only endanger the rest of us.

So I do the best I can to just keep her comfortable, and pray for the best. I come over, reach down, and slowly untie her latest bandage, filled with blood.

Rose groans in pain as I take it off. Once again, I curse that crazy who bit her.

I leave the bandage off, letting the wound air out, and go to mouth of the cave, and grab a handful of snow as I have done several times. I come back with it and kneel beside her and place it on Rose's wound. She winces and groans as I do. I'm hoping the snow will have a cleansing, cooling effect. I take a fresh bandage, dried by the fire, and delicately wrap it around her wound.

Rose opens her eyes and looks up at me. They are so small and afraid.

"Thank you," she says.

My heart breaks at the sound of her voice. She is so sweet, so courageous. If I were her age, I doubt I would be half as brave. Any other girl would be screaming and wailing.

I lean down and kiss her forehead and am alarmed to feel how clammy it is. My heart is breaking into a million pieces; I know this cannot end well. I don't see how it possibly can.

I want to scream at the world, at the injustice of it all. It's not fair. For such a sweet and beautiful and amazing girl like this to be taken away from us. I'm at a loss for words, and do my best to hold back tears and appear strong for her.

"You're going to be fine," I say, summoning the most confident voice I can.

She smiles weakly, as if seeing right through me. It makes me think of something someone once told me: the dying are granted the gift to see through all of our lies.

Bree, sitting on Rose's other side, reaches over and strokes back her hair. Bree looks more tormented than Rose; I've never seen her so upset, my entire life. It is almost as if she's the one who has been injured.

Penelope leans on Rose's chest and licks her face from time to time.

"Will you eat something?" I ask Rose.

"I can try," she says weakly. "But I'm not very hungry."

I pull over the sack and pull out a jar of jam and unscrew it. I can smell it from here: it's cherry. It smells delicious.

"Do you like cherry?" I ask her.

"My favorite," she answers.

I reach in with my finger, take a small scoop, and place it on her lips. She licks it, closes her eyes and smiles. I reach out with another, but she shakes her head no. "I've had enough," she says.

I hand the jar to Bree, but she shakes her head.

"Please, Bree, you need to eat."

"Give mine to Rose," she says, staring down with sadness.

I hold out a fingerful to Penelope, and she devours it without hesitating.

"It's ready," comes a voice.

I turn and see Ben has removed the pieces of cooked meat off the fire. He holds out the sticks and I take one and pass it to Bree. I take another, and hold it up for Rose. I lean over, hold up her head, and gently bring the food to her lips.

"Please Rose," I say. "You need to have something. This will help you get better."

"I'm not hungry," she says. "Really."

"Please. For me."

I can see she doesn't want to, but Rose does me a favor and takes a tiny bite from a piece of meat. She chews weakly, looking at me.

"You remind me of my mom," she says.

My eyes water up and it takes everything in me to hold back my tears.

"I loved her," Rose says.

"What happened to her?" I ask. I know I shouldn't. Whatever the answer is, it won't be good.

"I don't know," she answers. "They took me away from her. She tried to save me. But there were too many of them. I never saw her again. Do you think she's okay?" she asks.

I try my best to smile.

"I think she's fine," I lie. "And do you know what else?"

Rose slowly shakes her head.

"I know that if she was here, right now, she would be so proud of you."

She smiles.

I lower the food to her again, but this time, she shakes her head vehemently. "I can't," she says. "It hurts so bad," she says, squinting her eyes in pain.

I try to think of what else I can do for her. All I can think is to keep her comfortable. Maybe I should give her another sleeping pill.

I hurry over to the fire and grab the glass bottle with the melted snow in it, now water. I bring it back to Rose. "Drink," I say, as I slip a pill onto her tongue. She does.

I sit beside her and stroke her hair. I see her eyes already closing and feel like in a few minutes she'll be asleep.

I look over at Bree and see she hasn't touched her food.

"Bree, eat," I say. "Please."

"*You're* not eating," she says.

She's right.

"I will if you will," I say. "We need to. Our not eating won't help Rose get any better."

I reach over to the fire, grab my stick of meat, and take a bite. The meat is tough and plain, but I'm not complaining. It may not be that tasty, but as it fills my mouth, I realize how ravenous I am. I take bite after bite, barely able to slow down. I feel the nutrition spread through my body and can't remember how long it's been since I had real, fresh cooked meat.

Bree's hunger gets the best of her, too, and she finally eats. After every few bites she stops and peels off a strip for Penelope, who snatches it from her hand. In the past, Bree would giggle; but now, she remains somber.

Ben sits on the far wall, opposite me, and quietly chews. I see the remaining stick on the fire and look over and see Logan, still sitting guard by the mouth of the cave. I look down and see Rose is asleep beside me, so I get up, grab his stick and walk it over to him.

"Come sit by the fire," I say. "Staring into the dark isn't going to do anything. No one's on this island, and no one's touching the boat. We can barely see two feet in front of our face. Come on. Your not eating and not sleeping isn't going to help any of us. We need you strong."

Reluctantly, he gives in, standing, taking the strip of meat, and following me back to the fire.

I sit beside Rose and Bree, our feet to the fire, as Logan joins us. He sits and eats.

We all settle in and sit there for a long while in silence, the only sound the cracking of the wood and the whipping of the wind outside. For the first time in a while, I feel relaxed, as we each sit there, staring into the flames, each lost in our own world. I can't help but feel as if we are each just waiting to die, each in our own way.

Rose suddenly grunts and cries out in her sleep. Bree hurries over to her and grabs her hand, as Penelope whines.

"It's okay, Rose," Bree reassures, stroking her hair.

I can't stand to look; I can't stand to see her suffer.

"If we don't do something, she's going to die," I say quietly to Logan.

He grimaces. "I know," he says. "But what can we do?"

"I don't know," I say, feeling desperate and hopeless.

"That's because there's nothing we can do. We've covered hundreds of miles, and there is only rubble. You think if we head out there now, at night, in a blizzard, we're going to find a town in the next few miles, before our fuel runs out? A town that has the medicine she needs?" He slowly shakes his head. "If we go out there now, we're all just going to get stranded. If I thought we had any chance of finding what she needs, I'd go for it. But you know as well as I do that we don't. She's dying. You're right. But if we go out there, we'll all die, too."

I listen to his words, indignant, but at the same time, I've been thinking the same thoughts. I know he's right. He just saying what's on all of our minds. We're in an impossible situation. There's nothing we can do except watch her die. It makes me want to scream.

"Not that I want to sit here," he says. "We need to keep moving. We need weapons. We need ammo. And food. A lot of food. We need supplies. And fuel. But we have no choice. We need to wait out the storm."

I look at him.

"You're so sure we're going to find this place we're looking for in Canada?" I ask. "What if it doesn't exist?"

He frowns down at the fire.

"You find a better alternative to what we're looking for along the way, you tell me. You find a safe place with plenty of food and supplies, I'll stop. Hell I might even stay. I haven't seen it. Have you?"

Slowly, reluctantly, I shake my head.

"Until we do, we keep moving. That's how I see it. I don't need to find paradise," he says. "But I'm not planting myself in a wasteland either."

Suddenly, I find myself curious about Logan, about where his survival instinct came from. About where *he* came from. How he ended up where he did.

"Where were you before all this?" I ask softly.

He looks up from the fire for the first time, looks me directly in the eyes. Then he looks away. A part of me wants to get closer to him, but another part is still unsure. I'm still not quite sure what to think of him. Clearly, I owe him. And he owes me. That much is a given. We need each other to survive. But whether we'd hang around together otherwise is a different matter. I wonder if we would.

"Why?" he asks.

That's him. Always guarded.

"I just want to know."

He stares back at the fire, and minutes pass. The fire cracks and pops, and I begin to wonder if he's ever going to respond. And then, he speaks:

"Jersey."

He takes a deep breath.

"When the civil war broke out, I joined the army. Like everybody else. I went to boot camp, training, the whole nine yards. It took me years to realize I was fighting somebody else's war. Some politicians' war. I wanted no part of it. We were all killing each other. It was so stupid. For nothing."

He pauses.

"The bombs were dropped, and my entire unit got wiped out. I was lucky—underground when they hit. I got out, made it back to my family. I knew I needed to go back and protect them."

He pauses, taking a deep breath.

"When I got home, my parents were dead."

He pauses a long time.

"They left a note," he says, pausing. "They killed each other."

He looks up at me, his eyes wet.

"I guess they saw what the world was going to be like—and they didn't want any part of it."

I'm taken aback by his story. I feel a heaviness in my chest. I can't imagine what he went through. No wonder he's so guarded.

"I'm so sorry," I say. Now I regret having even asked. I feel like I pried.

"I was more sorry for my kid brother than for me," he says. "He was 10. I found him at home, hiding. Traumatized. But surviving. I don't know how. I was about to take him away somewhere when the slaverunners showed up. They had us surrounded and outnumbered. I put up a fight, wasted some of them. But there was nothing I could do. There were just too many of them.

"They made me a deal: they'd let my brother go if I joined them. They said I'd never need to capture anyone—only to stand guard at the arena."

He pauses for a long time.

"I justified it to myself. I wanted my brother to live. And after all, I heard that there are far worse arenas out there than Arena One."

The thought fills me with panic: I had never imagined anything worse could be out there.

"How is that possible?" I ask.

He shakes his head. "There's all sorts of sick things out there," he says. "Gangs. Cannibals. Mutants. And other arenas that make One look like nothing."

He sighs.

"Anyway, I gave my little brother two guns, fully loaded, two weeks' worth of food, my motorcycle, and sent him away, on Route 80, heading west. I told him to head to our uncle Jack's house, in Ohio, if it was even still standing. At least it was a destination. I made sure he hit the highway, and was going in the right direction. That was the last I ever saw of him."

He sighs.

"The slaverunners took me away, made me one of them, and I stood guard in the arena. For months, every night, I watched the games. It made me sick. I saw new people come and go every night. But I never saw anyone make it out of there alive. Never. Until you came."

He looks at me.

"You were the only one."

I look back at him, surprised.

"When I saw you fighting, I knew my time had come. I had to leave that place. And I had to do whatever I could to help you."

I think back and remember when I first met him, how grateful I was to him for helping us. I remember our trip downtown, his nursing me through being sick, how grateful I was to him again.

"You said something to me once," I say. "I asked you why did it. Why you helped me. And you said I reminded you of someone." I look at him, my heart pounding. I've been wanting to ask him this forever. "Who?"

He looks back into the fire. He's quiet for such a long time, I wonder if he'll answer me.

Finally, in a quiet voice, he says. "My girlfriend."

This floors me. Somehow, I can't imagine Logan with a girlfriend. I envision him in a military barracks. I'm also shocked that I remind him of her. It makes me wonder. Who was she? Did she look like me? Is that why he did it? Does he see her when he sees me? Or does he really like me?

Instead, I can only summon the courage to ask, "What happened to her?"

Slowly, he shakes his head. "Dead."

I've asked too much. In another time and place, they would be harmless questions; but this is not a harmless age we live in, and here and now, even the most innocuous question leads to lethal answers. I should've remembered what I learned years ago: better not to ask anyone anything. Better to just live in the silence, in the wasteland. Better not to talk at all.

EIGHT

I open my eyes, looking around, trying to figure out where I am. I'm sitting, leaning back against the rock wall of the cave, and I look around, and see everyone else lying around the fire, fast asleep. Something feels wrong.

I feel something crawling on my leg, and I look down and see a huge tarantula, making its way up my calf. I jump up with a start, brushing it off, freaking out. I feel more of them, all over me, and spin and turn as I frantically swat them off.

I look down, and see dozens of them, crawling all over the floor. Tarantulas cover the walls, swarms of them, making the walls seem alive.

I turn and look to the mouth of the cave. As I do, suddenly, a dozen slaverunners burst in. They're wearing masks and holding guns, as they charge right for us. There are too many of them, and they're coming in too fast, guns drawn. I'm unarmed, and there's nothing I can do. They found us.

They come right at me, and the closest one raises his gun to my head. My throat goes dry, a moment before I hear the gunshot.

I wake up gasping, swatting my arms and legs, trying to get the spiders off. I look around and realize, slowly, it was just a nightmare.

I'm in the cave, leaning against the stone wall, before the embers of the dying fire. Everyone is fast asleep—except, I see, for Logan, who sits by the entrance, stoically looking out, standing guard. It is daybreak.

I sit there, hyperventilating, trying to calm down. It was so vivid.

"You okay?" comes a soft voice.

I look over at Logan, who looks back with concern. Beyond him, the snow is piled high, at least a foot and a half, and it is still snowing. I can't believe it. The storm hasn't stopped.

I take a deep breath and nod back.

"Just a bad dream," I say.

He nods, and turns back to looking outside.

"I know what that's like," he says.

I stand, needing to shake out the cobwebs, and walk over to him. I stand at the mouth of the cave, and look out. The light of the breaking dawn is beautiful, with streaks of reds on the horizon against the thick gray clouds. The Hudson has turned to ice in places. A mist and fog settles over everything, and I feel as if we are in a surreal winter postcard.

It is very tranquil. I feel tucked in here, safe. I look over and see our boat, covered in snow, still bobbing in the water. Yes, it's treacherous out there, but at the same time, that means no one can get to us. It seems we have another day pass; clearly, we can't be going anywhere in this.

"Looks like we're not going anywhere today," I say.

"Looks like it."

I turn and look for Rose, my heart racing. It will be impossible for us to get out there and try to find medicine for her in this weather, the only drawback.

I hurry over and examine her. Her breathing is shallow, rapid. She looks more pale than the night before, and her bandage has turned green and brown, pus oozing out the sides. I can smell it from feet away, and my heart wrenches at the site.

I kneel down, and slowly unwrap it. As I do, she twists and winces, moaning softly. I unravel it, dripping with pus. Her wound has turned entirely black, festering, and I nearly gag. My heart breaks in pieces. I can hardly imagine the pain and suffering she is in right now. It looks incurable. I feel like crying, knowing what's on the horizon for her. I would give anything to be a doctor, to have a doctor here right now. It is like watching my own little sister die, helplessly.

I want to feel like I'm doing something, so I hurry to the mouth of the cave, grab some fresh snow, and gently place it on her wound. She winces as I do so. I take one of the fresh bandages I have left to dry by the fire, and wrap it around, doing the best I can.

I turn back and come over to Logan. I sit beside him, looking out at the snow, and my eyes well up.

"It's bad, huh?" he asks.

I nod, not looking at him.

"You're doing everything you can," he says.

"No I'm not," I say.

He doesn't respond.

I think back, wondering how we could have prevented it. I should've been more vigilant that night, when the mutants attacked. I never should've let Ben stand guard. I knew he was too fragile, too unstable. I can't help feeling as if it's all my fault.

"It's not your fault," Logan says, surprisingly, as if reading my mind. "It's his," he says, gesturing with his head back to Ben, sleeping along the back wall.

Logan refused to allow Ben to stand guard the night before, still not trusting him. I can feel his anger and resentment towards him, but I know it is not helpful. Yes, Ben fell asleep. But even if he was awake, who knows if things would have gone down differently.

"You shouldn't be so hard on him," I say. "He just lost his brother."

"That's no excuse. He should've stayed awake, or if he couldn't, he should've woke one of us. It's his fault she got bit."

"You're right. He should've stayed awake. But even if he was awake, do you really think things would've gone down differently? You think Ben would have stopped them?"

"Yes I do," he says. "He would have at least woken us. I could've responded sooner."

"We were outnumbered. They were fast. Even if he woke us, I don't know that would've made a difference."

Logan shrugs.

"Anyway, anger and blame won't help us now," I say. "Ben is sorry. We need to stick together. You guys need to get over your thing and get along."

"I don't need to get along with anybody," Logan says.

I look at him, wondering if he thinks his whole life is an island.

"Keep telling yourself that."

*

The fog comes rolling in off the Hudson as I walk with Ben, our boots crunching in the snow, traversing the island in the afternoon, looking for food. The blizzard is still raging, worse than ever, the wind whipping at us in occasional gusts. It is incredible. I feel like it hasn't stopped snowing for days. The snow reaches my knees, making each step an effort. When the wind blows, I can see maybe a hundred feet; when it doesn't, and the fog gathers, I can barely see ten. Between the fog and the snow, I feel like our hunting today is a futile effort. I think Ben thinks so, too.

But we have to try. We know that other deer is out there, and has nowhere to go. We have to find it, get at least one more good meal in all of us before we leave. Bree desperately needs the protein, and Rose.... Well, my heart sinks as I think of her.

It's hideous weather out here, my feet and face numb—but in some ways, it's still better than being in that cave. With Rose dying, the cave has become small, tense, claustrophobic, filled with the stench of death. I had to get out. And I think Ben did, too. Logan, of course, wanted to stay put and stay guard, watching the boat. I don't think he'd ever trust Ben to stand guard again.

Ben holds the bow and arrows slung over his shoulder, and I have only my hunting knife. If we spot the deer, of course Ben is our best hope. But even with his skill, I don't see how he'd possibly be able to hit. It is probably a lost cause—yet still, a welcome distraction.

Ben and I walk in silence, neither speaking to each other. But it is a comfortable silence. I feel that he's come out of his shell since yesterday. Maybe he feels more confident, maybe a little bit better about himself, after bringing in that deer. Now he realizes that he is not useless.

"Where did you learn how to shoot like that?" I ask.

He looks at me, startled; it is the first words we have spoken, breaking a long silence.

We continue for several more steps before he answers.

"When I was younger," he says, "before the war. Day camp. Archery was my thing. I'd stay on the range for hours and hours, long after everyone left. I don't know why, I just always loved it. I know it's silly," he says, and pauses, looking embarrassed, "but it was my dream to compete in the Olympics. Before the war, that was what I lived for."

I'm surprised by this; I hadn't expected this from him, of all people. But I do remember his shot, and it was extraordinary.

"I'd like to learn," I say.

He looks at me, eyebrows arched in surprise.

"I'll teach you," he says.

I look at him and smile. "I think it's a little bit late for that."

"No it's not," he says firmly. "It's never too late."

I hear the seriousness in his voice, and am surprised to see how determined he is.

"I want to teach you," he insists.

I look at him, surprised. "Now?" I ask.

"Why not? We've been out here for hours, and there's no sign of the deer. It's not like we'll lose him if we take a few minutes."

I guess he has a point.

"But it's not like we have a practice range here," I say. "We don't have any bulls eyes or anything."

"How wrong you are," he says with a smile. "Look around. Everything in front of you is an archer's target. Actually, trees make some of the best targets."

I look around, and have a whole new appreciation for the forest.

"Besides," he says, "I'm tired of walking. I wouldn't mind taking a break for a few minutes. Come here," he says, gesturing.

My legs are getting tired, too, and I actually would love to learn. I hate relying on other people for things, and I like learning anything that can make me self-sufficient. I'm doubtful over whether I can really pick up the skill, especially in these conditions, but I'm willing to give it a try. Plus, it's the first time Ben warmed up to me, and I feel like he's starting to come out of his trauma. If this helps him, then I'm willing to do it.

I walk over to him, and he removes the bow from his shoulder and hands it to me.

I hold up the bow with my left hand, and hold onto the string my right, testing it. It is heavier than I thought, its large wood frame weighing down my arm.

Ben comes around behind me, reaches out, and puts his left hand over my left hand, over the handle of the bow. As he does, I feel a chill. He has caught me off guard. I didn't expect him to come so close, or to put his hand over mine. The feel of his touch is like an electric shock.

He reaches around with his other hand, and places his right hand on my other hand, on the string. I feel his chest rub against my back.

"Hold it like this," he says. "Support your shoulders. If your grip is too high, you'll never hit your target. And hold it closer," he says, pulling it closer to my chest. "Align your eyes on the notch. You're too tense. Relax."

"How am I supposed to relax when I'm pulling on the string?" I ask.

But I can't relax for another reason: I'm nervous. I haven't had a boy this close to me in years. And I find myself realizing that there is something about Ben that I actually do like. That I've always liked, since I met him.

"The paradox of archery," he says. "You have to be tense and relaxed at the same time. You're pulling on a string attached to a piece of wood, and that tension is what's going to make the arrow fly. At the same time, your muscles need to be lithe to direct it. If you tense up, you'll miss your mark. Let your shoulders and hands and wrists and neck all relax. Don't put your focus on the bow, but on the target. Try it. See that tree, the crooked one?"

A gust comes in and the fog lifts for a moment, and in the distance I spot a large, crooked tree, standing by itself, about thirty yards away.

Ben takes a step back, letting go of me, and I find myself missing the feel of his touch. I pull back the string and take aim. I close one eye, and try to focus on the notch at the end of the wood, trying to align the arrow.

"Lower the bow a little bit," he says.

I do so.

"Now take a deep breath, then slowly let it go."

I breathe deep and as I breathe out, I let go. The string snaps forward, and the arrow goes flying.

But I am disappointed to see that it doesn't hit the tree. It misses by several feet.

"I told you this was a waste of time," I say, annoyed.

"You're wrong," he answers. "That was good. The problem was, you didn't plant your feet. You let the bow carry you. Your strength is in your feet, and in your hips. You have to be rooted. Plant yourself. Try again," he says, handing me another arrow.

I look over at him, worried.

"What if I miss?" I say.

He smiles. "Don't worry. I'll find the arrows. They can't go far."

I take another arrow and set it on the string.

"Don't pull it back all at once," he says, gently. "That's it," he adds, as I begin to pull it back.

The string is more taut this time—maybe because I'm nervous, maybe because I feel more at stake. As I hold it back, I feel the bow quivering, and it's hard to stop.

"It's hard to steady it," I say. "My aim is all over the place."

"That's because you're not breathing," he says. "Relax your shoulders, lower them, and pull it in closer to your chest."

He comes up behind me and reaches over and puts his hands on mine. I feel his chest against my back, and slowly, I stop quivering a little bit less.

"Good," he says, stepping back. "Okay, take a deep breath, and release."

I do so, and let it go.

It is exhilarating to watch the arrow go flying through the air, into the thick blizzard, and to watch it hit the tree. It doesn't hit it in the center, as I was hoping, but it hits, along its edge. Still, I hit it.

"Great!" Ben yells, genuinely excited.

I don't know if he's just being kind, or if he's genuine; but either way, I'm grateful for his enthusiasm.

"It wasn't that great," I say. "If that was a deer—especially a moving deer—I never would've hit."

"Give yourself a break," he says. "That was your first shot. Try again."

He reaches out and hands me another arrow. This time, I place it on the bow, more confident, and pull it back. This time, I pull it back more easily, more steadily, remembering everything he taught me. I plant my feet and lower the bow. I aim for the center of the tree, and pull back breathe deep as I let go.

Before it even leaves, somehow I know it is a good shot. It's weird, but before it even hits, I know it will.

And it does. I hear the sound of arrow striking wood even from here—but a fog rolls in, and I can't tell where I hit.

"Come on," Ben says, trotting off excitedly towards the tree. I follow him, equally curious to see the result.

We reach the tree and I can't believe it. It is a perfect strike. Dead center.

"Bingo!" he yells out, clapping his hands. "See? You're a natural! I couldn't have done that my first time out!"

For the first time in a while, I feel a sense of self-worth, of being good at something. It feels real, genuine. Maybe I do have a shot at archery—at least enough to catch dinner once in a while. That shot might have been a fluke, but either way, I feel I can get this over time. It is a skill I know that I can use. Especially out here.

"Thank you," I say, meaning it, as I hand him back the bow.

He takes it, as he pulls the arrows out of the tree and puts them back in his quiver.

"You want to hold onto it?" he asks. "You want to fire on the deer, if we ever find it?"

"No way. If we do find it, we get one crack at it. I don't want lose dinner for everyone."

We turn and continue on, heading farther into the island.

We walk in silence for several more minutes, but now it's a different silence. Something in the air has shifted, and we are closer to each other than before. It's like the silence has shifted from a comfortable one, to an intimate one. I'm starting to see things in Ben that I like, things that I hadn't seen before. And I feel like it's time to give him a second chance.

We keep walking, cutting through the woods, when suddenly, to my surprise, the island ends. We've reached the small sandy beach, now covered in snow. We stand there and look out the Hudson, now just a huge white wall. It's like staring into a wall of fog. Like staring into nothingness.

And there, to my shock, standing on the beach, leaning down and drinking the water of the Hudson, is the deer. It is not even twenty feet ahead of us, not even aware of our presence. It is wide out in the open, almost too easy of a shot. A part of me doesn't want to kill it.

But Ben already has the bow in hand, an arrow in place, and before I can even say anything, he pulls it back.

At the slight noise, the deer lifts its head and turns, and I feel it looking right at me.

"NO!" I scream out to Ben, despite myself.

But it is too late. The deer starts at my cry, but the arrow is already flying. It flies at lightning speed and hits the deer in the neck. The deer takes a few steps forward, stumbles, then collapses, the pure white snow immediately turning red.

Ben turns and looks at me, surprised.

"What was that about?" he asks.

He stares at me, his large, light-blue eyes filled with wonder. They are lit up by the snow, mesmerizing.

I have no idea how to respond. I am embarrassed. I look away in shame, not wanting to meet those eyes.

"I don't know," I say. "It was stupid. Sorry."

I expect Ben to tell me that I'm stupid, that I almost lost us dinner, that I should have kept my mouth shut. And he would be right.

But instead, he reaches out with one hand, and takes my hand in his. I look up at him, and he stares down at me with his large soulful eyes, and says:

"I understand."

*

The mood is somber as we sit around the fire, staring into the flames after our meal. Night has fallen, and unbelievably, it's still snowing. There now must be three feet piled up out there, and I think we are all wondering if we will ever leave this place.

Of course, we shouldn't be complaining: for the first time in a long time, we have real shelter, fire, warmth, no fear from attack, and real food. Even Logan has finally relaxed his guard, realizing that no one could possibly reach this island in these conditions. He's finally stopped sitting guard, and sits with the rest of us, staring into the flames.

Yet still, we are all morose. Because beside us, lying there, groaning, is Rose. It is obvious she has reached the point of no return, that she could die at any moment. All the color has left her skin, the black of the infection has spread across her shoulder and chest, and she lies there, pouring with sweat and writhing in pain. Bree's eyes are red from crying. Penelope sits on Rose's chest, whining intermittently, refusing to go anywhere else. I feel as if I am on a death vigil.

Normally, I would gorge myself on the fresh meat, but tonight I eat half-heartedly, as do the others. Bree didn't even touch hers. Even Penelope, when I handed her a piece, refused to take it. Of course, Rose wouldn't take a bite.

It breaks my heart to see her suffer like this. I don't know what else to. I gave her the remainder of the sleeping pills, three at once, hoping to knock her out, to alleviate her pain. But now she's in so much pain, it's not doing her any good. She cries and moans and squirms in agony. I sit there, stroking her hair, staring into the flames, wondering when this will all end. I feel as if we're all stuck in some interminable suffering that has no end in sight.

"Read me a story," Bree says.

I turn and see her looking up at me with red eyes.

"*Please*," she pleads.

I put one arm around her and hold her tight; she rests her head on my shoulder, crying softly.

I close my eyes and try to remember the words of *The Giving Tree*. They usually come to me, right away—but tonight, I'm having a hard time. My mind is jumbled.

"I…" I begin, then trail off. I can't believe it, but I'm drawing a blank. "I'm sorry. I can't remember."

"Then tell me a story," she says. "Anything. Please. Something from before the war."

I think back, trying hard to remember something, anything. But I'm so tired, and so frazzled, I draw a blank. Then, suddenly, I remember.

"I remember one night, when you were young," I begin. "You were maybe four. I was eleven. We were with mom and dad. It was a summer night, the most perfect, beautiful night, so still, not a breeze, and the sky filled with stars. Mom and dad took us to an outdoor carnival, I don't remember where. It was some kind of farm country, because I remember walking through all these cornfields. It felt like we walked all night long, this magical walk through open farms, up and down gentle hills. I remember looking up and being awed at all the stars. There were so many of them and they were so bright. The universe felt alive. And I didn't feel alone.

"And then, after all this walking in the middle of nowhere, there, in the middle of these country fields, there was this small town carnival. It lit up the night. There were games, and popcorn, and cotton candy, and candy apples, and all kinds of fun things. I member you loved the candy apples. There was this one stand, where the apples floated, and you'd dunk your head in the water and try to bite one. You must have tried a hundred times."

I look down and see Bree smiling.

"Did mom and dad get mad?"

"You know dad," I say. "He gets impatient. But you were so insistent, they waited. They weren't mad. By the end, dad was even cheering for you. Telling you how to do it, giving you direction. You know how he is."

"Like we're in the Army," she says.

"Exactly."

I sigh and think, trying to remember more.

"I remember they got us all tickets for the Ferris wheel, and the four of us sat together, in the front. You loved it. You didn't want to get off. More than anything, you loved the stars. You were really wishing it would stop while we were at the top, so you could be closer to the sky when you looked. You kept making mom and dad do the ride over and over again until finally, you got what you wanted. You were so happy. You're so good with the sky: you pointed out the Milky Way and the Big Dipper and everything. Things I didn't even know. I'd never seen you so happy."

Bree has a real smile on her face now, as she rests her head on my shoulder. I can feel her body starting to relax.

"Tell me more," she says, but now her voice is a gentle whisper, falling asleep.

"Later, we went into a hall of mirrors. And then into a freak show. There was a bearded lady, and a 600 pound man, and a man who was two feet tall. He scared you.

"dad's favorite game was the guns. He made us stop at the BB guns, and he fired again and again. When he missed a target, he got mad, and blamed the manager for the faulty gun. He insisted that he never missed a shot, that there was something wrong with the gun, and he wanted his money back. You know dad."

Thinking of it now, I smile at the thought of it. How little something like that would matter now, in this day and age.

I look down, expecting to see Bree smile back, but find her fast asleep.

Rose grunts and squirms again, lying by the fire, and this time, it seems to really upset Logan. He gets up, walks to the mouth of the cave and looks out the snow, ostensibly watching our boat. But I know he's not watching; there's nothing to see out there. He just can't take her pain and suffering. It's upsetting him, maybe more than anyone.

Ben sits opposite me, staring into the flames, too. He seems to be coming out of it more and more. I'm sure he must feel a sense of self-worth for feeding us both these nights.

I sit there in silence, staring at the fire for what feels like hours, Bree asleep in my arms. I don't know how much time has passed, when Ben speaks:

"What happened in New York was horrible."

I look up at him, surprised. He looks right at me, his large soulful eyes staring, and I can see that he wants to speak, that he wants me to know. That he is ready. He wants to tell me everything.

NINE

"I caught the train my brother was on," Ben says, "and it took me deep in the tunnels. It stopped at a huge mining station, deep underground. Hundreds of boys chained together, working like slaves. I looked everywhere for him. Everywhere. But I couldn't find him."

He sighs.

"I snuck up to one of the boys and asked him. I hid in the shadows as he asked around. I described him perfectly. Finally, word got back to me. They said he was dead. They were positive. They saw one of the slaverunners get mad at him for not moving fast enough, and they said they beat him with a chain. They saw him die."

There is a long silence, and then a muffled cry, and I see Ben wiping away his tears. I hardly know what to say. I can't comprehend the guilt he must feel.

"I never should have left him alone," Ben says. "Back in the mountains. I left him alone, just for an hour. I didn't think they'd come. I hadn't seen them in years."

"I know," I say. "I never thought they would, either. But it's not your fault. *They* are to blame, not you."

"The worst part of all of this is not seeing it for myself," Ben says. "Not seeing him dead. Not knowing for sure. I can't explain it, but I don't believe he's dead. A part of me still thinks those boys might have mixed him up with somebody else. I know him. He wouldn't die. Not like that. He's strong. Smart. Smarter than me, stronger than me. And tougher than me. I think he escaped. I really do. I think he worked his way back up the river. I think he's going to come back to our house, and wait for me there. Back in the mountains."

I look at Ben and see a frenzied look in his eyes, and realize that he has taught himself to believe this fantasy. I don't want to ruin his fantasy. I don't want to tell him that that is nearly impossible. Because in this day and age, we all need our dreams, as much as we need food or water.

"Do you think?" he asks, looking right at me. "Do you think he's still alive?"

I don't have the heart to say no.

So instead, I look back at him, and say, "Anything is possible."

Because a part of me knows that it's not helpful to live in fantasy—but another part of me has learned that, sometimes, fantasy is all you have.

*

I open my eyes, disoriented. I don't understand what's happening. The floor of the cave is lined with thousands of brightly colored flowers, purple and whites and pinks. I look down and see I am lying on a bed of flowers, see sunlight pouring into the cave. Outside, it is warm, balmy, a beautiful spring day, with gentle breezes coming off the river. Beyond the entrance to the cave I see lush trees, flowers everywhere, birds chirping. The sun is so bright and strong, it is like a light shining in from heaven. As I look all around me, I notice there is a soft white glow in the air; a great sense of peace has come over me.

I sit up and see, standing before me, Rose, light radiating behind her. To my shock, she looks perfectly healthy and happy now, a big smile on her face.

She steps forward and wraps her arms around me in a huge hug. She kisses my cheek and whispers: "I love you, Brooke."

I pull her back and look at her and kiss her on the forehead, so happy to see her healthy again.

"I love you, too," I say.

I can feel the warmth and love radiating off of her. She slowly pulls away. I tried to hold onto her, but she releases my hands, and I feel her slipping away.

"Rose?"

Before my eyes she starts to float away. She drifts up into the air, smiling down at me.

"Don't worry," she says. "I'm happy now."

She becomes more and more translucent, until she blends into the light. She floats up out of the cave, outside, into the sky, higher and higher, all the while, her face looking down at me, smiling. I can feel the intense love from her, and I feel just as much love for her. I want to hold her, I don't want her to go. But I feel her leaving.

I wake, looking all around in the cave. I wonder if I'm dreaming this time, and it takes me a minute to realize that this time, I'm truly awake.

Sunlight floods the cave, and it is much warmer than yesterday. The snow is piled high but already melting, and light bounces off of it. I remember being up all night with Rose; she was shaking, trembling, burning up from fever all night long. But I didn't let her go. I rocked her and whispered in her ear that everything would be okay.

Now I look over, and see that Rose is still in my arms. I slowly lean back, look at her—and my heart freezes to see that her eyes are open. Frozen open. I watch for several seconds, before I realize that she is dead.

I look around and see everyone sleeping, and realize I'm the first one to wake.

I hold Rose tight, rocking her, my eyes flooding with tears. Penelope, in her lap, whines and whines, and begins to bark. She licks Rose's hand, and barks again and again.

Others in the cave wake. Bree wakes and hurries over, and I brace myself. She leans over and looks down at Rose's face. And then suddenly, her face crumples into tears. She starts hysterically crying.

"ROSE!" she wails. She wraps her arms around her, holding her tight. She sobs and sobs.

Ben and Logan sit up and look over, grave expressions on their faces. I see Logan wipe away a tear then turn, not wanting me to see.

Ben, though, lets the tears fall freely from his face. I feel the wet on my cheeks, and realize I'm still crying, too. But, strangely, I also feel a sense of peace. My dream had been so real, so vivid—I feel like it really happened, that Rose was actually with me. I feel that she really said goodbye, and that she's in a peaceful place now.

"I dreamt of her," I say to Bree, trying to console her. "I saw her. She was happy. And smiling. She's in a good place now. She's happy."

"How do you know?" Bree asks.

"She told me. She's happy. She loves you."

This seems to make Bree feel better. Her crying slows, and she gently pulls back.

I look outside, and realize we'll never be able to bury Rose in this weather. Even with this warmer day, the ground, I'm sure, will be frozen solid. It will have to be a river burial.

I figure that the sooner we do it the better. We have to move on. We *need* to move on.

"Do you want to help carry her?" I ask Bree, wanting to involve her.

I stand, grab Rose's arms, and let Bree take her legs. Together, we walk her out of the cave. Ben and Logan and Penelope follow.

We walk out into the soft snow, up to my calves, into the shining light, and I am momentarily blinded. It is like a summer day. Birds are chirping, it is probably twenty degrees warmer, and much of the snow has melted. The storm has passed. It is as if it never was.

Penelope gets lost in the thick snow, and Logan reaches down and lifts her.

"Where are we bringing her?" Bree asks.

"We can't bury her," I say. "The ground is frozen, and we don't have any shovels. We'll have to bury her in the river. I'm sorry."

"But I don't want to put her in the water," Bree says, her face crumpling up as she begins to cry again. "I don't want her to be eaten by fish. I want to bury her here, on this island."

Logan, Ben and I all exchange a worried look. I don't know what to say. I understand how she feels. And I don't want to make things even worse for her. Then again, it's just not practical. But knowing Bree, she won't give in. I need to find an alternate solution.

I look out at the river, and am struck with an idea.

"What about the ice?"

Bree turns and looks out at the river.

"See those huge floating chunks of ice? What if we place Rose on one of those? Let it carry her downriver? She will float away, carried on the ice. Like an angel, floating away. Eventually the ice will melt, and the river will take her. But not yet."

I brace myself, hoping Bree will agree.

To my great relief, slowly, she nods back in agreement.

We all walk down to the water's edge, and as we get close, I watch and wait for one of the occasional large blocks of ice to float down river. They are far and few between, but occasionally, they do come. One floats by, but it is a good fifteen feet out in the water—there's no way I can reach it.

We wait and wait, and finally, one huge block of ice, about six feet long, breaks off from the others and drifts our way, as if being led by a magical current. It is a couple of feet out in the water, and just as I'm trying to figure out how I'm going to wade out and get it while holding Rose, suddenly Ben and Logan take action. They hurry past me, wading out into the water, each grabbing one end of it. Their boots get soaked and I'm sure the river is freezing, but they bear it stoically. It is nice to see them working together for a change.

They pull the ice close to shore, and together, we all set Rose down on it. She looks like an angel lying on top.

While we hold the ice, Bree stands over her, looking down.

"I love you, Rose," she says.

Penelope barks.

Finally, after several minutes of silence, Bree steps back. The four of us gently push the huge block out into the river.

We all stand on shore and watch as the block of ice catches in the current and begins to float away, down river, Rose's tiny body spread out on it. I was right: she does look like an angel, floating there amidst all that white. I hope that wherever she's going, she's going to a place of peace.

Logan is already eyeing our boat. He goes over to it, and starts scooping the snow out, preparing.

"We should go now," he says, getting the snow out with both hands, wasting no time.

"I want to leave, too," Bree says. "I *hate* this place. I never want to come back here."

"Go where exactly?" Ben asks. I'm surprised. It's the first time he's asked about any of our plans, or shown any concern.

"What do you care?" Logan snaps. "You haven't said anything before."

"Well, I'm saying something now," Ben says. I can feel the tension between them.

"We're heading north," Logan answers. "Like we always have. To Canada."

"There are four of us here," Ben says. "And I don't want to go to Canada."

Logan looks at him, dumbfounded. I am shocked, too.

"Like you said, there are four of us," Logan says. "That means majority rules. I want to leave, and so does Bree. That's two of us. Brooke?" he asks, looking at me.

Actually, now that he asks me, I'm not so sure. A part of me feels that we have a good thing going on this little island. It's hard to get to, hard to be ambushed. We have a cave, shelter from the wind and elements. A part of me wonders if we can live here. It would be boring, but safe, protected. When we run out of food, we could take the boat to shore and hunt. Capture food, bring it back here. And maybe we could farm something here in the summer. And fish.

I take a deep breath, not wanting to cause a rift.

"I don't know what's out there," I say. "It might be safer to continue north. But it might be more dangerous. Personally, I think it might be safest to just stay here. I don't see why we should be in such a rush to leave. I don't see how the slaverunners can find us here. If you're worried about their spotting the boat, we can drag it ashore, hide it in the trees. I think it can get a lot worse for us out there. I vote we stay put."

Logan looks blindsided.

"That's ridiculous," he says. "We'll be out of food in days. Maybe we can find more, maybe survive here a few weeks. Then what? The slaverunners are still after us. And this is just a measly strip of land. What if there's a city out there? A real city, that has everything we need to live forever?"

"We have everything we need right here," I say. "Food. Shelter. Safety. What more do we need?"

Logan shakes his head. "Like I said, majority rules. I vote to leave. So does Bree. You vote to stay. Ben?"

"I vote to leave, too," Ben says.

I'm surprised by this.

Logan smiles. "There you have it," Logan says. "We're leaving."

"But I vote to head south," Ben adds.

"South?" Logan asks. "You crazy?"

"I want to go back to my old house," Ben says. "In the mountains. I want to wait there for my little brother. He might come back."

My heart falls to hear this. Poor Ben, clinging to his fantasy.

"There's no way we're going back there," Logan says. "You had your chance. You should've said something before."

"Do what you want," Ben says. "I'm going back home."

The four us stand there, at a standstill. There is no majority vote here. All of us are torn, all wanting something else, none giving an inch.

Suddenly, a cracking noise pierces the air. A tree branch falls right near us, and it takes me a moment to figure it out. The noise comes again, and another branch falls, and that's when I realize: it was a gunshot. We are being fired upon.

TEN

Another shot, and a bullet flies right past me and hits the ground, only a few feet from where I stand.

"TAKE COVER!" Logan screams.

We all run back to the cave, as another shot rings out, chipping a branch a foot above my head.

We make it back to cave and stand huddle inside, looking at each other, shocked.

"What the hell is it?" I ask.

"A sniper," Logan says. "Somewhere on shore. It's not coming from the island—the angle is too steep. He must've been waiting for us." Logan turns and looks at me. "You still want to stay here?"

He has a point. But I don't care about who was right or wrong now; I just want to get us all out of here, quickly and safely.

"So now what?" I ask.

"I only have a few shots left in my pistol," Logan says. "There's no way I'd hit him. He's too far. That's a long-distance rifle. He's got us pinned here."

Ben crosses the cave, grabs the bow and arrows. He wears a new expression—tough, fearless—one I haven't seen before.

"Where are you going?" I ask.

But he just struts out of the cave without hesitating, into the open.

"Ben!" I yell. "Don't! You'll get killed!"

But Ben keeps walking, and as he does, another gunshot rings out, missing him by a few inches.

Ben keeps walking, doesn't even flinch. It is unbelievable. He struts with his chin up, determined, walking right out through the trees, towards the direction of the gunfire. It is as if he is suicidal.

And then it occurs to me: maybe he *is* suicidal. Maybe he feels so overwhelmed with guilt about his brother, that a part of him *wants* to die.

I hurry to the mouth of the cave, as we all do, and stand there, watching.

"He's going to get himself killed," I say.

"That's his choice," Logan says.

Ben walks through the trees, gunfire hailing down all around him, barely missing him in the tree cover. He reaches the shore, and stands there, out in the open. Gun fire hits the sand near him, just missing.

As if he has all the time in the world, Ben slowly removes the bow from his shoulder, takes out an arrow, and studies the far shoreline. On the horizon, on the other side of the Hudson, high up on a cliff, there is a lone gunman, aiming down with his rifle. The stock of his rifle glistens in the sunlight.

More shots ring out, but Ben doesn't flinch. He stands there, boldly. I wonder if this is courage, or suicide. Or both.

Ben places a single arrow on the bow, pulls it back, and takes aim. He holds it there for several seconds, waiting, aiming. Another gunshot rings out, missing him, but he doesn't flinch.

And then, finally, he lets go the arrow.

I see the arrow sail through the air, high across the Hudson, a good hundred yards. It is a thing of beauty. I'm amazed.

I'm even more amazed to watch as it finds its target: it lodges right into the chest of the lone gunman. After a moment, he falls face down, dead.

I look over at Ben in shock.

Ben walks back to us. He stands at the mouth of the cave, holding his bow and arrow, and we stand there, staring back at him. No more gunshots hail down. It wasn't the slaverunners. It must've been a lone, crazed gunman. A survivor.

Ben stares back at us wordlessly, and for the first time I can see the warrior in his eyes, a whole different Ben than I've seen before. I can also sense that a part of him had indeed wanted to die, had wanted the gunman to kill him, had wanted to join his brother. But he didn't get his wish.

At the same time, it seems like the episode was cathartic, like it exorcised something within him. Some sort of guilt about his brother or Rose. As if he faced death, and now he's ready to live again.

"I'm ready to leave," he says. "Let's go north."

*

The four of us sit silently in the boat, each lost in our own world, as our boat continues up the Hudson. Logan is steering, and we have been driving for hours, winding our way slowly upriver, avoiding chunks of separating ice. We all keep our eyes peeled forward; none of us dare look back.

We all left behind too much back there. Since the shooting, Ben doesn't talk about going home. I have nothing more to say, either. Obviously, it wasn't safe to stay there, after all. That shooter may have been a stray—or there may be more where he came from.

The mood now is much more somber. We all feel the absence of Rose. Penelope sits in Bree's lap, shaking, and I feel like we're all in mourning for a lost comrade. I think her passing also reminds us all of how close we came. It could've been any one of us—by pure happenstance it just happened to be her.

I don't think any of us really believe we will live for long. Each day is like looking our own mortality in the face. It's not a matter of *if* we will all die. But when.

A part of me has given up caring. I just look ahead, focus on the far north, on the distant goal of Canada. I hold it in my mind, and try not to let it go. Whether it's real or not, it doesn't really matter anymore. It's something. A destination. It beats our aimlessly wandering, heading God knows where, for God knows what. It's comforting to think that we're heading some place that might one day be home.

Ben surprised me back there—he surprised all of us. I was sure that he was going to get killed. Whatever his motive, his actions were brave, and he took out the sniper and saved us all. I think Logan has a new respect for him. I certainly do. And I think Ben, sitting a little taller, has a new respect for himself. It's like, finally, he's a member of our team.

Bree, on the other hand, has withdrawn into herself, ever since Rose's passing. Her eyes seem sunk, hollow, and she seems more out of it than I've ever seen her. It is as if a part of her died with Rose. She clutches Penelope as if she's holding a piece of Rose, and looks off into the water as if she's bearing the sorrows of the world. I can't stand to see her like this. But I don't know what else to say.

Logan, beside me, is quiet, and I can see the concern in his face. He stands over the wheel, checking the gas gauge every few seconds. We are now officially in the red. He keeps scanning the shoreline, as do I, for any signs of a town, a station—anything. But there is nothing. We'll be out of gas soon. And we'll be stranded. What I would give now for just a gallon of gas. I don't know what we'll do without this boat, if we have to leave it.

Suddenly, I spot something coming towards us in the river. At first I wonder if I'm seeing things, but then I see it's real. I grab my gun, even though there's no ammo left, and brace myself.

"GET DOWN!" I scream to Bree.

She and Ben jump down, looking out over the rail. Logan looks over at me, not understanding, then he looks out and sees it, too. He squats down, and reaches over and grabs his gun.

Coming right at us is another boat. It is a huge, rusted metal boat, maybe a hundred feet long and half as wide—it looks like a mini barge. It floats towards us, between the chunks of ice, crookedly, on an angle. That is when I realize that something looks wrong with it.

As it comes into better view, I see what it is. And I relax.

It is a ghost ship. Its entire hull is hollowed out, and I can see right through it. It is incredible: a huge, empty, rusted shell, floating down the river. It creaks and groans as it bounces in the river, sandwiched between large chunks of ice, leaning. It drifts our way and Logan turns us away, to keep us a good distance from it.

We float right past it and I look up, amazed by its size, as it blocks the sun. It is eerie. It is like looking at an old pirate ship. I wonder who piloted it, wonder how many months it's been floating down this river. It is other-worldly, this strange relic, this vestige of a world that once was. It makes me wonder if there is anything left in the world anymore.

None of us say anything as it passes. I relax my guard, realizing there is no danger.

But I hear a noise and I look down, as our boat starts to slow. At first I wonder if we ran out of gas. But that's not what it is. We suddenly stop moving, our boat groaning. We are stuck.

I look down, trying to figure out what happened.

"Did we hit a rock?" I ask. "Aren't we too far from shore?"

Logan shakes his head, looking down grimly.

"Ice," he answers.

I lean over the boat, and see it. There, all around us, are huge chunks of ice, boxing us in. So much of it has gathered around us that we can no longer move. I can't believe it.

"Now what?" Ben asks, also leaning over.

"We need to break out," Logan says.

"We need some kind of tool," Logan says. "Like a saw. Or a hammer."

I remember the hammer I salvaged from my dad's house, and rummage through my sack and pull it out. I lean over the edge and hammer at the ice.

But it hardly does a thing. The ice is too thick, and my hammer is too small.

I lean back, exhausted.

"Nice try," Logan says.

I look all around the river, and realize we are sitting ducks out here. This is bad. It could take hours for the ice to thaw. And the current is now bringing us back downriver.

Logan, Ben and I all exchange a nervous glance; clearly, none of us have any ideas.

"What about the anchor?" Bree asks.

We all turn and look at her. She stands there, pointing. I follow her finger to the back of the boat, to the small anchor on an iron chain. Bree's right. It's a brilliant idea.

Logan hurries over and hoists it. I am impressed by his strength: it must weigh thirty pounds, solid iron.

"Stand back," he says.

He leans over the edge, winds up the chain and anchor, and brings it down hard on the ice. It hits with a cracking noise, and I watch as the ice cracks and splits in several parts. Logan does it again and again, and soon, the huge chunks of ice break free.

He drops the anchor and turns to Bree with a smile: "Smart thinking," he says.

I come over and put my arm around her, and she smiles proudly.

"Don't know what us grownups would do without you," I say.

Logan guns it and we break through the remaining ice, back into open water. We are moving, but more slowly than before, Logan doing his best to avoid the floating chunks. I stand beside him, watching the horizon.

"See that up there?" he asks, pointing.

I squint, and in the distance I see, on the shore, the remains of what looks like a gas station. It is a small, crumbling dock, with the remnants of rusted gas pumps. It looks like it once fueled boats. It sits on the periphery of a sprawling town, dilapidated, like all the towns we passed.

"I say we give it a shot," he says. "Probably empty, but we need to try. We're running on fumes."

"Could be risky, getting that close to shore again," I say.

"We have no choice," Logan says. "It won't be long until the river freezes over for good. And if the pumps are empty, we can scavenge that town."

Ben and Bree are standing beside us, looking too.

"Any objections?" Logan asks.

We are all silent. It's probably a waste of time, but he's right: it's not like we have a choice.

Logan turns us towards the dock. We pull up to it, my heart beating in anticipation, and I silently wish and pray that there is gas left in these pumps. All we need is *some* gas, in just one pump. Just a few gallons. Something. Anything.

Come on.

Logan pulls up expertly beside the dock, aligning the nozzle. He jumps out, our boat rocking, as he lands on the dock two feet away.

He lifts the rusted nozzle, inserts it into the boat, and pulls the lever. My heart stops as I hear a swooshing noise. Then silence.

Logan tries again and again. He leans back and bangs the pump. But nothing happens. It is empty.

We all look away, grimacing. We know what that means.

"What now?" Ben asks.

"We have no choice," Logan says. "We've got to see if we can find some gas. We've got to check this town out. A canister, anything. Maybe even siphon it off an old car, if we can find any. The boat's useless to us now."

He's right. I know he's right, but I hate to admit it. I don't want to leave the safety of the boat, don't want to go back on shore. But I know that it's useless without gas.

"Let's do it," I say.

I jump off the boat, the dock bobbing as I do, then turn for Bree and pull her up. Ben lingers, reluctant to leave the boat, then finally jumps off and joins us. Logan reaches down and drops the anchor.

"What about the boat?" Ben asks.

Logan shakes his head.

"Can't take it with us," he says. "One of us could stand guard, but that'd be a waste of time. Don't worry about it," he says. "It's useless without gas. It's not going anywhere."

As we all follow Logan towards town, I check back over my shoulder, and look one more time at the boat. I don't know why, but I have a sinking feeling that I'll never see it again.

ELEVEN

We walk down the snow-lined rubble, right down the center of Main Street, and I look at the apocalyptic town spread out before us. It is the largest town I've seen in years, stretching for dozens of blocks, as far as I can see. On either side of us are crumbling, burnt out buildings. The devastation is tremendous. It reminds me of some of those photos I saw of cities bombed out after World War II.

The snow, while melting, is still up to our shins, and various objects stick out, like neglected toys. I see the hull of a burned out car, its wheels covered in snow, its top rusted right through. Beyond it, I see a broken wheelbarrow.

We are all tense, on guard, as we continue deeper into this town that once was. I hope and pray we can find fuel. All we need is one house, one store, one room—just one thing left uncovered. Who knows? Maybe we can even find more than fuel? Maybe food, weapons, ammo.

We come to the first store that looks like it might hold anything, and I stick my head through the open frame where there was once a window. I look inside, and see nothing but ruin.

I am about to move on, but Bree suddenly enters. She must spot something, because she steps across the threshold and into the store, and kneels down and reaches into the rubble. She pulls up something, gleaming in the light. I'm amazed she spotted it. She holds it out before us, and we all examine it. It's an old, rusted tin. It looks like it was once a candy tin. She opens it, and I'm amazed: inside are several red sucking candies.

We each reach in and grab one. I pop one in my mouth and am overwhelmed by the sweet, sugary taste, which rushes through my blood. It tastes like cherry, and is sweet and sour at the same time. It is incredible.

"Nice find," I say to Bree.

"Can I give one to Penelope?" she asks, who squirms in Bree's arms.

"Better not to," I say. "She might choke."

We continue on, each now more invested in scanning the rubble carefully. But despite Bree's initial find, we come up empty. We enter store after store, block after block, and I am beginning to feel hopeless.

"I don't see how anything could be left that wasn't already picked over," Ben says. "We're wasting time."

"We have no choice," Logan says. "We need to find gas."

"Well we can't make gas appear just by willing it to," Ben says. "If there's no gas, there's no gas."

"There must be an old gas station somewhere," Logan says. "Maybe an old body shop."

"Don't you think scavengers would've raided it?" Ben asks, annoyed.

I can't help feeling Ben's right. Maybe we are wasting time.

Logan stops and stares Ben down, equally annoyed.

"You have any better ideas?" Logan asks.

Ben hesitates. Clearly, he's stumped, too.

"Maybe we should split up," he says. "Cover more ground."

"Fine," Logan says without hesitating. "You go that way and I'll go this way."

They both turn and look at me, as if wondering who I will go with.

I feel torn, like a child divided between parents. I don't want to offend either one. But as I look at them, I can't help but feel that Ben needs my help more, and that Logan is more able to take care of himself. So I turn and head off with Ben.

"Let's all meet back here in an hour," I say to Logan. "Holler if you find anything."

I notice a hurt look on Logan's face, as he turns and heads off in his own direction, and I can't help feeling as if I betrayed him. But before I can say anything, he's walking away. Ben's right, anyway. We will cover more ground this way.

Bree sticks with me, and the three of us head off down a side street. As we go, I turn side to side, looking at all the different stores. I look everywhere for any sign of an auto shop, of a garage. I don't find any.

But as we turn down another street, I look over and can't believe my luck: I see a faded sign which reads: "Guns." The windows are a shell, and I am sure that this was the first store that was raided when the war broke out. But I enter anyway.

I rummage through the rubble, looking for anything we can salvage. Of course, all the glass display cases have been shattered, and all the guns are missing. On the floor, I see a few stray bullets. I lean down and pick one up and begin to examine it, when suddenly, I hear a distant noise, like a cry.

I immediately turn, and my heart stops to see that Bree is not in here. It's just me and Ben. I am shocked: I could have sworn she followed me in.

"Bree?" I ask, frantic. "Where is she?"

Ben stares back at me, wide-eyed, and before he can respond, I take off, bursting out the store.

Back in the street, I look all around, and see, in the snow, Bree's footsteps. I also see Penelope's paw prints, and I realize what happened: Bree must have put Penelope down, who must have ran off. Bree must have chased her.

I hear another cry, and I'm sure it's Bree.

I sprint down the street, following the trail. I am flooding with panic as I imagine the worst possible scenarios.

"BREE!?" I scream, frantic.

I turn the corner, and stop short at the site. There, at the far end of the street, is Bree, Penelope beside her. She stands frozen in shock, daring not to move. Because standing opposite her, towering over her, is a huge, vicious, emaciated bear.

The bear roars as it stands over Bree. It looks like it hasn't had a meal in years.

I watch in horror. There is little I can do: Bree, at the other end of the block, is too far for me. There is no way I'll be able to reach her in time.

Ben runs up beside me.

"Where's the bow!?" I scream to him. "Shoot it!"

"I didn't bring it!" he says back, frantic.

"BREE!" I scream. "Step back slowly!"

But Bree doesn't listen. She must be too frozen in fear.

I break into a sprint. The bear closes in, and there is nothing I can do. It will be too late. I am going to have to watch my little sister get killed before my eyes.

"BREE!" I scream.

The bear approaches her, and as it does, suddenly, I see motion.

Behind the bear, Logan turns the corner, comes running out, an old crowbar in hand. He charges, putting himself between Bree and the bear, winds up, and hits the bear just in time, just as its claws are coming down. Somehow, he also manages to push Bree out of the way at the last second.

Bree goes flying, tumbling in the snow, and the bear's claws slash Logan's thigh instead. Logan screams out in pain, as his blood squirts everywhere, darkening the snow red.

Logan switches hands with the crowbar, wheels around, and cracks the bear across its jaw. The bear yelps, turns, and flees down the side street.

"Logan!" I yell, as I run for him.

He sinks to his knees, collapsing, grabbing his thigh with two hands. My heart breaks as I can already see how badly injured he is.

I run to him, kneel down and grab him, draping one arm around his shoulder. Ben, to his credit, kneels down and props up Logan with his arm. The two of us pick him up, holding him. He is heavy, much heavier than I thought.

Ben reaches down, tears a strip off his shirt, and ties it around Logan's wound, tight. The bleeding slows, but drenches the rag quickly.

"We have to get back to the boat," I say. "Can you walk?"

Logan looks dazed, confused.

"I don't know," he says.

We prop him up, and he walks with us. He's hobbling badly, and I can feel his weight on me. I look at the injury and see how deep the claws punctured, nearly all the way to the bone. Logan's blood trails us on the snow.

Bree, right beside us, is crying.

"I'm sorry," she says. "I'm so sorry. It's all my fault."

"You didn't do anything wrong," I say back to her.

As we hurry back down the streets, I wonder what our next move should be. I have no idea. I know we have to get back to the boat, provide Logan some comfort. This town was a waste of time. And I feel that being out in the open is just too dangerous. Once we get back to the boat, somehow I'll know what to do.

As we turn the corner and the river comes into view, suddenly, I freeze. I can't believe what I see.

My mouth goes dry and heart drops into my throat. I'm too numb to move. To speak. I feel the world spinning out beneath me.

Because there, in the distance, on the water, I watch our boat being taken away. It is being tugged from shore by a large speedboat, all-black. They are not slaverunners—they look like some sort of pirates. They cut our anchor, and tied our boat to the back of theirs, and now they tug it away, at high speed. It is already halfway across the river, going God knows where. Our boat is gone.

We are stranded.

TWELVE

The four of us are still in a daze as we walk north, through the woods, alongside the Hudson. We walk beside the river, on snow-covered train tracks, and I watch the water as we go. A part of me refuses to believe our boat has been stolen.

But it's been hours, and it's starting to sink in that it's gone for good. That we are stranded, on foot. And our boat, our only means of transportation, is gone.

After we discovered the boat was gone, we all spent time brushing the snow off the shells of vehicles that lined the streets, some of them on their side, twisted, burnt out. It was a desperate move, and a waste of time. Of course, none of them had any keys, and most of them didn't even have engines—just gobs of metal, vestiges of cars. None of them remotely worked.

We knew we couldn't stay in that town. We figured our safest shelter might be somewhere in the woods, close to the river. So we walked.

Now here we are, completely on our own. I can't believe how stupid we were to leave the boat unguarded. But then again, who would've imagined that something like that would happen? We were too lax. We should have anticipated it.

But as I think about it, I realize that even if we did stay with the boat, there was probably not much we could have done. That was a large group of armed, professional pirates. Survivors. They probably would've just mowed us down with their guns. And with our boat basically out of fuel, it's not like we could've taken it anywhere else. Maybe we got lucky that they took it while we were away. Maybe if we had put up a fight, we'd all be dead right now.

The grim reality of not having any transportation or shelter starts to sink in, to weigh heavily on all of us. We all walk slowly, our feet crunching in the snow, which is hardening. The temperature has dropped at least ten degrees and the wind has picked up; the snow is now freezing and turning to ice. A deep cold is starting to settle in my bones, to pierce right through me. I look at the others and see it is piercing through all of us. We are all huddled over, rubbing our hands, desperate for warmth.

Making matters worse—much worse—is Logan. He was hurt bad, and Ben and I have to help him walk, his arms slung over our shoulders. It is slowing us down, and I am very concerned for him. Up until now, he was always our backbone, our strength; now, he is a liability. I can't help feeling that the odds are turning against us. The idea of reaching Canada at this point is almost laughable. We'd be lucky to make it the next mile.

We are getting farther and farther from any remnants of civilization, deep into the woods, and I'm starting to feel that our chances are grim. We're nearly out of supplies, there is no sign of shelter, it's getting dark out, colder, and soon we'll have to stop for the night. Even Ben's bow and arrow, left on the boat, is gone.

Hunger sets in, eating away at my stomach, stabbing me with sharp pains. I am feeling weaker with each step, especially with Logan's weight pressing down on me.

As we continue down the train tracks, I look out at the river and see it has frozen over—one big sheet of ice. It is incredible. Even if we were in our boat now, we couldn't get anywhere, anyway.

I can't go on much longer, and I sense that Ben and Logan can't, either. In the distance, I spot a particularly thick copse of trees, forming a wall from the elements. We head for them.

As we enter the patch of trees, I feel they provide some protection from the wind. I stop, and the others turn to me.

"I think we should rest here," I say. "It's almost dark."

"Good idea," Ben says, slowly removing Logan's arm from around him.

Logan winces in pain as he does. I look down at his leg: it is already swollen. Luckily, it doesn't look quite as infected as Rose's had; maybe the cold weather has helped. But still, it is a very bad injury.

"Are you okay?" I ask Logan.

He nods quickly, wincing, and Ben and I lower him down to the ground. He sits heavily, his back against one of the thick trees, and breathes out sharply in pain as he does, his face bunching up into a million wrinkles. But he never cries, or complains. Not once. He is a real trooper.

"I'm starving," Bree says.

I kick myself for leaving our food on the boat; the only thing I had thought to take with me was a single jar of half-eaten jam. I pull it out of my pocket now. It is raspberry, Bree's favorite, and as I unscrew the lid, Penelope whines, too. I reach in, take a huge scoop out, and put it into Bree's open palm. She eats slowly, savoring it, then reaches over and gives some to Penelope.

I hold the jar out to Ben, then to Logan, and they each tape take a finger-full, savoring it. Finally, I do the same, taking the last scoop of our last jar. It melts in my mouth, and is the best raspberry jam I've had in my life. I close my eyes, trying to savor every second of it. What I would give right now for a dozen jars like this.

I look at the empty jar longingly. We are out of food. It is going to be a long, hard night.

*

Hours have passed since we've curled up here. Night has fallen, and the four of us sit in the snow, our backs to the trees, freezing. We all huddle against the wind and the cold, which seems to get worse with every minute.

Thank God, after hours of effort, I was able to start a fire. I used the last of the matches that I salvaged from dad's place, lit the last candle, and used the shelter from the wind, to light the kindling I'd found. I built a small pile, but even so, it took nearly all the matches to get something going.

Now there is a small fire before the four of us. We are all so cold, we literally hover over it, raising and rubbing our palms. Every passing gust of wind threatens to blow it out, and I get up every few minutes, and put more sticks on. The fire is fighting to stay alive. Just like the four of us.

It helps a lot, but provides little warmth in these awful conditions. I've never been so cold in my life. The cold seeps into my hands, my feet, my nose. It's hard to think straight. I have to keep opening and closing my limbs, trying to keep my whole body from freezing over. I feel if I fall asleep, I will never wake up.

I can't imagine how much worse it would be without the fire. I know that having a fire here is not the safest thing—it could attract the wrong kind of attention. But we are past the point of caring. If tomorrow's like this, I don't see how we could make it through another day. We will be frozen by the end of it—if we don't starve first.

I look over at Logan, and he looks delirious. He sleeps, wincing in pain, and his leg looks stiff, frozen solid. I don't know how we'll be able to drag him tomorrow.

I lay with one arm over Bree's shoulder, rubbing her as she leans into me, resting her head on my shoulder. I take some solace in the fact that, if we all die, at least we will die on our terms. Not as slaves, or prisoners. But together. Free.

Well, at least we had a nice run. I think of how far we came, how much we accomplished—escaping from the slaverunners, getting as far as we did. It is something, at least.

At least we have survived. And that is what I've learned. Every day of survival is a victory. That in itself is what we live for. And my hundreds of days of survival have been hundreds of small victories.

"Can you read me a story?" Bree asks.

I try to think, try once again to remember the words to *The Giving Tree*. This time, to my surprise, the words come back to me.

"Once, there was a tree, and she loved a little boy. And every day the boy would come, and he would gather her leaves, and make them into crowns and play king of the forest," I say.

I feel Bree relax in my arms as I continue to recite the book from memory. Amazingly, it all comes back to me, line after line, and I recite the whole thing to her. I reach the ending:

"'Well, an old stump is good for sitting and resting. Come, Boy, sit down. Sit down and rest.' And the boy did. And the tree was happy."

I feel Bree fast asleep in my arms. It is a gift, falling asleep in this weather. I hope that she dreams of things, other worlds, other places, other times.

I look over at Logan, and see he, too, is asleep, in a fitful, painful sleep. Then I look over at Ben. He is awake, his eyes open wide, staring into the flames. I wonder what he is thinking of. His brother? What he could have done differently?

I cannot help but think back to that moment, in Penn Station, before we parted ways. When he leaned in and kissed me. Why had he done it? Had he really meant it? I'm no longer sure how he feels.

"Ben?" I ask softly, my teeth chattering.

He turns and looks at me. His eyes are sunken, as if they've just been through a war.

A part of me thinks we might not all make it through this night. If we don't, I want to know how he really feels about me.

Now that he's looking at me, I don't know how to ask. I am nervous. But I force myself. After all, I have little left to lose.

"When you kissed me, back in the city," I say. "Why did you do that?"

I look at him, searching into his eyes, waiting for his reaction. I don't know why, but for some reason, now, here, of all places, it is suddenly important to me.

He opens his mouth and closes it several times. He looks flustered, as if he doesn't know how to respond.

"I… I…um…" He looks down, then up again. "I'm sorry," he says. "I wasn't in my right mind."

His words hurt me.

"So you're saying you didn't mean to?" I ask.

My heart is sinking. He looks down, then back up at me.

"That's not what I'm saying," he says. "I did mean to do it. I meant to do it. I wanted to."

"So then why are you sorry?" I ask.

He looks at me, confused.

"Aren't you upset that I kissed you?" he asks.

I think about that. I was surprised at the time. But not…upset. And now, as I think about…no, I'm not upset.

In fact, I want him to do it again.

But I'm nervous, and my words are starting to fail me. So instead, I shake my head.

Slowly, he gets up, snow crunching beneath him, and takes a few steps over to me.

He sits in the empty spot beside me, against the same tree, and looks into my eyes. He reaches up with one hand and places it on my cheek.

My heart is pounding.

And then slowly, Ben leans in and kisses me.

At first, I hesitate.

But then, I meet his kiss, kissing him back. My heart is pounding in my chest, and for the first time in as long as I can remember, I'm no longer aware of my surroundings, of the cold, the hunger, of the million things that are wrong in the universe.

I think only of Ben. And of my wonder that he can transport me from this place, this time, with just a single, magical kiss.

THIRTEEN

I awaken at dawn, slowly peeling open my eyes, colder than I've ever been. The cold is unfathomable. I feel as if someone has thrown me into a meat locker and slammed shut the door, and not let me out for a week.

The fire is long-extinguished, now ashes, covered in ice. I look up and see that the entire ground is covered in ice—and that all the trees are covered in ice, too. Everything, down to the smallest branch, hangs with ice. I can't believe it. An ice storm.

The world is as beautiful as it is cold, everything frozen, shining in the early morning light. I feel as if I've wakened in Superman's palace.

I try to move, and feel my body covered in ice, stuck to the tree. I raise my arms and shoulders, and I break off small particles of ice. Ben has fallen asleep beside me, leaning against the same tree, and Bree is asleep on my other side. Two feet away is Logan, lying exactly as I left him, against his own tree. Everyone is asleep but me. They all look frozen. In fact, they all look dead, and for a moment, I wonder if they have all frozen to death.

My heart beats wildly as I sit up. I shake Bree. Penelope wakes, looking up at me, her eyes sleepy, then, finally, Bree opens her eyes, too. I flood with relief. We're not dead, yet.

I reach over and shake Ben, then get up and shake Logan. Thankfully, they each wake, although they all look frozen, half dead. I know we can't lay here anymore.

"We have to get up," I say. "We have to keep moving. If we don't, we'll freeze to death. Let's go. On your feet," I say, summoning my toughest voice, needing to mobilize them.

I help pull them up, and slowly, each of them begins to rise, the sound of ice cracking as they gain their feet. Logan tries several times, but can't seem to get up on his bad leg, which is covered in ice. I'm hoping the ice helped reduce the inflammation, at least. I bend down and drape one of his arms over my shoulder, and Ben takes the other. Together, we hoist him onto his feet. My back reels as I do so: he feels like he weighs a thousand pounds.

Logan groans as he gets to his feet, and he wobbles, unsteady.

"I can't stand," he says.

"We'll walk you," I say.

I look at Ben, he nods back, and together, we begin to walk Logan, he leaning heavily on us, limping on one leg. Bree hurries up beside us, holding Penelope. I take one last look back at our little campsite, at the frozen fire, at the sparkling woods all around us. I'm glad to leave this place.

We hobble through the woods, the four of us, walking into the breaking day, each stiff and exhausted. We reach an open clearing, and find the train tracks and continue alongside them, our feet crunching with every step on the ice. It must be ten degrees. I've never been this cold in my life. It is a mind-numbing cold, one that prevents me from thinking clearly.

"Where are we going?" Bree asks, finally shattering the silence.

I'm wondering the same thing myself. All I know is that we are heading north, to some remote town in Canada that probably doesn't even exist. With each step, I feel more and more the futility, the impossibility, of our mission. We are slowing down with each step, too, and I'm seriously doubting if we will even survive to nightfall.

"I don't know," I answer Bree, truthfully.

I look for shelter as we go, but see none. Nothing but endless trees and train tracks, and the frozen river to our side. No sign of any towns at this point, no boats, no old houses—nothing. We are in the midst of a vast stretch of wilderness, and we walk and walk. With every minute, it's getting colder, harder, and my legs ache even more.

"Stop," Logan says.

Ben and I stop and turn and look at him. He is groaning in pain, his face drawn, too pale. He looks like a walking corpse.

"I can't go on anymore," he says. "Leave me here. You'll be faster without me. I'm not going to make it anyway."

"We're not going to leave you," I say.

Logan pulls his arms off of our shoulders, and suddenly collapses down to the ground. He lies there, not moving.

"I can't go on," he says, lying there.

We all exchange a worried look.

"Leave me," he says. "I'm serious."

I don't know what to do. I know that I can't leave him. But if he refuses to walk, I can't force him to.

I realize he's right: we're not getting anywhere. He is slowing us down. But at the same time, I don't care. I think back, remember when he helped me. He wouldn't let me die, for any reason. And I'm not about to let him die. Especially since he hurt himself saving Bree's life.

"We can stand here all day if you want," I say down to him. "We're not leaving you. If you can't walk, we'll make camp here."

Logan weakly shakes his head, too tired to argue back.

As I stand there, listening to the wind howl, feeling colder than I ever have, trying to figure out what to do, suddenly, I hear a noise.

Ben and Bree must hear it, too, because at the same time, we all turn and look at the horizon.

I stand there and watch the horizon, and wonder if my ears are playing tricks on me. First, there is a low rumbling, like the sound of an engine. At first I wonder if it's a slaverunner boat, racing up the Hudson somehow, despite the ice, coming to get us. But then I realize the engine sounds different. Like some kind of vehicle. Maybe a truck.

I look all around, and see no signs of a road. Yet somehow, the sound is getting stronger, closer. I even begin to feel the ground tremor beneath me.

"A train!" Bree yells, excited.

The second she says it, I realize she's right. I can't believe it. I have no idea how it's possible. A train? Running? I haven't seen a running train in years. But then again, I've never been on this side of the river.

But a train to where? From where? Operated by whom? It doesn't seem possible.

Sure enough, as I continue to look, there, on the horizon, there begins to appear a large, rusted, freight train, moving right towards us, on the tracks. It chugs along, moving slowly, kicking up huge clouds of exhaust.

I realize this could be what we need. It could be a godsend. If we can get on that train somehow, maybe it will be heated—or if not heated, maybe at least protected from the elements. Whatever it is, it has to be warmer than being out here. And we could get on it, and rest, and wherever it's going, it is, at least, heading north. And who knows? Maybe it's actually going some place civilized?

We have no choice. Here we'll freeze to death.

"Logan, you have to get up!" I yell at him. "There's a train coming! We have to catch it!"

"No," he moans.

Ben jumps into action: he reaches down, and with all his might, he picks Logan up. He grabs him by his shoulders and drags him to his feet, Logan moaning. I come over and help, and we manage to get him up.

Logan opens his eyes and looks at me.

"Logan, please," I say. "You saved me once. Let me save you. Let *us* save you. Please. Survive. We don't want to be without you."

Logan's eyes open for a moment, then he nods, relenting.

We stand to the side, as the train comes towards us. Luckily, it's going slow, probably about five miles an hour. My guess is that they're conserving gas.

But it's perfect for our purposes. It will give us a chance to actually jump on it, and to get Logan on board.

We wait as it passes, watching, and I see that it is about twenty cars long. The cares are made of an old, weathered wood, and some of the doors are open, revealing empty cars. I wonder again what its purpose is.

We get into position, and I drag Logan close to the tracks.

"Logan, you have to help us," I say. "When we get close, Ben will jump up and open the door. He'll pull you up and I'll push. Bree, when Ben jumps up, you jump up with him and get inside. Everybody ready?"

We all turn, as the next car comes.

"NOW!" I scream.

Ben jumps up into the car, turns and reaches out a hand. Beside me, Bree jumps up with Penelope, easily getting into the car. I shove and push Logan with all I have, and Logan does his best to make one last effort, as he grabs Ben's hand and pulls himself. Ben, to his credit, yanks Logan with all that he has. I gave him one final shove, and he goes head first into the car. His legs are sticking out, but he's in.

The car has gone past me, so I race to catch up. My legs are moving slowly, stiffer than I thought, and I slip. The train is getting farther away.

"Brooke!" Bree screams out.

I regain my footing, and force myself to run faster, the cold air cutting my lungs.

My dad's voice rings in my head.

Come on soldier. Come on!

I run through the pain bursting through my frozen limbs, breathing hard. I run faster than the train, catch up to the car, then reach out and grab Ben's hand. I step up on the iron latch, and he yanks me in. I go tumbling into the train car.

I sit up, look around, and can hardly believe it. We are in. We made. All four of us. Penelope barks.

I burst into laughter, victorious laughter. It is contagious, and we all sit there, laughing. We have made it. We are out of the cold, and we are moving.

It is much warmer in here, compared to the bitter cold outside. This is the break we needed, what we needed to de-thaw. To rest. Even better, it gives us a vantage point from which to view the countryside as we go, allowing us to look out for any towns—or anything—as we pass.

"We made it," I say.

I look down and see Logan smiling, lying on the floor. Bree and Ben sit close by.

"The question is, to where?" Ben asks. "Where is this train going?"

It is the same question I'm wondering myself.

"Wherever it is," Ben says, "it can't be good. I'm guessing that the only people organized enough to run a train must be slaverunners."

"It could be some sort of government or military unit," I say. "Maybe even that town in Canada Logan was talking about."

But even as I say it, I know it's unlikely. I know that Ben is probably right.

"And what if it's not?" he asks.

"The way I see it, it gets us out of the cold and gives us a vantage point to scout the countryside. If we pass any towns, any shelters, any structures, any boats—anything good—we can always just jump. Being stranded in the wilderness wasn't exactly helping us."

Ben shrugs, unconvinced.

"It's risky," he says. "We don't know who's running this. Or what's waiting for us."

A part of me knows he's right; but at the same time, I don't see what choice we have. We just have to ride this train out, see where it takes us.

And hope and pray for the best.

*

I open my eyes, immediately alert. Something is wrong. I look around and see Bree, Logan, Ben and Penelope, all lying asleep in front of me. Muted afternoon light comes in through the slats in the wood. Everything seems peaceful enough. But I know something is wrong. I can feel it.

And then I realize: we are not moving. The train has stopped.

I try to get my bearings, to remember. I'm sitting exactly where I put myself when I came in, right along the slats of the train door, so I could look out. I remember sitting here and watching the countryside pass, for hours. I looked out on one side, and Ben on the other. We promised to let each other know if we saw anything worth jumping for. But I watched for hours, and saw nothing. There was nothing but wilderness, and desolation. Snow and ice as far as the eye could see. It was a barren wasteland: like crossing the face of the moon.

And then, at some point, I must've fallen asleep. So stupid of me. I should've stayed awake, on guard. But as I look around, I see the others have all fallen asleep, too. We were just so tired.

And now, we are stopped. I don't know why. Or where. I look out and see nothing but wilderness.

My heart is pounding, as I wonder what the destination could be. Should I wake everyone? Should we jump out now?

Before I can decide, I hear a noise. At first, it is faint, then it grows more distinct. Approaching us are footsteps in the snow and ice. The crunching gets louder, as several sets of steps approach. I brace myself, wondering who it can be. I have a feeling that whoever it is, it can't be good.

I look around at the others, my first instinct to protect them. I reach down to my waist, feel my knife, and place my hand on it, ready to use it if I have to.

"Ben," I hiss.

He doesn't respond, asleep.

"Ben," I hiss again.

Finally, he opens his eyes, blinking several times, disoriented.

"We've got company."

Ben sits up, alert. Logan, now awake, too, slides his pistol over to Ben, who takes it.

Suddenly, the train door slides open, light flooding into the car. The light is blinding, and for a moment, I can't see what's happening. I kneel to the side, out of sight; luckily, Ben, Logan and Bree are off to the side, too. We all hide in the dark corners, and there is no way that anyone could spot us without looking carefully. My heart is pounding in my chest, as I wonder who it could be.

I hear the muffled cries and groans of several people, and moments later, bodies are hurled across the threshold, into the car

One after the other, bodies land on the floor with a thud, in the car with us. They are bound and gagged, hands tied tightly behind their backs, their feet tied together, and they hit the floor hard, squirming. I realize that someone must be throwing them in.

They are captives. But to whom? And why? And where are they taking them?

I brace myself, wondering if anyone will follow, if I will have to fight.

But the train door slides closed just as quickly, and slams shut with a bang. I hear a new sound, one which makes my heart drop: it is the sound of a heavy metal bolt, being slid into place. And then, I realize: we have just been locked in.

The train starts up again, and we begin to move.

I am overwhelmed with conflicting emotions. A part of me wants to get out immediately, as a kickback reaction, to break open the door. I hate being locked in, anywhere. And now I feel like a prisoner.

But another part of me forces myself to stay calm, to figure out what's going on. And possibly to wait. After all, there are no good options out there, either.

Ben drops the gun, and I lower my knife. The four of us exchange a wary glance, staring at our new guests.

"Brooke?" Bree calls out nervously.

"It's okay, Bree," I say out confidently across the car.

The six captives turn at the sound of our voices; they squirm up, and look over my way. Enough light comes into the slats so that I can make them out. They are our age. Teenagers. Emaciated. They look tired, sickly, freezing. They look like the walking dead. They stare back at me with desperate, hollowed-out eyes. One of them, a girl with stringy brown hair clinging to her face, has managed to get her gag free.

"Please, help me," she whispers out to me, her voice hoarse. "Please, untie me. I beg you."

I look over at Ben, and he nods back.

"Don't do it," comes a voice.

Logan is sitting up, struggling with his leg. "Don't untie them."

"Why?"

"You don't know them. You don't know how they'll react."

"I'm not going to hurt you," the girl hisses at Logan.

"I know she won't hurt me," he says. "But they might draw attention we don't need."

I look between her and Logan, debating. Logan is such a cynic; I don't share his views. And I can't help feeling terrible for her.

I hurry to her, and use my knife to cut the ropes behind her wrist. I then cut the ropes tying her feet together. She immediately leans forward and rubs her wrist and ankles, breathing hard, tearing off her gag.

She surveys the train car, looking frenzied, wide-eyed.

"You have to get out while you can," she says in a rush, frantic. "You don't understand. You don't understand what they'll do to you."

She looks all around, like a crazy person, as if looking for a way to escape.

"Who is they?" I ask. "Who are you? Where are they bringing you?"

"I have to get out," she says, jumping to her feet. "I can't let them take me."

"Take you where?" I ask, growing increasingly alarmed. She darts her head all around, then suddenly, she stands and sprints across the car.

"Wait!" I scream, worried for what she will do, worried that she will draw attention to us. Logan was right. I shouldn't have untied her.

But it's too late. She darts across the car, and runs to the small door that connects the two cars. She tries to pry it open, but it won't give.

She leans back, and kicks at the wood with her bare feet. She kicks again and again, even though she's cutting her own feet. Whatever it is she's running from, she's truly desperate. She throws her body through the wood and finally shatters it. A gust of freezing air enters the car.

"Stop!" I yell, running to her.

But I can't get her in time. She jumps in between the cars, and then jumps down, landing barefoot in the snow and ice.

She doesn't seem to care. I watch her, and she keeps running, sprinting as far away from the train as she can.

Suddenly, the train slams to an abrupt stop, sending me flying across the car and slamming my head into the wall.

I turn and look between the slats, and see her running across the field. Then I see a slaverunner. He steps up, holds out a gun, and fires.

"No!" Bree screams, standing beside me, also watching.

He has shot her in the back, and she lands face first, dead.

The slaverunner turns and stares at our car. I feel as if he's looking right at me.

"I'm sorry," Bree says. "I shouldn't have screamed."

My heart sinks to see the slaverunner begin to approach our car.

"We have to get out of here," I say urgently.

"They're coming!" Bree screams, still watching through the slats. I turn and look: slaverunners. Tons of them. They're coming right for our car. We're finished.

I was so stupid. I shouldn't have freed the girl.

"We have to surrender!" Ben says. "They'll kill us."

"No!" I scream, determined to never be captured again. "We won't surrender. When they open the door, fire!"

I hold my knife, ready to hurl it.

Suddenly, the door is unbolted, rolls back.

As the first sign of them, Ben fires. To his credit, he hits the first slaverunner right in the chest. He falls face first, into the car.

As he does, the slaverunner's handgun comes spilling out of his hand, sliding across the floor towards me. I pounce on it.

I take a knee, my back to the far wall, and open fire. I take out one after the next. Ben takes out more himself. The bodies are piling up. I can't believe it, the damage were doing.

I am wondering how much ammo I have left, when suddenly the wall opens up behind me. I had no idea there was a sliding door on the other side of the car, too, and now I realize that my back wasn't against a wall, but against a door. It opens behind me, and I feel hands grab me, yank me backwards.

The world and the sky go hurling past me, as I go flying through the air, and land hard on my back in the snow. I feel my head and back hit the ice hard, feel the wind knocked out of me.

Dazed, on my back, I look up at the blue sky, at the clouds, and then see several slaverunners standing over me, scowling down through their masks. Before I can react, one of them raises his boot.

The last thing I see, coming right down for my face, are his thick, rubber treads.

And then my world goes black.

FOURTEEN

I wake with a splitting headache. The entire right side of my face is swollen, and I can feel a huge lump on my head. The pain is so strong that for once, I don't feel the hunger, or the cold. It feels like a combination of a really bad hangover, and having been punched hard in the face.

That is when I remember: the slaverunners. Our fight. That boot coming down on my face.

In a sudden panic, I try to figure out where I am. I hear the familiar sound of the train moving on the tracks and feel an icy wind blowing in, and I realize I'm back in the same train car. Except now, things are different: I'm lying on my side, on the floor, and as I try to move my hands and feet, I realize I'm bound. My hands are tied tightly together behind my back with a coarse linen rope, and my feet are tied at the ankles. I squirm, try to move, but cannot. The rope cuts into my skin hard. They have tied it well.

I lift my head, looking all around, desperately trying to see who else is in here with me. I look first for Bree. There are several bodies strewn about the car floor, and at first, I can't tell who is who. There are at least ten of us in here. We're now just like first group that was thrown in here: bound. Helpless.

I'm flooded with panic as I wonder if Bree is still with me, if she's dead or alive. I look all around, in every direction, moving my body as best I can, and finally, with relief, I spot her. She is bound, too, lying there. I'm relieved that she's here, and even more relieved to see that her eyes are open, and she's staring back at me. Rolled up against her stomach is Penelope, shaking, cowering.

"Bree? Are you okay?"

She nods back, but her eyes are opened wide, and I can see the fear in her face.

"Are you hurt?" I ask. I survey her body, see no signs of injury, and as she shakes her head no, I feel even more relieved. We're lucky. I killed several of them. And all they did was bound me and the others in return.

But as I think about it, I realize maybe we are not so lucky. If they chose to bind us, to take us somewhere, instead of kill us, there must be a good reason. And that can only mean that they're bringing us somewhere to torture us. Or to use as sport. Or worse: to make us fight in another arena.

My stomach drops at the thought of it. I look around in the car, and I spot Ben and Logan, both bound. I also look over the other kids, everyone bound, lying on the floor, not moving. I can't believe I have ended up in this position again. A prisoner. I can't imagine being brought to another arena. I close my eyes for a moment at the pain, trying to block it all out.

The train ride gets bumpy, my head hits the hardwood, and jolts me awake. I realize I've drifted off.

Suddenly, I hear a loud banging on the car door. I'm confused, because the train is still moving. The banging comes again, from both sides, like hail smashing against the wood.

I roll over, up against the car door, and lift my neck, peering through the slats. I can't believe what I see.

The train slows as we enter the remnants of a city. It is a vast place, the buildings burnt out, just piles of rubble. The streets are filled with garbage, refuse, and to my surprise: people. Mutants. Biovictims. Their faces are warped and melted, their bodies emaciated. They look crazed, as if an entire mental asylum had let all its prisoners at once. They look as if they'd tear us to pieces if they could. For once, I'm happy that these train doors are bolted shut.

Mobs of them start hobbling towards the train, throwing rocks at us as we go. Some come right up to the door, slamming it with sticks. They are chanting and screaming, and I'm trying to understand what is happening.

As we pass through the city, through block after block, I realize we are being taken somewhere for these peoples' enjoyment. That we are the sport. The sound of objects striking the car is deafening.

I try to figure out what city we're in. We've been going so far north, for so long, I am guessing we must be far upstate New York. As I look out, at the city outline, I think I recognize what was once Buffalo. I see rivers in the distance, crisscrossing through the city, and am surprised to see several motorboats on them. Slaverunner boats, well-guarded, dozens of soldiers, everywhere.

That tells me something. We are being brought to them. And that can only mean one thing: a new arena.

The banging grows so loud that I fear they will smash our car doors in. At just that moment, our train suddenly dips down, like a roller coaster ride. I feel my stomach plunge. Suddenly, the city goes black. The tracks have descended, have dipped down into a tunnel, beneath the city. Now all I see are the red emergency lights of the tunnel, which we pass every twenty feet or so. Our destination can't be far.

I roll across the car, beside Bree. I want to make sure she is okay.

"It's okay Bree," I reassure. "Just stay close to me. Do you understand? Whatever happens, just stay close to me."

She nods back, and I can see she's trying to be brave, but she's nodding through silent tears.

Suddenly, the train stops. There comes the sound of our car being unbolted, the lock slid back.

Penelope barks.

"Go Penelope!" Bree screams.

She looks back at Bree and whines, not wanting to leave.

"GO! RUN! ESCAPE!" Bree screams fiercely.

Penelope finally listens, and just as the car door is opening, she turns and bolts, jumping out. She goes so fast, she flies under the radar of the slaverunners, disappears beneath the tracks. I hope she runs far from here.

We are not so lucky. Several pair of steel boots step up, into the car, and I look up, and see the faces, through the masks, staring down.

Now, we are at their mercy.

*

A slaverunner walks right for me and takes out a huge knife. I lay there, bound and helpless, and close my eyes, expecting him to stab me. I brace myself. The knife gets closer, and he leans over, and I see the blade coming down. I flinch.

But to my surprise, he doesn't cut me; instead, he slips the knife between my feet and slices the rope binding my ankles together. All around me, slaverunners are doing the same to the others. They want us to walk. They are taking us somewhere.

I'm hoping they will also free the ropes on my wrist, but I'm not so lucky. A slaverunner grabs me from behind, by the back of my shirt, and pulls me roughly to my feet. It feels good to be standing again, and I rub my ankles together, trying to soothe the rope burn. The ropes are still way too tight my wrist, bounding my shoulders, and while I can walk, I can barely move otherwise.

The slaverunners take the gags out of the other prisoners' mouths, as well. As soon as they do, a girl a couple years younger than me, cries out, frantic.

"Where are you taking us!? Where are we going? Where are we?"

A slaverunner reaches out and backhands her hard across the face. She cries out and falls back, crashing into some empty boxes. Another slaverunner yanks her to her feet.

Lesson learned. Don't talk back.

We are herded off the train, and down onto the floor of the train tunnel. My boots crunch on the gravel. At least it is dry here, no snow. But it is dark, lit only by the emergency bulbs, and it is cold, drafts whipping through the empty tunnels. We are all herded together, and I make sure I stay close to Bree. We are poked and prodded and we begin marching down the tunnel, going deeper into the blackness. I wonder where they are taking us.

We are pushed and shoved down tunnel after tunnel, a ragtag group, scores of slaverunners behind and in front of us. I walk with Bree on one side and Logan and Ben on the other. Logan is suffering, I can see, limping badly on his leg, and Ben and I do our best to prop him up between us. The other captives march like sheep, not even trying to resist.

We turn a bend, and stop before a stone wall. Before it is a single torch, and beneath that, I can barely make out the outline of a steel door. A slaverunner steps forward, unlocks it, and yanks it open.

I'm kicked hard in the small of my back and go flying, with the rest of the group, tumbling into the room. I land hard on the ground, rolling in the dusty, dirty floor, then hear the steel door slammed behind me.

But my hands are bound so tightly behind my back, it is hard for me to get leverage to get back on my feet. I lie there, beside Bree and Logan and the others, and look up, trying to figure out where we are.

We are in a huge, cavernous room, the walls lit by torches, high up. It is like a large cave. The first thing I notice is the noise. And the second is movement.

I look up, blinking dust out of my eyes, and see dozens of people swarming about the room. Kids. We are the only ones tied down, the new kids, thrown down on the floor.

As I watch, several of the other kids race forward towards us, and suddenly start kicking the teenage girl on the ground a few feet away from me. She cries out, as they kick her in every direction. Several kids get down and start rifling through her pockets, looking for whatever scraps they can find.

Just as I'm about to cry out in protest, I feel a kick, hard in my stomach. I look up and see a kid standing over me. I feel others rummaging through my pockets. Then I feel another kick.

I buckle like crazy, trying to break free, but my hands are bound tightly. I manage to swing around and with my free foot, kick one of them hard in the face: a scraggly boy, around 15. I connect hard on his jaw, and he goes down. But I immediately get another kick in my ribs. There are just too many of them.

I look over at Bree, and see, thankfully, that they haven't reached her yet. But as I watch I see a boy ran up behind her, maybe 11, with sandy brown hair and green eyes. Even in this light, I can't help noticing that he looks different than the others—noble, intelligent, kind. He is good looking, too, with freckles spread across his face.

So I'm surprised to see him pull out a knife, with that sweet angelic face of his, and aim it right at Bree's exposed back.

"BREE!" I scream out desperately.

As I watch, from several feet away, the boy lowers his knife and, to my surprise, slashes the ropes bounding her wrists. He is freeing her.

I feel another kick in my ribs, right before I see Bree yell to him: "Free her!" pointing at me.

The boy slips in between the others, and a moment later, I feel the knife cutting the ropes off my wrists.

That is all I need. A moment later, I jump to my feet and tackle the person in front of me hard, a 17-year-old, skinny boy. I drive him back several feet, and slam him down hard on the ground, knocking the wind out of him. I jump to my feet, spin around, and kick another boy hard in the face, knocking him out.

Then I spin again, like a wild woman, ready to face the others.

But now that I am freed, and have inflicted some damage, the others seem wary of me. Of the dozen or so, only one steps forward to challenge me. A boy, missing an eye, maybe 15, but wide and fat. He scowls as he charges, reaching up with his dirty palm to smack me across the face.

I dodge at the last second, and he goes world whizzing past me. As he does, I lean back and kick him hard in the small of the back. He goes flying forward, face first, and lands on his fat stomach. Not taking any chances, I run up behind him, and kick him hard between the legs while he's down. He groans in pain, and stops moving.

I turn to face the others, but now, they are afraid. They all back off, starting to dissipate. I see that Logan and Ben are still tied down and I hurry over to them, looking for the boy that freed us. I don't know who he is, where he went, or why he did it—but now I can't find him. I stand over them protectively, and the other kids in the room back away.

I realize that these other kids are prisoners, just like us. I can't understand why they'd welcome us like this.

"They do this with all the newbies," comes a voice.

I turn to see the boy standing there, holding the knife.

"They're just trying to raid you. To take what they can. And to test you. After all, you're their competition. They want to show you who's boss."

"Competition?" Bree asks, stepping forward.

I can see by the way she's staring at this boy that she likes him. And I can see by the way he stares back that he likes her, too. He lowers his knife.

I hurry over to him. "Can I borrow that?" I ask.

He looks at me warily, reluctant to let his weapon go.

I gesture to Ben and Logan, still tied up on the ground. The boy turns, not wanting to give up his knife, and instead hurries over to them himself and cuts their ropes.

Ben quickly gains his feet; he is shaken, but not hurt badly. Logan, though, just turns over. I can see from the pain in his face that is unable to make his feet. His swollen leg looks worse.

It is warmer in here, much warmer than outside. With all the body heat in this room, and all the torches, it must be close to 60 in here. I welcome the reprieve; we need to thaw out. It's not good for Logan's leg, though. I can't help but think of Rose, of how she ended up. I pray to God the same fate does not await Logan. It's so strange to look at him now, lying there, so helpless—when just days ago he was our beacon of strength, the backbone of our mission.

"Yes, your competition," the boy continues, returning to Bree's side. "Think you're down here alone?"

"Where's here?" I ask. "Where are we?"

"You're in the cage, just like all of us. We're the entertainment now. Tomorrow, the games begin. You'll be in it, just like the rest of us. We'll all die together."

I turn and survey the room, look at all the faces. They're all kids, teenagers, just like us. They're all emaciated, survivors, rounded up from the countryside by the slaverunners. Some look sicker than others. Only a few of them are anywhere near fit. I realize with a sinking feeling that we are heading back into another arena, will soon be made to fight to the death. To kill one of the kids in this room.

I only spot one person who seems strong, and I'm surprised to see it's a girl. About my age, my height—but with a more muscular build than me. In fact, she's almost built like a bodybuilder. She wears tight, camouflage pants and a tattered green shirt, and for some reason she stands across the room, her back against a wall, and stares right at me with her big black eyes. It is a piercing, intense stare, and I wonder what I've done to get on her bad side. She looks like a formidable opponent.

"Don't be scared of her," the boy says, catching my look. "That's my sister."

I turn look at the boy, and see no resemblance.

"She's just watching out for me."

I turn and look down at the boy, and remember how he helped us. I'm so grateful.

"Thank you for saving us," I say.

He smiles back and shrugs. He is cute, innocent, with his freckles across his nose.

Brooke approaches him. "Yeah, thanks," she echoes.

He turns and looks at her, and smiles back, seeming to be transfixed by her.

She looks away, and I could swear that I see her cheeks flush.

"Want to introduce us to your sister?" I ask.

"Sure," he says.

There's a sweetness to this boy, a happy-go-lucky attitude, that surprises me, as if he is unfazed by all of this.

As we turn and follow him, Ben and I dragging Logan. Bree hurries up and walks alongside him.

"What's your name?" he asks her.

Bree turns and looks at me, as if for permission, and I nod back.

"Bree," she says. "What's yours?"

"Charlie," he says, holding out his hand.

Bree waits a moment, then shakes it.

"Charlie," she says. "That's a funny name."

"Why?" he asks.

"I don't know, it just is."

"My sister is going to be mad," he says to me, as we get closer. "I'm just warning you. She gets mad when I talk to people. Especially if I help them. She wants us to keep to ourselves."

We get closer, and she comes into view, standing beneath a torch: she stands against a wall, arms crossed, and with her sleeveless shirt, I can see her huge muscles bulging in her shoulders and arms. She looks like a rock, like part of the wall itself. She's a humorless person, with a warrior's face. The opposite of her little brother. He was right: she is scowling.

"Get over here," she snaps at Charlie.

He hurries over, and stands at her side, facing us.

"Your brother saved us," I say to her. "Thank you."

"He should've let you die," she says.

She scowls back, meaning every word of it.

I am surprised by her response. I've never met such a hard person; she's harder than Logan ever was.

"We're not running a charity here. It's every man for himself. And if I have to kill each one of you in the games, I will," she says. "Don't think that you're getting on my good side."

"I don't even know what the games are," I say.

She stares back, cold. "You will."

"Don't be so mean to them, Flo," Charlie says.

"What games?" Ben asks, stepping forward.

She surveys him, looking him up and down, coldly summing up the competition. She looks like she decides he isn't worth the bother.

"The reason we're down here," she says. "We're bait. Everyone dies."

"Except for you!" Charlie chimes in proudly. "Tell them! She's the only who ever survived. This is her second go."

I survey her with a new respect. Somehow, I'm not surprised.

But her scowl only deepens.

"I'm not stupid enough to think that means I'll survive again. The new arena starts tomorrow. They'll watch us kill each other, until they're satisfied. Winning didn't get me anywhere. I'm right back here, where I started. There is no prize for the winner. Just a prolonged death."

"What about escape?" I ask.

She stares at me as if that's the dumbest idea in the world.

"Don't you think if it was that easy I would've done it already?"

We stand there, in the gloomy silence, and I ponder this news. It is bleak. She's right: if there were a way out, I'm sure she would have found it. We are stuck.

"Or someone else would have," Flo adds. "They bring in this riffraff by the trainloads. This rooms is always filling with them. I hate them. I hate them all. They're so stupid. They don't realize what's ahead of them. Some of them try to escape. They don't get far. It doesn't really matter: we're all going to do either way. In here or out there."

I look over and see Charlie sneaking behind his sister; he reaches out and hands Bree something furtively. She reaches out and grabs it.

"Charlie don't!" screams Flo, slapping his hand hard. But it's too late. He is caught red-handed, as he gives Bree a small piece of chocolate.

"What's the matter with you!?" she snaps at him.

"I just want to give her a small piece," he says.

"These people don't care about us," she scolds.

Charlie looks down, in shame.

You're wrong, I want to say. *I do care about you. And especially about Charlie, who I already love like a brother.* I will have a soft spot in my heart for him forever for helping us, and for giving Bree that piece of chocolate. *Your heart has become too hard*, I want to say to her. *You might be surviving, but you're already dead inside.*

But I don't say any of these things, because I recognize a part of myself in her. And it scares me. She is almost like the version of myself that I might have become, if I stayed along such a hard road. I remember what happened when I helped that man back on the Hudson, and a part of me gets her, and respects her—yet dislikes her at the same time.

"You can have it back," Bree says, reaching out to hand it to Flo.

Flo looks down at her, and for a millisecond, I think I see her expression soften.

Then it hardens again.

She turns her back, grabs Charlie, and yanks him around, to walk away with her. They disappear, towards a darker side of the cavernous room, clearly signaling that her time with us is done.

I watched him walk into the blackness, already missing Charlie, already feeling as if we've lost a friend.

Bree turns and holds out the chocolate to us all.

"You guys share," she says.

Ben shakes his head, and I shake mine, too, despite the pain in my stomach.

"It's yours," I say.

"Logan, what about you?" she asks. "You have to eat something."

"That's a good idea," I echo, and Ben and I each prop him up.

He looks back at her weakly and shakes his head.

But Bree breaks off a piece of her piece, and puts it in his mouth. She shoves it into his mouth, and he chews. His eyes light up, for the first time in days.

"That's the best chocolate I ever had, kiddo," he says to her.

My heart breaks at the sound of his voice, to hear how weak he has become. I think of the irony: we have come all this way because of him, and he sustained his injury while saving Bree. I feel awful. And Bree does, too.

"I need to sit," Logan whispers.

We all head to a far wall, dragging Logan with us. We find a spot against the stone where we can all sit, flickering beneath a torch, our backs to the wall. It is a good vantage point: we can survey the entire room, see what everyone's up to, make sure no one sneaks up on us.

We settle in and wait, and a heavy silence blankets us. I can't help but feel as if we are all waiting for our deaths.

*

We sit there, the four of us, our backs against the wall, looking out, watching. I don't know how much time has passed. The activity in the cave seems to have quieted down, with most of the others sitting or lying down along the sides of the cave. Few people in here cross from one side to the other, interact with each other. Most are wary and cautious, and keep to themselves. I feel as if we're in prison, and I trust no one. Especially after the reception we received.

I look over at Bree, sitting to my right, and Ben beside her. They each sit with their eyes wide open, looking shell-shocked. I look to my other side and see that Logan's eyes are closed. His breathing is shallow, and I worry for him. I reach out and brush the hair from his eyes, place my hand on his forehead. He is cold and clammy. He groans from the pain.

"Shhh," I said. "It's going to be okay."

I look down at his leg, see his wound festering, and wish there was something I could do. Some medicine, antibiotics—bandages, at least. But I have nothing. I remember the time he nursed me back to health, in the city, when I was so sick. He brought me back. He found me medicine. I feel terrible that I can't reciprocate.

I run my hand again and again over his forehead, trying to soothe him.

Slowly, his eyes flutter open. He looks at me. Weakly, he smiles. Then he closes his eyes again.

"You're not half bad," he whispers, eyes closed.

I can't help but smile back.

I feel Ben looking over at us; I can't help but feel that he is jealous that I'm giving Logan all of this attention. I don't want him to be. And I do have feelings for Ben. But I can't ignore Logan in his time of need either.

I lean back and close my eyes for a minute and wonder how we got here. I can't believe that I am in this position once again, about to enter another arena. I messed up somewhere along the way. I try to think of what I could have done differently. I should've been more careful, more guarded. Maybe we never should have stopped at my dad's after all. Maybe if we stayed on the river, like Logan said, if we never stopped, things would have gone differently. Maybe we just had to keep going. But to where? That's the million-dollar question. There seems to be nothing left in this world. Nothing, except for violence and evil and arenas, clustering in what's left of the big cities. This is what our society has come to.

I get another sharp hunger pain, and I am feeling lightheaded. I've never been this hungry in my life, and I seriously don't think I can make it through the night without another meal.

As I'm thinking this, a set of boots appears before me from out of the shadows. A large teenager, maybe 19, broad, stocky, stops before us. He looks down, puts his hands on his hips, as he looks us all over carefully. He especially looks Bree over, up and down, as if she is a thing of prey. He smiles, an evil smile.

"The new kids," he states.

My anger rises, especially as I see how he looks at my sister.

"What do you want?" I ask sharply.

Slowly, his smile drops.

"All business, huh?" he says. "I like that." He licks his lips. "Well, sweety, I came here to do you a favor. To make you a deal. You want food, right? You all do, right?"

He looks left to right, examining us.

"Well," he continues, before we can respond. "I've got some. Good food. Fresh fruit. A lot of it. As much as you can eat."

I look over this creep: he is broad and stocky and looks well fed, much better fed than the others. He looks strong, a fierce opponent. And shady, slimy. I hate the way he licks his lips at me.

"Like I said," I repeat, an edge to my voice. "What do you want?"

He smiles.

"I want to trade," he says, his cold black eyes locking on mine. "Food for sex."

I can't believe it; I am too shocked to even respond.

"You'll do," he says, looking at me. "I'll bring you back in an hour, when I'm done with you, and I'll give you enough food for all of you."

As he smiles at me, proud of himself, I've never been more disgusted in my life. I want to get up and kick him, but it's not worth the energy. Instead, I just turn my head, waiting for him to go back to the rock he crawled out from. He doesn't even deserve a response.

But then, he turns and looks at Bree.

"Or, if you give me a go with the young one here," he adds, "I'll give you twice the food."

Something snaps in me, and without thinking, I react. I push up on my palms off the ground, swing back my leg, swing it across, and kick him hard behind both of his knees, sweeping them out from under him. He lands flat on his back, hard.

Without pausing, I jump to one knee, lean over him, and take my thumb and forefinger and dig them deep into pressure points on his throat.

He looks up at me, his eyes bulging, gasping for air. He grabs my hand, trying to remove it, but I have him pinned down, and the strength that overcomes me keeps him there. I think of what he said about Bree, and I want to tear him to pieces. I make him struggle for every breath.

"I'm only going to say this once," I growl, through clenched teeth. "You come near my sister again, or even look her way, and I'm going to kill you. Do you understand? I will kill you."

Slowly, he nods, and I let go. He sits up, gasping for air, then jumps to his feet and trots away.

He turns back and looks at me as he runs.

"You're dead!" he screams out, in a whiny voice. "Tomorrow, in the arena. I'm going to get you. You're dead!"

And with that, he disappears into the darkness.

I turn and look at the others. Bree looks scared, and Ben sits there, fists clenched.

"You okay?" he asks.

I nod back, breathing slowly, my heart still pounding. I lean over, and kiss Bree on the forehead.

"Was he going to hurt me?" she asks.

"Don't worry, love," I say. "No one's ever going to hurt you. Not while I'm around."

I slowly lean back, and I see Logan grinning at me.

"Nice move," he says, his voice hoarse. "Of course, I would've swept him differently."

I can't help but smile back. I am about to answer, say something witty, but my thoughts are interrupted.

A loud buzzer sounds, and I look over and am surprised to see a huge hole open up in the ceiling of the cave. A bright spotlight shines straight down, and suddenly, all the other kids are on their feet, racing, running towards the light in the middle of the room. I don't understand what's happening—until suddenly, I see something fall from the ceiling, land on the floor. It pours straight down, and I don't understand what it is. And then I realize: food.

Slop is being poured down, straight down to the dirt floor, buckets and buckets of it. It looks like oatmeal, and it hits the dirt floor with a splat.

It is gross-looking, but the other kids are racing for it, pouncing on it, grabbing it by the handful and shoving it in their mouths.

Up above, leaning down over the edge, are dozens of faces of humans, laughing at the spectacle. They throw more buckets in, and some of it lands on the backs of the kids as they eat on all fours. They laugh harder.

I waste no time. As gross as it is, it's feeding time, and my stomach decides for me. Ben and Bree also jump to their feet, not needing any prodding.

We all rush to the center, and reach the pit of kids who are elbowing each other out of the way; I get closer, and people viciously elbow me left and right. After taking some hard bruises, I get to the center, get down on all fours, and grabbed a handful of the slop. I cram it into my mouth, and chew it.

It is slimy, and perhaps the grossest thing I've ever eaten. It tastes like raw barley, barely cooked. But it is food, and I grab handful after handful. I look over and see Ben getting a handful, but see Bree getting edged out. I grab a handful for her and put in her hand; then I grab two more and do the same.

As I'm looking over at her, I spot something: a few feet away is Charlie, on his hands and knees, grabbing a meal. He doesn't see the person creeping up behind them—a skinny boy, maybe 16, with curly black hair and lots of acne. He creeps up behind Charlie, and in one quick motion, he reaches down and grabs the knife from his sheath.

He then raises it up high, and I see that he's taking aim: he's about to plunge it into Charlie's back.

Without thinking, I leap into action. I tackle the kid, a second before he stabs him. I drive him down hard to the ground, and the knife goes flying. I spin him over, planting his face in the ground, and twist his arm behind his back, all the way, nearly breaking it. He screams out in pain.

Charlie, beside me, looks down and realizes what I've done.

I look over at the floor, for his knife, and am surprised to see it's already gone. I look up, and see Flo standing there, holding it.

"Let him go," she says, coldly.

I lift my knee off the kid's back, and back away. This is her fight now.

Flo grabs the kid by the back of his head, and without hesitating, reaches the knife around and slashes his throat, quick and clean, muscles rippling in her arms and shoulders. The kid hardly has time to scream, as blood pours out of his neck. He dies.

Flo stands erect, looking all around her to see if anyone will challenge her. Nobody does; they quickly turn back to eating. I see the remorseless look in her eye, and finally realize she is a natural, trained killer.

Flo takes two steps forward, and puts the knife back into Charlie's sheath firmly. She grabs him by the shoulders and looks him in the eye.

"Never leave yourself exposed again. Do you hear me?"

Charlie nods back, dazed.

Flo turns and looks at me. Slowly, her scowl subsides.

"You saved Charlie's life," she states.

I shrug. "I just reacted."

She looks me up and down, nodding, as if with a new respect.

"I owe you one," she says. "And that's not something I take lightly. Follow me. All of you. Leave the food. I've got plenty."

I turn and look at Ben and Bree, who look back quizzically; we all follow her.

I grab one more handful of slop for Logan, and hurry over to him. I reach out and put one in his mouth. "Chew," I say.

He chews. Then Ben and I lean down, pick him up, and begin to drag him across the cave, to Flo's corner.

Flo and Charlie have set up camp in the far corner of the cave. We follow her to the farthest reaches of it, twisting and turning, until we reach it. I'm impressed by their setup. I guess this is what Flo gets for being the victor. It is a large section of the cave, surrounded by stone on three sides so her back is guarded from every direction. She has a nice fire going, and a large chest filled with slop.

Bree walks over to Charlie, and he to her, and I can see that they're happy to be reunited. They each take a handful of slop and chew.

"It's not as bad as it seems," Charlie says. "You get used to it."

"I think it's awful," Bree says. "But I'm so hungry, I would eat anything."

"I remember once, when the world was good, I had a stack of pancakes," Charlie says. "Five of them, with butter and maple syrup and whipped cream. Oh my God. It was the best thing I ever had. Can you imagine eating that?"

"Charlie, stop," Flo reprimands. "That's not helpful."

"It's ok," Bree defends him. "I actually like it. I haven't thought of pancakes in forever."

"Living in fantasy is how you get yourself killed," Flo snaps.

I think about that. On the one hand she's right. But on the other hand, what's so great about reality? Isn't fantasy all we have left?

We set Logan down beside Flo's fire, and as we do, she looks at his leg.

"I have medicine," she says.

My heart leaps as I look at her.

"Spoils to the victor. When you win, they give you a box of stuff. Food, mostly. But some meds, too. Basic stuff. They want you in shape for the next round. I've got some syringes with stuff in them. I'm guessing it's for wounds, for healing. Maybe penicillin, or something like it."

"Please," I say. "I would give anything."

She reaches into her chest and pulls out a fresh, unwrapped syringe and throws it to me. I tear it open, examine the clear liquid. I hope it's what he needs.

I hurry over to Logan, kneel by his side, look at him. He is sweating.

"You want me to try?" I ask. "I don't know what's in it."

"Do it," he says, weakly. "I have nothing to lose."

I lean over and insert the needle as gently as I can into his leg and inject the serum. He winces.

"They gave me some treats, too," she adds. "Does someone like marshmallows?" she asks, looking at Bree.

Bree looks up at her, eyes open wide.

"You're joking," she says.

"She's not," Charlie says. "She's really got them. She must really like you. She hasn't even given one to me. She said she was waiting for a special night."

"This is it," Flo says. "Tomorrow, they begin. This could be our last night."

"I don't understand," Bree says to Charlie. "If you have food here, why were you in the pit, fighting for slop with the others?"

"Flo wants me to fend for myself," he answers. "She says it makes me stronger."

Flo reaches into her bag, takes out a handful of fat marshmallows, and puts one into each of our open hands. She hands out sticks, and we place them on the sticks and roast them over the fire.

The smell of roasting marshmallows makes me salivate. I pull mine out, nearly black, and chew slowly, savoring each bite. It fills my every pore. I would eat a thousand more if I could.

My thoughts drift to tomorrow, the arena. My stomach drops, as I wonder what's in store for us.

"Tell us what it's like," I say to Flo, who sits opposite the fire, chewing. "The arena."

Flo is silent a long time; finally, she shakes her head.

"Tomorrow, they'll come for us early," she says. "Be ready. The first day of fighting, it's not what it seems. It's more about survival than fighting. You won't understand until you see it for yourself. But there are ways to live, and ways to die. I'll give you some good advice. Don't go for the bridges. And stay away from the edges. Don't try to escape. That's the mistake most people make. They want to escape. Stay calm. Don't think about fighting, or winning. Think about surviving. Just remember: things are not what they seem."

I'm grateful for her advice, but as I try to take it all in, I find it confusing and overwhelming. Her advice is too ambiguous; I'm not really sure what she's talking about.

"I don't really understand," I say.

"You can't," she says. "But once you're there, you will."

"I'm going to escape," Charlie says, as he sits beside Bree, roasting her marshmallow for her, and chews his. The site makes me think of summer campfires, when we would lie under the stars for hours, when everything was safe.

"What do you mean, escape?" I ask.

"I'm going to find a way out of here. The train tunnels. I saw, coming in, where they go. When they first brought me here, I slipped out. I ran for a while before I got caught. I saw where they lead. There's a back exit. Outside the city. I saw their boats. I know how to get there."

My heart leaps at the possibility.

"Stop talking nonsense," Flo snaps at him harshly.

Charlie's face falls, and there is a tense silence.

"I'm just trying to tell them—" Charlie begins.

"I've heard enough of your stories," Flo said. "It's ridiculous. You can't escape here. Even if you made it out, they'd hunt you down and kill you in two seconds. That's a sure death. Fighting in the arena, at least it gives you a chance. And where would you go anyway? You think there's some great world out there waiting to be found?"

Charlie looks down to the floor, disappointed; but then he looks back up, eyes filled with hope.

"You remember what dad said? About that town? In Canada?"

Immediately, I am on high alert, and sit up straighter. Logan and Ben and Bree do, too. I am shocked. Is this town for real? Or is it just a persistent rumor?

"Charlie," I say. "What did you just say?"

He turns and looks at me, unsure. "About Canada?""

"How do you know about it?" I ask. "Is it true?"

"No, of course it's not," Flo snaps.

"Yes it is!" Charlie insists.

"It was just another one of dad's fantasies," Flo says.

"No it wasn't!" Charlie says. "He knew it. He was there. He wasn't lying. All we have to do is get up the river. To Canada. We can find it. I know we can. He said it was by the river."

Charlie seems so certain, and his story does seem to line up with Logan's. It makes me wonder if maybe that town really does exist.

Flo shakes her head.

"Like I said," she says, "you can either live in fantasy or reality. And you can die in either, too."

I think about that.

"Well if we're going to die either way, why not live in fantasy?" I ask her.

She locks eyes with mine, and I can feel the coldness in her eyes, and it goes right into me, like a winter breeze. I force myself to look away, seeing death in those eyes, and knowing that, soon, it's coming for me, too.

*

I lay awake in the darkness, late into the night, Bree curled up in my arms, Logan beside me, Ben on the other side. Sitting next to Bree is Charlie, and their heads rest on each other's. A few feet apart is Flo. Everyone is asleep, except for me. And Flo. Her eyes are wide open, staring into the dying flames of the fire. Cold, hard, unflinching. I see that being awake is her natural habit of being. A warrior to her last breath, always on edge.

Me, I want to sleep, but I can't, because my mind won't stop racing. I keep trying to think about tomorrow, about what it will be like. If only I could be prepared, it might go better. But Flo doesn't seem to want to tell me any more and I have to just appreciate what she's already told me. I turn her words over and over in my mind. *Don't go for the bridges. Stay away from the edges….* I don't know what it all means.

I'm determined to survive. I'm determined for Bree to survive, Ben, Logan. I look over at him, and he seems more relaxed than before, and I have a good feeling that the medicine helped. I won't know until the morning.

At least it is warm in here, and we have been fed. Ironically, the slaverunners catching us probably saved our lives. I know that another day in the wilderness and we would have been dead for sure. Ironically, they've given us life. At least for now.

I look at Bree, curled up in my arms. I want so badly to protect her, to shield her from all this, to force the slaverunners to keep her out of it. But I know it's useless. I rack my brain, thinking of what I can do. But I keep reaching dead ends.

I sit there for hours and hours, knowing I should sleep, knowing that I need rest for tomorrow. But I can't. I try as hard as I can, and a few times, I feel my eyes getting heavy, my chin nodding—but then I immediately lapse into fast, troubled dreams, of dad, yelling at mom. And I wake quickly, on guard, finding nothing but blackness and silence.

As I stare into the blackness, I could swear I see my dad's face, becoming more vivid, staring back at me. It is hard and firm, as it used to get when he was trying to make me tough.

"Brooke, you're a soldier," he says. "Just like your dad. A Marine. You may not wear the uniform, but that doesn't mean you don't have a Marine's heart. A Marine's valor. It means you don't give up. And if you die, you die. But you die like a Marine."

It is as if I feel him right here, with me, in the room. In some strange way, it's comforting. I feel less alone. For the first time in years, I miss him. I really miss him.

I hear you, dad, I say back in my head. *And I love you.*

FIFTEEN

I open my eyes to the sound of groaning metal. A steel door creaks open, light floods the room, and I realize I've fallen asleep. I jump to my feet, awake, alert, ready to fight.

I stand there and see that Flo is already on her feet, fists clenched, looking at our new guests. There, at the entrance, are dozens of slaverunners, wearing their face masks and each carrying a black uniform in their arms. They march into the room, and as they do, the dozens of kids slowly get to their feet in every direction. They all know what's coming. The time has come.

A loud buzzer sounds, and whoever's left sleeping gets to their feet. One slaverunner marches up to each kid, and several of them approach us. One marches right up to me, and shoves into my hands a black bundle of clothing. I look down at it, surprised.

"Your uniform," Charlie explains.

Flo, standing a few feet away, says, "Put it on. Over your clothes. If you don't, they'll beat you down."

I hold mine up, wondering how one size fits all, then realize it is made of a flexible, spandex-like material. It is supposed to be tight.

They've handed me a set of pants, and a jacket. It is all black, and tight, except for the jacket, which is thickly padded, like a military uniform. he jacket has is a bright-yellow X across it. Like a target. This does not bode well. At least it will keep me warm.

I reach down and slide the pants on over my boots, over my pants, then put the shirt and jacket on and zip it up. Mine is tight and snug, and actually feels good. The thick padding hugs me, and I feel like a warrior going into battle. All around me, all the other kids put them on, too. The whole room, dressed in tight black uniforms with yellow Xs across our chests. We are all walking targets.

I make sure Bree does the same, and help Logan into his. I'm thrilled to see that Logan is better; the medicine worked. His skin color has returned, his eyes are bright, and he is able to get on his own feet. He hobbles, but not as badly.

"Whatever you gave me worked," he says to me. "Thank you."

"Thank Flo," I say. "I didn't do much."

"Thank you, Flo," he says to her.

She turns and looks at him, unsmiling.

"Don't thank me yet," Flo says. "You'll be dead soon enough."

Just like Flo. Refusing to drop her edge, even for a second.

A slaverunner gets behind me and prods me hard in the small of my back, making me stumble forward. All of us are prodded, and we begin to march for the exit. Finally, we are leaving this place. A part of me hopes I never return.

Bree, Ben, Logan, Charlie and Flo march beside me in the winding subway tunnels. The six of us make our way with the dozens of other kids through the cold and dark tunnels, our footsteps echoing. I feel like I am marching helplessly towards my fate. I wish there was something I could do. Anything. I need to think of a strategy, some sort of plan. I don't want Bree separated for me. Or Ben. Or Logan.

"Once we get out there, we should act like a team," I say to everyone, including Charlie and Flo. "Stick together. No matter what. If anyone attacks us, we can watch each other's backs. Bree, do you hear me? I want you close to me. By my side, no matter what."

Bree looks up and nods, and I can see the fear in her eyes.

"That won't last," Flo says. "You'll see, once you're out there. It won't work. It's every man for himself. I'm not watching after you guys. I'm watching after myself. And Charlie."

Her eyes and jaw harden, defiant. I don't know what to say.

"Does that mean we're enemies?" I ask her.

"I like you," she says. "All of you. But I'm out to win. To survive. Not for you to live. Not at my expense. And not at Charlie's. I don't want to kill you. And I owe you a favor. So I'll give you one good piece of advice: stay away from me. Far away."

We turn the corner, and before us, the tunnel floods with sunlight. An exit to outdoors. A cold wind slaps me in the face, and I hear the muted shouts of a mob.

I am shoved hard one last time and we all go stumbling out of the train tunnel, into the outdoors. I squint at the blinding light, and the cold stings my face. Still, it is good to be outside, to be out of that dark tunnel, and to have fresh air.

My senses are assaulted by so many things at once. The air is filled with the cheers and screams of what seems like thousands of people. I pry open my eyes and see we are on a wide, dirt road, and on either side, behind a fence guarded by slaverunners, stand hundreds of mob members, biovictims, jeering at us. They are dressed in rags, and their faces are mutilated. Mutants, grotesque people. They raise their fists and snarl, and the excitement in the air is palpable.

My heart is pounding in anticipation as we go. The slaverunners poke and prod, and one jabs me hard in my ribs with the butt of his gun. It is cold out, but not as cold as the day before. In fact, it is quite warm for a winter day. I'm thrilled to see that the snow has virtually melted, and at least my uniform is keeping me warm. I feel snug and secure in it, sheltered from the elements, and its hard plastic padding makes me feel invincible. I feel like wheeling around and cracking the slaverunner hard across the face, stealing his gun, mowing them down, and making a run for it.

But I know if I do that, Bree, Ben, Logan and the others won't get far. I look around and see dozens of slaverunners trained on us, their guns at their hips. It would be a massacre.

We clear a small hill, and as we stand at the top, the vista is spread out before me. I see, in the distance, the arena to which we are being lead.

My heart stops at the daunting site: thousands of crowd members are spread out around a huge, circular canyon, cliffs dropping off hundreds of feet. The canyon is spanned by four rope bridges, spaced out evenly in the circle, and all leading to a small, circular piece of land in the canyon's center. This round, circular stretch of land, maybe a hundred yards wide, is connected to the mainland only by the four rope bridges. Otherwise, there is a steep plummet off the edge.

The spectators cheer wildly at the site of us coming over the hill.

My throat goes dry as I realize where they're taking us. They're going to prod us over a bridge, onto that circular piece of land in the middle. Once we're on it, there'll be no way off without crossing one of those four bridges back to the mainland. The drop-off is hundreds of feet deep. It is like a vast canyon, except with a large piece of land in its center.

This doesn't bode well. We will all be stuck together on that small landmass and forced to fight each other to the death, or fight each other to cross one of the bridges to get back to the mainland. Otherwise, there is no way out.

It is a cruel set up for an arena. All your opponents have to do is push you off the edge, and you're dead. It leaves no room for error. None at all. And I don't like heights.

Not to mention, no one's given us any weapons. What is it they'll expect us to do: fight to the death with our bare hands?

I gulp, worrying for Bree, for Logan, for Ben, even for Charlie. I'm not worried for Flo. Somehow, I feel she's invincible.

The suspense builds as we are marched closer, and the crowd roars louder. As we get within feet of it, approach one of the bridges, a narrow rope bridge only a few feet wide, I can see over the edge. The drop-off is dizzying, at least a hundred feet. One slip will mean instant death.

"Brooke, I'm scared," Bree says beside me. She is looking out over the edge, and I grab her by the shoulder and pull her close.

"Don't look," I say. "Just follow me. Stay close. You'll be okay."

A slaverunner prods me hard in the back, making me stumble, and this time, I've had enough: my reflexes kick in and I wheel around and shove him back. Immediately, another slaverunner steps up and backhands me hard across the face, then a third one shoves me again. I get the picture. I stop resisting, and continue forward with the others.

"You're wasting your energy," Flo chides.

She's right. I need to focus. I continue with the others, like sheep, as they prod us all onto one of the rope bridges. It sags and sways as they do, and I find myself grabbing on to the rope railing.

The crowd cheers as we all step foot on the bridge, herded towards the land mass in the center. I try not to look over the edge as the rope swings; it feels too flimsy to hold us. I reach down and hold Bree's hand, and she dutifully holds my hand and the railing. Logan is limping, and Ben, behind me, to his credit, helps prop him. It is big of him to overcome his jealousy to help him. It's strange: only a few days ago, those two were rivals. Now, they are helping each other.

Behind us, Flo walks, so stable that she doesn't even need to hold the railing. She reaches out with one hand and grabs the back of Charlie's shirt, by the neck, guiding him. She reminds me of a wolf, holding a pup in its mouth. Her game face is on, wearing a steely look of death, and I fear for anyone who gets in her way.

I step onto the land mass with relief, happy to be off the flimsy bridge. We are all herded towards the center of it. It is wider here than I thought, spanning about fifty yards at its widest. But dozens and dozens of kids are herded onto it, and soon it gets crowded. Everyone naturally flocks towards the center, as far away from the edges as they can get. The slaverunners, finished, turn and march across the bridge, back to the mainland. As they do, the crowd cheers again. Now we are alone out here.

We all stand here, dozens of us, huddled together in the center of this land mass, all nervous, unsure what to do.

Just as I'm wondering what will happen next, the crowd quiets. A path parts in the mob, and a group of slaverunners comes forward, bearing on their shoulders a huge, golden throne, borne by rods. On the throne sits a single man, with long hair, falling down to his shoulders. A long scar runs from the corner of his lip to his chin, making him look like he's scowling. He stands and holds out his arms: he is huge, muscular, wearing a sleeveless vest, even in this cold. He looks like a mountain. I can't tell his ethnicity: maybe a cross between Native American and Hispanic. He's one of the fiercest looking men I've ever seen.

As he stands, the thousands of mutants fall silent. It is obvious that he is the leader.

"Brothers and sisters, I present to you our newest batch of contestants!" he bellows out in his low voice.

The crowd goes crazy. They stand before a metal railing, waist high, at the edge of the canyon, and bang on it. A loud noise rises up, and I see that each of them holds a rock, which they bang on the metal.

The leader holds up his arms again, and the crowd quiets.

"There are two ways to victory, contestants," he says to us. "One is to make it back to the mainland. If you can cross a bridge and come back here, you will be safe forever. The other, of course, is to be the last one standing."

The crowd roars.

The kids around me all turn, looking at the bridges or summing each other up, jittery. It is like being in a corral of horses before a storm.

The leader throws his arms wide one last time:

"Let the death games begin!"

The crowd, screaming, bangs its rocks on the rail.

I run through in my mind Flo's words. *Stay away from the bridges. Stay close to the center. Nothing is what it seems.*

Now I have a better idea of what she's saying. But is it true advice? Or was she just lying to me to have an advantage?

Before I can figure it out, before I can strategize, suddenly, all hell breaks loose.

I feel something hard hit me on the side of my arm, and I wheel around to see that the hundreds of spectators are throwing rocks at us. Luckily, they're far enough away that most of them miss. But a lot of rocks are landing close, and a second rock hits my leg. It hurts like hell.

Panic ensues. All around me, the dozens of kids gathered in the center begin to sprint for the bridges. They take off in all four directions, for the four equally spaced bridges around the circle, and I spot Bree begin to run with them. I reach out and grab her.

"No," I say. "Stay here."

I can see on Ben's face that he wants to run for it, too.

"But you heard him!" Ben says frantically. "We have to make it to the mainland. We have to beat the others!"

"No!" I yell back. I look over and see Flo standing still in the center, holding Charlie by the shoulders. I hope she knows what she's doing.

"But the rocks!" Logan yells, dodging one that narrowly misses his head.

Before I can respond, suddenly, I'm tackled hard from behind, and find my face planting on the ground.

I spin over to find one of the teenagers on top of me. He holds a rock up high over his head, a large, sharp rock, and begins to bring it down for my face. It is the boy from last night. The one that wanted to sleep with Bree.

He has me pinned down, and I can't react in time. I flinch, as he brings it down.

Suddenly, right before he kills me, he stops in midair. His eyes open wide, frozen, and he collapses, limp, to the side.

I look over, and see a sharp rock jutting out the back of his neck, blood oozing from it.

I look up, and see Flo standing over him, scowling down.

"Now we're even," she snaps.

I can't believe it: she has just saved my life.

All around me in the chaos, not only are kids running for the bridges, not only are rocks flying in every direction, but also a group of kids has decided on another strategy: to kill the others.

I see one kid grab another from behind, and hurl him over the edge of the cliff. I hear him scream as he goes flying over, shrieking to his death. This same kid is grabbed from behind by another, and hurled himself. With another shriek, he plummets.

On the far side of the circle, I see another kid attacking others from behind; he kicks one hard in the back and sends him over the edge.

Another kid grabs a rock and smashes another kid in the back of the head. He collapses.

Now I realize that Flo was right. Stay in the center. Far from the edge. It makes sense. But why not run for the bridge?

I look over and see Flo lying face first on the ground, holding Charlie down. Before I can figure out why, another rock whizzes by my head, and I turn and realize the crowd has circled around, found a place that is in closer range. Now, tons of rocks hurl by us.

"Get down!" I scream at the others.

Bree is slow to react, so I reach out and grab her and pull her down in the dirt. It is lucky timing: a rock whizzes by where her head was moments ago. Logan grabs Ben and pulls him down, saving him, too, from a large rock aimed at his head.

I look up and see that one of the mercenary kids, having just hurled another kid off the cliff, turns and sets his sights on us, in the center. He charges, and I see he has his sights set on Bree.

I don't wait. Even though rocks are whizzing overhead, I grab a large rock, stand, and charge him. I want to meet him mid-charge, before he gets anywhere near Bree. We charge each other, head on, and he swings his rock right for my face. I duck, and at the same time, smash my rock into his gut.

He drops to his knees and I smash his nose, breaking it. He collapses.

I feel footsteps charging me from behind, and realize, too late, that I left my back exposed. I turn just in time to see another one charging me and about to bring a rock down on the back of my head. I can't react in time.

Suddenly, I hear a whizzing noise, and just as I prepare for the blow, instead I see the boy fall beside me. I look over and see Bree standing there, and realize she has thrown a rock with perfect aim, and hit him square in the head. It was a hell of a throw, and she saved my life. I'm impressed.

I run back over to Bree and hit the ground beside her.

The spectators cheer and scream, as they continue to throw rocks our way. Their scream morphs into an excited roar, and I look up and see the first group of kids has reached one of the bridges. A dozen of them stampede one of the rope bridges, all charging at once. They run across it single file. Soon they are halfway across, the bridge swaying wildly.

At the midway point, one of them gets the idea to attack the others; he grabs one kid from behind and throws him off the bridge.

He plunges to his death, screaming. The bully grabs another one and tries to throw him—but this kid grabs the edge of the railing as he goes over, then reaches up and grabs the bully's ankle and yanks him off with him. Together, the two of them go plunging down, screaming, to their deaths.

The dozen or so kids left on the bridge continue to run across it, getting close to the other side, to freedom. The spectators throw rocks like crazy, now aiming at them. One kid gets hit so hard that he loses his balance and falls plunging off the bridge.

But the others are making good time, and it looks like they're going to make it. I can't believe it was that easy. Was Flo wrong? Should we have went with them?

Then, everything changes. The crowd parts way as a group of slaverunners marches up, holding torches. Without hesitating, they hurry forward and set the rope bridge on fire. They then hurl the torches to the far side of the bridge, setting it on fire from both sides.

In moments, the rope bridge, destabilized, on fire from all directions, swings erratically. It is horrific. There is nowhere for these kids to go. Flames rise in both directions, and some of the kids are already on fire themselves. They scream and yell, trying to get the fire out, running over each other. But it is useless.

One of them jumps off the bridge, choosing suicide. Others try to put out the flames, but suddenly, the bridge collapses. The 10 or so of them left go plunging, all in flames, all screeching, down to their deaths.

The crowd cheers like crazy.

Flo was right. Her advice saved our lives.

I look over at the other three bridges, and now I wonder. A dozen kids are already charging onto one of the other bridges. They race onto it, stumbling over themselves, seeing who can get there quick enough.

But as they are halfway across, something goes horribly wrong. The ground is slipping away where the bridge was attached to the landmass. Roots and dirt go crumbling, then suddenly, one of the two ropes snaps.

The bridge swings wildly side to side and the kids all screech as they try to hold on. A few of them fall off.

Then, the other rope snaps. The bridge, attached only by the far side, goes swinging wildly, heading towards the cliff wall. Whichever kids manage to hang on go flying at full speed, smacking right into the wall. It is a horrific sound of breaking bone.

They drop like flies, plunging to their deaths, no one left.

All that remains of the bridge is a long line of rope, attached at the far end, going straight down the cliff. The crowd roars.

I look over at the other two bridges and wonder what could be in store. As I watch, a dozen kids race onto it, running at full speed, trying to cross. But they have just witnessed what happened on the other two bridges, and now they're not so sure—they hesitate, stopping halfway, debating whether to go back. Some of them rush forward, stampeding the others, while others try to run back.

On the mainland, suddenly, the crowd parts and two slaverunners step forward with huge machetes. They raise them high, the crowd egging them on, and the kids on the bridge open their eyes wide in fear. They turn and try to make it back.

But it's too late: the slaverunners bring down their machetes, cut the ropes. The bridge plummets and swings. All the kids go hurling and screaming, plunging to their deaths as the rope smashes into the rock wall of the land mass.

I turn away from the grisly sight. Aside from our small group, huddled on the floor in the center of the land mass, I look around and see there are now only about fifty of us left. The others lie on the ground, too, some covering their heads, all doing our best to avoid the hurling rocks. We all look over at the remaining bridge. It is our only way out. But it looks too good to be true. None of us seem to want to try. It is just another cruel trick? Do they want to see us all dead? Is there really no other way out?

The crowd cheers, and I see a huge, satisfied smile on the face of their leader. I wish I could kill them all.

"Is that bridge a trick?" I ask Flo, who's lying a few feet away from me.

"What do you think?" she snaps back, cynical.

Of course, I know the answer myself. It can't be that easy. Or could it? Maybe it's some sort of sick reverse psychology.

Apparently, several of the other kids have the same idea. They suddenly jump to their feet and race for the final bridge. There must be ten of them, brave souls. They race for it at full speed, one of them tackling the other from behind as they go, apparently still thinking that killing each other off is the way to go. Another punches the other, and one throws another off the cliff.

The others continue to run, hit the bridge single file, and I'm shocked as I see them race across it easily, making good time. There's nothing wrong with this bridge, and I'm kicking myself now. It looks like they will make it. They were the brave ones, the ones willing to risk when others weren't—and they are being rewarded for it.

Then, everything goes wrong. The kids are only feet away from the mainland, when they all stop. I can't understand why; they stand there, frozen, as if glued to the bridge.

As I look closely, as I hear their screams, I realize what has happened: thousands of small blades popped up from the bridge, through their feet, through their hands on the railings. The kids are pierced with knives, blood gushing from them as they are literally stuck to the bridge. I am so grateful we didn't go for it.

I swallow hard, and look around. There are only about forty of us left. All the bridges are gone, and the crowd is screaming like crazy.

"KILL! KILL!" the crowd chants at us.

I look at our opponents, and they look back. At the same time, it seems to dawn on everybody that the only way left is to kill each other.

A wild look starts to come on the faces of the survivors, as I see them getting ready, grabbing rocks, preparing to fight. Then, it happens. Seemingly all at once, the forty or so kids jump to their feet, and charge each other. The crowd goes wild.

I jump to my feet, sheltering Bree, as kids charge and hand-to-hand fighting erupts all around us. I watch Flo step up, take a rock, and smash a boy in the face right before he can hit Charlie. Then Charlie reaches down, grabs a rock, and chucks it at a tall boy racing towards Flo. It is a perfect strike, right between the legs, and the boy drops to his knees, groaning. In the distance, I see a boy pick up a girl over his head, race towards the edge, and hurl her off the cliff. She goes down screaming.

The crowd is screaming like wild.

I suddenly feel someone approaching me from behind, and I turn and spot it just in time. A large boy charges and jumps up on my back. But I bend over as he does, and in one smooth motion, flip him. He lands flat on his back, the wind knocked out of him. I step up and kick him hard once in the face, knocking him out.

I see Ben tackled hard from behind, driven to the ground; Logan, beside him, reaches around and elbows the attacker in the back of the head, knocking him off Ben.

But then Logan himself is kicked, right in the ribs, and he keels over. A second boy jumps on Logan, pinning him down.

Bree picks up a huge rock and brings it down on the back of Logan's attacker. He rolls off of him. I'm surprised by Bree's fierceness.

Logan rolls onto his back. He breaks free of his second attacker, knees him in the gut, and throws him off. He then manages to reach around and grab him in a chokehold, choking him until he passes out.

Dozens more of kids are fighting all around us, and many more are racing our way. Rocks are still hurling through the air, and a rock from a spectator hits a kid hard in the temple, knocking him out. The crowd screams like wild.

I realize quickly that this is a no-win proposition. We can't survive long like this. Soon, we'll all be dead. There has to be another way out. There *has* to be. There has to be a way to reach the mainland without killing each other.

I look again at the four downed bridges, studying them—and suddenly, I see a pattern. Two of them—the way they collapsed. One was severed from our side, the rope still attached at the mainland, and one was severed from the mainland, the rope still attached to our land mass. The rope dangles straight down, like a ladder down to hell. I get an idea.

"FOLLOW ME!" I scream to the others. "I see a way out!"

"What are you talking about?" Flo screams.

But there is no time to explain. I grab Bree and sprint for one of the downed bridges. Logan hobbles behind me, Ben helping him, and Flo reluctantly prods Charlie, and they follow me, too.

"You better know what you're doing," Flo warns.

The six of us race towards one of the collapsed bridges, dodging flying rocks and other kids. Luckily, the kids are preoccupied with each other—but I do get hit hard by a rock, in my hip. It hurts like hell.

As I reach the precipice I hit the ground and slide my body right to the edge. I look straight down, and see the two ropes, dangling straight down, all the way to the bottom of the canyon, a good hundred feet below. Heights. I hate heights. But I take a deep breath and force myself to look. They cut the ropes on the mainland, but they are still holding here. I test them, yanking hard. They don't give.

I look over, to the far side of the canyon, and look at the other destroyed bridge. The ropes gave way on our end, but not on the far side. We could climb down her and climb on up on the other side.

I turn and see that some of the other kids notice us and head our direction. Rocks whiz by my head and I know we have to act quickly.

Flo looks over the edge, too, seeing what I'm thinking.

"So, we can climb down," she says. "Then what? That doesn't get us out."

"They had to design this arena with a way out," I say. "Otherwise it wouldn't be a game. Don't you see? It's all a game to them. We just have to figure out how to break the code. This whole place was designed with a way to get to the other side. These two bridges, they collapse in two different directions. There's a reason. It left a way out. We can climb down this rope, and climb up the other."

"That's crazy," Flo says. "What if they cut the rope on our way up?"

"Or what if one of the kids cuts it on our way down?" Ben asks.

"That's the chance we have to take," I say. "I don't think they will. The other kids want a way out, too. And the gamemakers—don't you see? They want survivors. They want to prolong this. We are their entertainment."

The other kids are charging, getting closer know. They know something is up.

"We have no time to lose," I say. "I'll go last and guard our backs. Bree, you go first. Then Charlie."

I grab Bree, pull her over, position her so she'll go down feet first, hold her hand, and make sure she grabs firmly on the ropes.

She looks back up at me, eyes wide in fear.

"I'm scared," she says.

"Don't be scared," I assure her. "You'll be fine. Now go!"

Bree hangs there, frozen in fear. I am sweating: I don't know what to do.

Suddenly, Charlie appears. He slides over to her and looks at her sweetly.

"It's okay," he says. "I'll go with you. Just follow me. We can do it together. One rung at a time."

Bree seems to relax as Charlie climbs down with her. They start to climb down together, and I am relieved.

Next, I prod Logan to go, then Ben.

Flo finally seems to be on board—but she stops and looks back over her shoulder. Several kids are running for us, now just twenty yards away. She reaches down, grabs a rock, and throws it at one of them. She hits him, and he goes down. But the others still charge.

"What about the rest of them?" she asks.

"Go," I say. "Watch over them. I've got this."

She looks at me with something like admiration, then, she surprises me. For the first time ever, she smiles.

"You're not half bad," she says.

Before I can thank her for the closest she'll probably ever come to a compliment, she gets on the rope and begins to quickly descend.

I turn just in time: two kids are charging right at me. One of them lowers his head, and I can see he is aiming to tackle me, to drive me off the edge.

I force myself to stay disciplined, relaxed. I wait. Just like my dad taught me.

Then, at the last second, I squat all the way as far down as I can, ducking under him, and as he is about to hit me, I spring up, using his momentum to throw him over my shoulder. His momentum carries him flying over the edge. He plummets down, screaming.

I can't react fast enough, though, for the other one. He tackles me, driving me down to the ground hard. He has me right at the edge, and before I can react, he reaches over and chokes me, holding my head backwards over the cliff. I look over and see nothing but a sharp plummet between me and the canyon below. He has all the leverage. I have none.

I'm slipping and sliding, about to go over. He grimaces down, flashing his orange teeth. I realize that he will kill me. This is how I will die.

I'm running out of air, and quickly sliding of the edge, and I have few options. I realize I have to make one last desperate move.

I reach back, over the edge, and just manage to grab, with one hand, a huge root, sticking out the side of the cliff. I wrap my legs around his waist, then slide my body backwards, over the edge of the cliff, grasping the root for dear life. I pray it holds.

I swing over the edge hard, taking him with me. I let go of my legs and he goes flying, screaming, plummeting head over heel down to his death.

The root is quickly giving way, dirt flying everywhere; I manage to swing around just in time and grab the edge of the rope ladder. As I do, the root gives way. Another second and I would've been dead.

I hurry down the rope ladder, and as I do, I feel something hard hit me on the shoulder. I turn and see the spectators are going crazy, hurling rocks at all of us as we climb down. Another rock hits me hard in the back, and each one hurts more than the next. I just hope and pray that Bree can hang on.

I am about halfway down the cliff when I feel the rope move. I look up and see a group of kids at the top, watching us, getting the same idea. They get onto the rope and begin to climb down, too. I was right: they didn't cut it. They wanted out, too. I just hope the rope can hold us all.

I look down and see the others have already reached the canyon floor. I move double time, and scramble down to the bottom. There is a ten foot drop down to the ground, and I hesitate for a moment. I know this is going to hurt.

I let go. I fall through the air and hit the dirt hard. It hurts, but I am ok.

The others are down there, waiting for me. They all made it safely.

"Let's go, move!" I yell, and we sprint across the canyon floor, running for the rope dangling down the cliff on the far side. Stones hail down on us, but we are moving fast and they mostly miss.

It is odd being down here—like being in the bowels of the earth. I look up and see the steep cliffs on either side, and I realize what a huge climb it will be to get back up. I hope and pray that this works.

I reach the other dangling rope bridge, and stop and look straight up. It hangs straight down the cliff. I yank hard on it. It's sturdy.

"It's risky," Flo says, breathing hard as she comes up beside me. "They might cut it, when we're halfway up. Or burn it. Our shower us with rocks. Or anything."

"I don't think they will," I answer, facing her, catching my breath, too. "I think a part of them wants us to make it. After all, they need entertainment for tomorrow."

She looks up, unsure, as the others catch up beside us.

"Besides," I add, "we have no choice."

I reach down, grab Bree, and hoist her up onto the rope. "Climb," I say.

Flo grabs Charlie, and the two of them climb up together.

Next comes Logan, then Ben.

Flo pauses. She turns and I turn with her to see what she's watching. A dozen kids are finishing their descent down the other rope, copying my strategy. They are charging right for us.

"Go," I say to Flo. "Protect them. I've got the rear."

Flo gives me a look of approval, then grabs the rope and scrambles up. I climb up right after her.

As I do, one of the kids below reaches up and grabs my ankle. A lanky teenager with broad shoulders, she yanks hard and pulls me down, keeping me from climbing. My hands are getting tired, palms burning into the ropes, and in a desperate effort to shake her off, I wind up with my other foot and kick her hard in the face.

It is a perfect strike, right on her nose. She lets go, and I continue to climb, as fast as I can.

I make good time, catching up to the others, and soon we are halfway up the cliff. I can hardly believe it: my plan is really working. For the first time I wonder if we just might make it.

And then come the rocks. We are all halfway up when rocks begin to hail down all around us. The spectators throw them like crazy, and now they come straight down at us, like missiles. They weren't letting us go: they were just waiting until we got closer.

I cover my head, as the others do the same, and do my best to withstand the torrent of missiles. I look down and see several kids climbing up the rope behind me—and I watch as one of them gets hit by a particularly large rock, right in the head. She loses her grip and goes tumbling, end over end, landing flat on the ground below. She is dead.

My heart floods with panic. We can't just stay here.

"Move!" I yell up.

We all start moving again, climbing up, despite the rocks. They come down hard, bouncing off my arms and shoulders.

I hear a cry, and look up and see Charlie lose his grip. He falls from the rope, goes tumbling through the air. Flo reaches out to grab him, but it happens so fast, she just misses his grip.

Instinctively, I reach out. As he goes flying past, somehow I am able to grab hold of his shirt. I grab hard and hold him by one hand, dangling in the air. I swing him over, bring him back to the rope, and he grabs on, behind me.

I breathe deep with relief: I have just saved him from instant death. I look up and see the visible relief on Flo's face, too, and the gratitude.

But there is no time to think about it: we are under fire, and we all continue to climb our way straight up. Somehow, we slog our way through the stones. We are close, just feet from the top, when the crowd parts ways and a slaverunner steps forward with a machete. He raises it high, and I can see he is aiming to bring it down on the rope.

My heart floods with panic. If he cuts it, we will all be dead.

I move quick. I reach into my back pocket, take out the knife that I found. I figure now is the time to use it.

I grab the rope with one hand, lean back, and throw it with everything I have.

It flies through the air, end over end, straight up. It is a perfect strike.

The knife lodges in the slaverunner's forehead, and he goes limp and falls off the edge of the cliff, hurling past us to his death.

The spectators love this. They cheer like mad as we continue up the ladder. Bree reaches land first. Then Logan, then Ben, then Flo, then Charlie. Then me. I collapse on the ground, exhausted, every muscle in my body about to give out, hardly able to catch my breath. I can't believe it. We made it. We really made it.

The spectators stand back, part ways as the leader appears, carried forward on his throne. He sits there, looking down at us all. He stares for a long time, and the crowd quiets. I wonder if he's going to have us killed.

Suddenly, he breaks into a wide grin. That is when I know that we have made it. We have survived the first day.

SIXTEEN

We all sit in the cave, each leaning against the wall, each trying to recover. I look around, at Bree, Ben, Logan, Flo and Charlie—we are a sorry bunch. We are covered in scrapes and bruises; I can feel my own body covered in large welts, and I see welts forming on the other's faces. I didn't realize how many rocks I'd been hit by until now, how many blows I'd sustained, until I sit here recovering, feeling the pain and swelling of all the lumps.

We sit here, still dressed in our outfits, our black battle gear with yellow crosses across our chests. As much as it is a sour reminder of the day's events, at least the padded gear is comfortable, and keeps me warm. It is too painful to even try to take it off. It hurts to even bend my knees. I'm stiffening up, and I suspect the others are, too. I can't see myself surviving another day of this.

As the six of us sit around the fire, somber, a buzzer sounds, and the large hole in the ceiling opens again. This time, instead of slop being dumbed down, six metal baskets are slowly lowered on ropes. I get up and hobble over to them, as do the others—except for Logan, who is too stiff to even get up.

As I reach the center of the room I look down and am surprised at what I see: in each basket is a wide array of delicacies: meats, cheeses, fruits. Fresh. I can hardly believe it. I grab mine, the others grab theirs, and I reach over and grab Logan's for him. The ceiling closes as quickly as it opened.

"I guess the good meals are reserved for the victors," Ben says, a smile on his weary face.

We head back to our corner of the cave, I hand Logan his basket and sit beside him, and Bree sits on my other side. I rummage through my basket of goodies, and the first thing I find is a Snickers bar. I tear off the wrapper and shove it into my mouth; I take bite after bite, hardly able to slow down. It is the best thing I've ever had. If I were to die this moment, I would die happy.

Next I eat a huge chunk of salami, followed by a hunk of hard cheese. I know I should eat slowly, pace myself. But I can't help it; I feel like I haven't eaten in years. All the others are doing the same, all devouring food.

I am grateful to the slaverunners for a moment—but then I realize they're just giving us food to sustain us for tomorrow's festivities. They want us in our best shape so that they can have a good arena, so that they can watch us kill each other.

As I sit there and look around, I wonder if it will be just the six of us tomorrow. If so, what will we do? I know I couldn't lift a finger against anyone here. Even Flo. I am so curious as to what tomorrow will look like.

I turn to Flo, who sits there eating, Charlie beside her.

"Will they put us in the same arena tomorrow?" I ask her.

She continues chewing on her hunk of salami, not looking my way, and doesn't respond until she's finished the whole thing. She takes a deep breath, and shakes her head, licking her fingers.

"It's always different. They have an infinite variety of arenas."

"Do you have any idea what will be next?" Bree asks.

Flo shakes her head.

"All I know for sure is that tomorrow will be worse. They always up the ante. Always."

"Worse?" Bree asks, unbelieving.

I can hardly fathom it myself. How can anything be worse?

Another buzzer sounds, and on the far side of the cave, a steel door opens. I can't believe the slaverunners would come back for us this quickly. Then I realize: they are not coming for us; they are bringing in fresh competition.

Dozens of kids are shoved into the room, fresh faces. The slaverunners poke and prod them, kicking and shoving them deeper into the room. Soon, the room fills up. The kids looked dazed and confused, probably the same way we looked when we arrived. Our competition for tomorrow.

I feel both relieved and stressed. Relieved, because the pressure won't be on the six of us to fight each other; stressed, because we now have dozens of new competitors. I notice Flo is staring back at them, summing them up. Her hand rests on her knife, and she is clearly on edge.

Several of the kids look our way; they see our baskets, our food, and perhaps smell it, too. A few of the bigger teenage boys begin to amble their way over to us.

Immediately I stand, as does Flo, ready to face them, to protect what's ours. They must realize that we are serious, because half way, they pause, as if deliberating.

"Give us some of your food," one of the boys, the largest, demands. He is cross-eyed, with a huge nose and thin lips. He must be at least six foot four.

"Pry it out of my fingers," Flo answers, her voice steel.

He stands there, uncertain, as he looks at his cohorts. I brace myself, preparing for a fight, but suddenly, another buzzer sounds and the ceiling opens. Buckets of slop come raining down, and all the kids turn and run for it. The new boy sneers at us, and then heads off with the others. But before he does, he points right at Flo and says, "I won't forget."

"I hope you don't," Flo says back.

The boy turns to the pit and jockeys with the others for a spot. I notice he is particularly aggressive, throwing others out of his way as he dives face first into the mush.

Slowly, we relax and sit back down. I watch these new kids in wonder. Where do they come from?

"Does it ever end?" I ask Flo.

She shakes her head.

"There's an endless supply of fresh meat out there," she says. "But don't worry—it will end soon for us. We're lucky we made it through today. We won't be so lucky tomorrow."

"There has to be a way out," I say. "We need a plan. Something."

"We can't continue on like this," Ben adds. "We'll be dead."

"We can escape," Charlie pipes up.

"Charlie, stop it," Flo snaps.

"Why stop?" I ask, sticking up for Charlie.

"He knows a few tunnels," Flo says. "What good will that do us? There's a four foot thick steel door between us and getting out of this room. There are a dozen slaverunners outside, all with guns. It's a waste of energy to think about it."

She has a point. But at the same time, the thought of going back to the arena gives me a hopeless feeling.

"What happens if they make us fight each other?" Charlie asks sadly, and looks at Bree.

It is the gorilla in the room.

"We're not here to make friends, Charlie," Flo says. "We are here to survive. You understand me?"

It is a harsh response. But at the same time, I wonder if, deep down, Flo is just trying to convince herself.

I wonder more about Flo and Charlie, where they came from, their background. But she stands and walks away, to a far corner, obviously wanting nothing more to do with the conversation. She is a hard person to know.

I use the opportunity to look over at Logan, and see how he is doing.

"You all right?" I ask. He doesn't look good.

He slowly shakes his head. I look down at his leg, which is more swollen than before.

"Can I look?" I ask.

He hesitates, then nods. I walk over and gently reach down and roll back his pants. I stop as I see the wound. It is worse. Much worse. It reminds me of the early stages of Rose's wound, turning black at the edges. My heart sinks: the medicine didn't do much good after all.

"I know," he says. He must see my expression. I wish I could hide it, but I can't. I feel awful.

It is just like Logan, to sum up the entire situation with two words. He knows his hours are numbered. He knows there's little more we can do. He knows there's nothing more I can say. I sit beside him.

"It's not that bad," I say, mustering my most confident voice. "You'll make it through tomorrow. I'm sure of it."

"That makes one of us," he says.

I want to distract him, to take his mind off of all of this. I notice Ben, sitting a few feet away, looking at me, and I feel that he wants to talk to me. But I can't help feeling that Logan's days are numbered, and I feel he needs me more.

I lower my voice as I turn to Logan, out of earshot of Ben.

"Logan?" I ask softly.

He turns and looks at me.

"You saved my life many times. You made me promise to hang on. I did it, for you. Now will you let me return the favor? Will you hang on? For me?"

He stares at me for a long time.

"Why do you care so much?" he asks.

His question catches me off guard. I look away, thinking. I search my feelings, and try to figure out the right way to phrase it. I turn and look back to him.

"Because you mean a lot to me," I say. "Because I care about you. Because I would be devastated if anything happened to you."

He looks into my eyes for a long time, as if searching to see if I'm telling the truth. It is easy for me to, because I am. I really do have feelings for Logan, too.

Finally, he nods, satisfied.

"OK," he says. "You got tomorrow. I promise you that. But you've got to find a way to get us out of here. You've got to."

His words echo in my head, as he closes his eyes and turns away.

You've got to.

*

I awaken to the sound of a loud buzzer, a steel door opening, and the room flooded with light, and realize that I've fallen asleep. I was so tired, so physically exhausted, that I must have let my eyes close on me after eating.

Dozens of slaverunners march in and round up everyone. We already wear the uniforms, but they dole them out to the newbies and drag everyone to their feet. Slowly, I get to my feet, my body creaking and groaning in protest. All the others do as well, except Logan. He sits there, in a lot of pain, and I have to help him stand. This doesn't bode well.

I make sure Bree is by my side as we are marched out of the room, down the now familiar tunnels. As we go I look in every direction for any signs of any escape routes, thinking about what Charlie said. As we pass deeper through one tunnel, he elbows me in the ribs. Wordlessly, I turn and follow his gaze; he nods, gesturing in one direction. I see a tunnel that veers off to the side, and realize he thinks that's an escape route.

As we are marched forward I realize it would be too risky to attempt any sort of escape now; it would also leave the others vulnerable to getting killed—especially Logan. But I file away that tunnel in the back of my head. Maybe another time.

Soon we are prodded outside, onto the familiar dirt pathway, the sun shining down on the winter day. It is another mild day, the snow entirely melted, and this time, the path veers off to the right. We march and march, until my legs grow weary.

We round a hill, onto a new path, and as we do, I see it is lined with hundreds of screaming spectators, jeering as we go. I can't help feeling as if this is a walk of death, our final steps towards execution.

The path twists and turns, and as we take one final turn, the new arena opens up before us. My heart stops.

Before us lies a giant mound of sand—more like a mountain. Its base is about a hundred feet wide, and it rises probably two hundred feet high, reaching a point, like a pyramid. It is comprised of smooth, fine sand. All around it stand hundreds of cheering spectators, in a broad circle. Their leader sits in his throne, hoisted above the others, smiling and watching.

At first, I can't understand what this arena is. But as I study it, it begins to become clear. With a sinking feeling, I realize the mountain of sand is the arena. Somehow, we're going to be thrown into that sand. But with what objective? To reach the top?

We are prodded and shoved, and soon we stand at the periphery of the mountain. The crowd quiets as the leader stands and holds out his arms.

"My fellow mutants," he booms, then pauses dramatically. "I present to you this day's contestants!"

There's a huge cheer.

The leader raises his arms, and the crowd quiets.

"There are six returning victors today, and for these, we salute you."

The crowd cheers as they look at us. I hardly think of myself as a victor.

"The object of today's arena, contestants," he booms, looking at all of us, "is to reach the top of the sand mountain. Whoever reaches the top wins, and will be spared from death. Yesterday's victors are granted the privilege of a brief head start. Step forward, victors!"

Bree clutches my hand hard, and I step forward with her, and the others. As we do, the crowd cheers wildly. We all walk towards the huge mountain of sand, and I don't know what to do. I follow Flo, as she leans forward and begins to climb up the sand. I put my hands into the soft sand, then my feet, and take a few steps. My feet sink, and it is hard to walk. For every two steps I take, I slip back one. It reminds me of a time when I was a child, trying to climb a steep sand dune.

"Something's fishy," Ben says. "It can't be this easy. Just climb to the top?"

"It's not," Flo says.

I turn and look at her. She has her game face on, looking stoically straight ahead.

"What tricks do they have in store for us?" I ask her.

She looks at me hard.

"You saved Charlie yesterday, so I'm going to give you one more piece of advice," she says. "Nothing is what it seems," she says. "Remember that. Don't be hasty. Don't race for the top. You let the others go before you. You hear me? Whoever tries to win will lose."

We are all climbing, about ten feet up the mountain, when suddenly, a buzzer sounds.

There is a huge cheer, and the dozens of new kids race behind us, climbing the mountain. They scramble up in all directions, all around us.

As a reflex I start climbing faster, as do the others; but I spot Flo hanging back and remember her words, and I put out my hand and stop Bree and Ben. Logan is going slower than the rest of us, so I don't have to stop him.

"What are you doing?" Ben asks.

"Let them go," I say.

"But if we don't reach the top we'll lose!" Bree pleads.

"Trust me," I say.

Ben reluctantly stops and lets a group of about a dozen kids pass him. We sit back and watch the others race up the mountain. I see two kids scramble past me and watch as one reaches out and grabs the other from behind. He yanks him backwards with a jerk and the other goes flying through the air and tumbles down the mountain.

As he tumbles there is a loud noise, and when he nears the base, long metal spikes rise up in all directions. He rolls right onto them and gets impaled by the spikes, screaming.

The crowd cheers in ecstasy.

Now I realize. Of course, it was not as easy as it seemed. The stakes have increased. This is no longer an innocent game of King of the Mountain. Falling back means falling to your death.

Suddenly, I feel a wrist grab my ankle, and look back to see a desperate girl, maybe 18, with long, greasy hair that clings to her face. She digs her fingers into my skin and pulls hard. I feel myself begin to slide backwards down the mountain. I am losing my grip, my fingernails slipping through the sand, and know that in a moment I will fall backwards and get impaled in the spikes.

Before I can react, I look over and see Bree reach out, grab a handful of sand, then turn and throw it right into the girl's eyes. The girl lets go of my ankle, grabbing her eyes. I pull up my leg and kick her hard in the throat. She goes tumbling backwards, and gets impaled on the spikes. The crowd cheers wildly.

I look over at Bree, amazed by her ingenuity and so grateful to her for saving my life. "Thank you," I say.

Other kids are scrambling up behind us.

"Let them go," I say to the others, wanting to avoid another confrontation.

Bree and I part ways from Charlie and Flo, creating a path in the middle. Several kids scramble past us, racing for the top.

But one of them stops and grabs Bree, apparently thinking he'll have an easy kill. He starts to yank her backwards when I reach out and grab his hand, pulling him off. At the same time, Logan swings around and elbows him in the chest, sending him toppling down the mountain. He gets impaled in the spikes, face first, and the crowd cheers.

I look over at Logan, impressed by his burst of energy. I had nearly written him off, but see his fighting spirit is still there.

Several more kids race past us, and I look up and already see one girl getting farther than the others, at least halfway up. But then something goes wrong. As I watch, her feet start to sink. Soon, she's in up to her waist—then her chest. Her hands are up, flailing, and I realize: she is stuck in a sand trap. Quicksand.

She screams as she sinks, her head getting lower. Soon, her screams are muffled, as she's completely swallowed up by the sand.

The crowd cheers.

I realize now how truly treacherous this arena is. It might be even worse than the last, and I start to wonder if there's any way out. I make a mental note of where she ran, to make sure we don't step in the same spot twice.

Some of the other kids hesitate, but another boy runs farther past where she was, until he suddenly stops, screaming in agony. A blade has risen up from the sand, impaling his foot. He stands there, stuck, screaming, trying to get out. But he can't. Blood pours from his wound, staining the sand red.

The crowd screams.

All around me, blades pop up, impaling many kids. In other places, more sand traps open, swallowing other kids. I realize this arena is a giant trap. Like a minefield. Flo was right: better not to rush. That "head start" for the victors was just a trick. Flo's advice, once again, saved our lives.

A buzzer sounds, and I hear something whirl in the air. All around me I spot objects landing in the sand, and for a moment, I wonder if it's a hailstorm. But then I get hit by something hard in the back, and I realize: the arena is now open for spectators to throw rocks. All around me, rocks are being thrown, hitting the sand everywhere. Several hit me in the back of the arms and legs. One barely misses my head. It is painful, and obviously meant to keep us moving.

We have no choice but to continue our way up the mountain.

"Drag your hands!" Flo yells. "Don't pick them up and drop them. If a blade is going to pop, you'll feel it beforehand, something hard in the sand. Pull back your hand."

It's good advice, and we all continue up, dragging our hands as we go. After several feet I feel something, and quickly retract my hand. A split-second later, a huge blade pops, missing me by a millisecond.

More rocks fly at me, and a large rock bounces off the back of my spine. It hurts like hell. I have an idea. I pick it up and grab it.

"Collect all the rocks!" I say to the others.

Bree, Ben, Logan and the others begin to collect the rocks.

"Throw them in the sand, before you move. It will set off any traps."

At the same we all start chucking the rocks ahead of us. We set off dozens of blades and we clear a path most of the way.

I save one rock, though, and turn around and aim for a spectator. I hurl it back, hitting him between the eyes, knocking him down. The crowd boos.

I turn around and smile to myself. It is a small satisfaction. It barely made a dent, but it sure felt good to give them a taste of their own medicine.

There are about thirty kids still alive, higher up on the mountain. These are starting to realize how treacherous it is, and some get a new strategy, stopping and wait for others to pass them. Others have yet another strategy: to retreat back down the mountain and kill off everyone below them. I guess they think that reaching the top is impossible and eliminating everyone else is the way to win.

Three kids scramble down right for us. One of them, running right at me, steps on a trap and a metal spike impales him; he drops to his knees and falls face first, dead. The other two, though, make it. One charges right down the mountain for me, his momentum carrying him, and before I can react, he tackles me hard.

I land flat on my back, and the two of us go sliding down the mountain, fast. I'm heading right for the blades at the base, and I need to think quick.

I arch my back and lift my legs up with all my strength, as if doing a backflip, and manage to use his momentum to send him flying over my head. Just in time: he gets impaled on the spikes at the base, and it just stops my free-fall.

But now I'm back down the mountain, rocks flying at me painfully, and I scramble back up as quickly as I can, trying to carefully retrace my steps. The other remaining kid dives into our group, aiming for Logan, going for the weakest link. He tackles him hard, and they go sliding down the mountain at full speed.

They are sliding for the spikes at the base, and my heart stops. It seems like in moments, Logan will be impaled. The crowd cheers wildly.

At the last second, Logan summons his strength. He reaches out, grabs the boy and spins around. As they reach the spikes, the boy gets impaled, back first, blood gushing from his mouth.

The crowd cheers.

But something is wrong. Logan is stuck, too, not moving, and as I look closely, my heart drops: I see that the spike has gone through the boy and into Logan's arm. Logan screams out, and the pain looks excruciating.

I scramble back down the mountain, as do the others, and hurry over to him and yank him out. The others help, and as we do, he shrieks. The steel slowly leaves his flesh, blood gushing everywhere. He's breathing hard, sweating, and I reach down and tear a strip off my shirt and use it as a tourniquet, tying it around his wound. It quickly fills with blood.

Flo and I each take one of his arms around our shoulders, and begin to drag him up the mountain, away from the jeering spectators and the flying rocks.

"Leave me," he grunts.

"No way," I say.

Together, we all hobble back up the mountain. I look up and notice there are hardly a dozen kids left, sitting there, higher up the mountain, probably waiting for us to pass them. They all seem scared to move on, not knowing what's in store for them.

And then, everything changes.

Another buzzer sounds, and high up, I detect a strange motion in the sand. At first I can't understand what it is. And when I do, I can't believe it.

Slithering out of the sand, in every direction, come dozens of brightly colored snakes.

The dozen or so kids higher up try to get out of the way, but it's too late for them. They try to dodge the snakes, running left and right, but the snakes dig their fangs into them. They scream out in agony, one after the other. The venom works quickly, and several of the kids lie limp; a few of the others impale themselves on spikes as they run.

The good news is that the snakes die on impact as they sink their fangs into the kids; it seems that using up their venom kills them.

The bad news is that there is one, particularly large, snake left.

It slithers its way down the mountain, right towards us.

No, I think. *Not a snake. Anything but a snake.*

Of course, the snake zeros in on me. I brace myself for the attack, flinching in advance, having nowhere to go.

But Flo leaps out from the side, grabs the snake by its head, and holds it there, squeezing hard with both hands. It squirms like crazy but cannot get out.

"Charlie, your wire!" she yells.

Charlie hurries over, takes a wire with two handles from his pocket and wraps it around the snake's throat, several times. He squeezes as hard as he can, and Ben hurries over and helps him. Finally, the snake's head is severed. The rest of its body slithers, uncontrollably down the mountain.

I look around and see that all the other kids are dead. We are the only survivors left. I can hardly believe it.

We grab Logan and we all head together up the mountain. We go single file, carefully following the trail of the dead bodies, other kids who paved the way for us, who already set off all the traps, and within moments, we reach the top, safe.

A buzzer sounds, and the crowd roars.

I can hardly believe it. We have survived.

SEVENTEEN

Back in our cave, at night, we all sit around the fire, completely exhausted. I lean my head back against the wall and close my eyes, and don't think I can ever open them again. Every bone in my body is aching and hurting. I can't believe what my body has been through these last two days. If someone told me I could fall asleep and wake up in twenty years, I think I would.

I just want this agony and suffering to end—not just for me, but for all of us. We are fighting for our lives, clinging to life, but a part of me wonders, what for? This will only end in all of us being killed. In some ways, we are just prolonging our agony.

I look around and see the exhausted faces of Bree and Charlie, Ben and Logan—and even Flo. It especially breaks my heart to see Logan, lying there beside me, looking like this. He was hurt the worst today of us all, and while I've been trying to staunch his new wound, it's barely working. He's lost a lot of blood, and he looks so pale, it's almost as if he's dead already. I've tried to wake him several times, but he just groans and turns away. My heart sinks, and I fear for him. If he doesn't get serious medical attention soon, I don't see how he can survive. Not to mention, it's just not possible for him to compete in tomorrow's games. I can't help but feel as if I'm sitting on a death vigil.

The rest of us hardly fare much better. We are all so beaten and broken and bruised and exhausted, not to mention, filled with dread for what might come tomorrow. Flo was right: they do up the stakes each day. I can't imagine how they can possibly up them again tomorrow. I feel certain that tomorrow will be our last day.

A buzzer sounds, the ceiling opens, and this time they lower twelve baskets, these overflowing with food and goodies. While yesterday we all jumped up for them, now, we all look at each other, all too broken to jump up and get them.

Eventually, we struggle to our feet and march across the room. My legs feel like a thousand pounds each as I pick up my two baskets, along with Logan's, and the others pick up theirs. We bring them back to the fire.

I am thrilled to see it is filled with goodies, foods, snacks and candies of all kinds. I can't believe that the slaverunners have managed to find and keep such an abundance of good food in this day and age, with the rest of the world starving. The thought of it makes me sick: they have so much while others have so little.

While yesterday I devoured my food, today I move more slowly, as do the others. A part of me has lost my appetite. I open one candy bar and take a bite; it is delicious, and I revel in the sugar rush. But I don't have the excitement of the day before.

I unwrap Logan's candy bar and put it in his mouth, trying to get him to take a bite. But he won't. I feel his forehead, how hot his fever has become, and grow increasingly worried. I wish there was something I could do.

"Logan," I say softly. "You have to eat. Please."

Eyes closed, he shakes his head in agony. Eventually, he opens his eyes just a bit, just enough to look into mine.

He just stares at me, his eyes into mine, for what feels like the longest time. He doesn't say anything, but in that stare, I feel him say things. *Thank you. I love you. I'm sorry.*

I want to say those things back to him, but I feel embarrassed, especially with others so close. I feel torn. On the one hand, I do have genuine feelings for Ben. Yet, I also have feelings for Logan, especially now, as I feel him leaving. I want to spend time with Ben, but I *need* to spend time with Logan.

I curl up beside Logan, hold his head in my lap, and gently brush his hair away, off his clammy forehead. I decide I need to distract him, to tell him a story.

"Once, when I was young, before the war, my dad took me hunting," I begin. I figure this is a story that Logan would like.

He perks up the slightest bit and I know he's interested. Encouraged, I continue.

"He gave me this huge, oversized rifle, and I was terrified to use it. We walked for hours, deep into the woods, looking all day for anything to kill. I really didn't want to be there. But I wanted to make him happy.

"Around sunset, I noticed this weird look in his eyes, a look I had never seen before. It was something like confusion. Maybe fear. He was always so confident, so in control, I didn't understand what was happening. That look, to me, was scarier than anything.

"I asked him what was wrong, and he finally admitted he was lost. He didn't know the way back. Now we were deep into the woods, and it was getting dark. I was terrified. I asked him what we were going to do. He said we were going to find a tree, go to sleep, and in the morning, find our way out.

"That terrified me more than anything, and I started to cry. He yelled at me, told me to be tough, that things could be worse. After a while I stopped crying and sat down next to him, against the tree. We sat there like that, silent, both of us against the same tree, all night long.

"The crazy thing was, he didn't say another word to me, all night long. As if he didn't have a single thing to say to his own daughter.

"I thought about that night for years, and for so many years I was mad at him. But now, looking back, I'm not mad anymore. Because now I realize that, for him, silence was speech. That was his way of being with me. He was telling me he loved me, in his own way. He just couldn't use his words."

I turn and look down at Logan, and he looks up at me, eyes open.

"In some ways, he reminds me of you," I say, nervous to say it.

Logan opens his eyes wide with one final effort, and looks up into mine. I see a slight smile at the corner of his lips, and I realize he liked the story.

Logan doesn't say anything to me either, but he slowly nods, and I can see the love in his eyes. In that moment, I can see he is just like my dad. He is talking to me. Even if he can't say the words.

*

It is late into the night, I don't know how late, and we are all sitting up, except for Logan, awake around the fire. After today's events, none of us can sleep. We all stare wide-eyed into the flames, each lost in our own world, each of us staring death in the face.

Hours ago, dozens of new recruits were thrown into the room. These new kids keep to themselves, on the far side of the cave, content with the slop dropped down for them. No one tries to come our way, which is just as well, because I don't know if I'd have the energy left to fight them off. Not that I even care about my food at this point. But I am curious as to why there are so few kids this time.

"Stragglers," Flo says. I look over and see she is watching them, too. She has an uncanny way of reading my mind. "It was slim pickings today for the slaverunners. That's bad news for us."

"Why?"

"They need to keep the games exciting for their crowd. When they don't have a lot of kids, they have no choice but to pit us directly against each other."

Instinctively, I feel that she's right. And it makes my heart drop. I can't stand the thought of it. I can't imagine being pitted against Bree, against Charlie, against Ben, against Flo. Against Logan. It is too cruel to even imagine.

"Well we found a way to stick together through all this," I say. "I think we can find a way tomorrow, too."

Flo shrugs. "I'm not so sure," she says.

I try to interpret her words, to understand her meaning. Is it a threat? Is she saying she'll fight us? A part of me feels that she might. She's a survivor, and she has Charlie to look out for. I can't put anything past her.

We lapse into silence, all retreat back into our own worlds, our game faces on, as I think about tomorrow. I know that we can't last another day. I have to come up with a plan. Something. I have to find us a way out of here.

I turn over all possible options in my mind, again and again, until my eyes grow heavy. I think of Charlie's tunnels, obsessively, feeling that is the key. But I am not thinking clearly, and cannot come up with any answers. The solution is just beyond my grasp.

*

When the buzzer rings on the morning of the third day, this time, my eyes are already opened. Bleary-eyed, I've been awake all night, my mind racing with the possibilities, with ideas of how to get out. The steel door slides open, and in march dozens of slaverunners.

I don't give them the dignity of dragging me to my feet, and instead stand before they can reach me. I walk over and wake the others, gently pulling Bree and Charlie to their feet. I see that Flo's awake, too, already standing. Ben gets up with an effort.

The slaverunners are in front of us, and I go to Logan and shake him roughly. It takes him a while to even open his eyes. He does not look good.

"Get up," I say.

He shakes his head no. He looks like he's half-alive.

A slaverunner hurries over and kicks him hard.

"Let him be!" I scream.

The slaverunner shoves me, and I stumble back into the wall, hard. Flo steps up and punches the slaverunner across the face. I'm shocked, and touched by her sticking up for me.

But she pays the price dearly, backhanded hard by another slaverunner, the sound of his hand slapping her flesh echoing in the room.

She goes to attack, but I step forward and get between them, holding her back.

"It's OK, Flo," I say to her, seeing the violence in her eyes and not wanting her to get hurt. "Let it go. Let's just get him on his feet."

I reach over with Flo and Ben and we all drag Logan to his feet. It's like pulling up an old tree. He groans out in pain, and Ben and I each drape an arm around one of his shoulders, helping him hobble. The six of us are then marched out of the room.

As they prod us out of the room, this time we are led down a different tunnel. We're all led to a huge steel door, and as it opens, to my surprise we enter a brightly-lit room, its walls lined with weapons. Hanging from the wall are swords, bows and arrows, shields, throwing knives, slingshots, spears, and all sorts of other weapons. I can't understand what's happening. I think of the damage I can do to the slaverunners with these, and feel as if I've walked into a candy store.

"Choose!" barks a slaverunner.

Suddenly, the dozen or so new kids race through the room, scattering, each bee lining for a weapon.

"It's fighting day," Flo says, and then hurries off to the wall. She goes for a large sword.

I hurry off with Logan and Charlie and Bree, and as we reach the wall, I prop Logan against it and hand him a big shield.

"If you can't fight, at least you can defend, right?" I ask him.

He nods weakly.

I grab a long spear and strap it to my back. Then I reach out and grab a long sword as well. While I'm at it, I see a nice throwing knife and grab that and attach it to my belt.

Beside me, Bree has chosen a slingshot. It is a good choice. She was always good with her hand-made slingshot, and this one comes with a bag of small rocks, and she ties it to her belt. Then, of course, she chooses the bow and arrow, which she is just as good at. Charlie chooses a strange medieval weapon: it is a long chain, with a handle on one end, and a metal ball on the other. Ben chooses a long sword, and nothing else.

Flo, holding her sword, turns towards me, and for a moment I feel what it would be like to face her. In some ways it would be like facing a mirror image of myself. It terrifies me.

A buzzer sounds and I look around the room and see the other kids are all well-armed. This doesn't bode well.

"Bree, Charlie," I say. "Whatever happens out there, stay close to me, okay? Don't go far off. This way I can look out for you."

"You don't need to look after Charlie," Flo chides. "I will."

She's territorial, and already has her game face on.

"Just trying to help," I say.

"Look after your own," she snaps back to me.

She has drawn a clear line in the sand.

"Charlie, come over here, with me," she commands.

Charlie looks back and forth between me and Flo, and seems reluctant to go to her. But slowly, he obeys, and walks over to Flo's side.

I can't help but feel as if we are now all adversaries. All fighting for survival.

*

We are marched down tunnel after tunnel for what feels like hours, entirely underground this time, passing red emergency lights every twenty feet. Rats scurry beneath my feet, and in the distance, I hear the muted rumbling of a train passing somewhere. I wonder how many trains passed through here today, how many slaves they are capturing from the countryside, to present to their games. It makes me sick.

I feel the winter wind whipping through, colder today, and I wonder when we will exit outside. Something is different today. This time, there is no end in sight to the tunnels. I don't understand it. Are today's games underground?

Logan is growing heavy as Ben and I carry him, and I can feel his life force leaving him. The idea of bringing him to these games, to compete with others, is crazy. He can barely stand.

I try once again to think strategy, to figure out a way we can all survive. But it is hard. We're surrounded by a dozen armed kids, all set on killing us, and I don't even know the playing field we'll be on. Just keeping myself alive will be a challenge, much less keeping the others alive, too. I worry for Bree, more than anyone. I have to find a way to protect her.

A huge steel door retracts, and as it does, the tunnel fills with sunlight. There is the muted roar of a crowd, and we are prodded forward. I raise my eyes against the blinding light, trying to figure out where we are.

As I am shoved outside, the steel door closes behind us, the winter wind hits me in the face and the roar grows louder. I look all around, and see no one. I can't figure out where it's coming from. Then the crowd roars again, and I look straight up.

I realize we're on the floor of a circular canyon, with steep cliffs rising straight up all around us, several hundred feet. At the very top, standing on the edge of the cliffs, behind a railing, are the spectators. They jeer down at us.

The walls rise straight up, for hundreds of feet, and I don't see how we can ever get out of here. Then I realize: there is no way out this time. I look around and see the dozen kids, armed to the teeth, standing with us on the floor of the crater. They have put us all down here, with no escape, to make us fight to the death. But why down here? Why not up high, on the ground?

I survey this arena, the canyon walls, and have an ominous feeling. I can't help but feel as if the slaverunners have some trick up their sleeve. I look up and about a hundred feet up, I notice thick ropes, dangling down from the top of the crater. But why do they stop midway? It doesn't make any sense. How are we supposed to get up there to begin with?

Before I can figure it out, suddenly, a voice booms through the air. The crowd quiets, and I look up and see the leader, staring down, his arms open wide, a smug smile on his face.

"Brothers and sisters!" he bellows. "I present to you the third and final day of Arena Two!"

The crowd screams out in response. He waits for it to quiet down.

"Today's objective is simple. There are eighteen of you down there. You will all kill each other. When there is one person standing, he or she will be the winner!"

The crowd roars at his words.

"Let the games begin!"

Suddenly, I sense motion all around me. The dozen kids all turn on each other, and on us—and a brawl breaks out.

The crowd roars, loving it.

This arena brings out the worst in the kids. I see vicious expressions on their faces as they charge each other in every direction.

I see one girl take her sword and stab a short boy in the back. He falls, stunned, the first casualty. The crowd roars.

I sense motion behind me and turn in time to spot an overweight girl charging me, bringing an axe down for my head. My survival instinct kicks in. At the last second, I swerve out of the way and swing my sword, chopping her ax handle in two. She goes flying past me with her broken handle, and as she does, I kick her hard in the back, sending her flying flat on her face.

The crowd cheers. She gets up with a snarl.

"I don't want to hurt you," I say, trying to talk reason to her. It's true. I don't want to kill anyone. I just want to get us all out of here.

But she won't listen to reason. She seems to think that the way to survive is to kill me.

She pulls a small knife from her waist and charges me, holding it high, screaming. I don't wait. I take the small throwing knife from my waist, plant one foot, reach back, and throw it at her. As she charges me, just feet away, my knife lodges perfectly in her forehead. Her eyes open wide as she stops cold, and falls flat on her back, dead.

The crowd roars.

But I am caught off guard. Before I can react, another kid charges me from the side, swinging a huge sledgehammer. I dodge it, and it misses by a fraction of an inch. I feel its wind race past me, and realize that in another second, it would've crushed my ribs.

This boy is quick and strong, and without pausing, he brings the sledgehammer up around his head, and aims to bring it down on my shoulder. I can't react fast enough, and realize that in another moment, he will break my arm.

A stone hits him in the side of the temple, and he staggers and falls sideways. I look over and see that Bree has used her slingshot. It was a perfect hit. Once again, she has saved my life.

Before I can process this, once again I'm caught off guard, as three more kids charge right for me. For some reason, they all seem to be targeting me. One of them brings a sword down for my back, and I hear a clanging noise, and turn to see Logan standing there, holding his shield, blocking the below. I am amazed: he has just saved me.

Logan stumbles on his bad leg, but manages to hold onto the shield, and uses it to block several blows. He then swings around and cracks the teenage boy hard across the face, knocking him back. I lunge forward with my sword and stab the boy in the heart, finishing him off. He goes down, and the crowd roars.

Another boy charges me from the side, holding a spear, about to hurl it at me. Before I can react, I feel something whiz by my ear, and see it lodge into his throat. An arrow. He falls, dead, dropping his spear harmlessly before he can hurl it. I look over and see Ben standing there, having just fired.

Another boy grabs me from behind in a chokehold; he has thick forearms, and he squeezes hard. His arms are the worst weapons of all: he's squeezing the life out of me. He's also using me as a human shield, so the others can't help me. I don't know how I will get out of this one.

Then I feel him stagger, off-balance, and fall. I don't understand why, but I break out of his grip, gasping for air. I look down and see a metal chain ball wrapped around his ankles, squeezing them together. Charlie has thrown them, tripped him up. I take my sword and plunge it through his heart. The crowd roars.

"Charlie!" Flo snaps, summoning him back to her side. Busy fighting, she leans back and kicks a girl hard in the chest, then swings her sword and cuts off her head. The crowd roars like crazy.

I look all around us, and can't believe the carnage. The fighting went so quickly, was such a blur. All around us are littered bodies. The other dozen kids are all dead. The six of us have won. Despite Flo's warnings, we worked as a team. And now we are the lone survivors.

The crowd roars and stomps like crazy. It seems we have beaten the system.

We all stand there, looking at each other, each out of breath, holding our weapons. Now there is no one left to fight but each other. And, of course, none of us would hurt each other.

Or would we?

I look over, and see Flo staring back at me, hard eyed. I see her summing us all up, surveying all of us as if we are her final competition.

The crowd quiets as the leader steps forward.

"There can only be one survivor. If you won't fight each other, then we will kill you all."

We all stand there, frozen in an awkward tension. Flo huddles beside Charlie, and Logan, Ben and Bree stand closer to me. Ben has his hand on his bow and arrow, and Bree on her slingshot. I can see that a part of Flo wants to be the only victor, for Charlie's sake. But I think another part of her is divided. After all, I have saved her, and Charlie. And now I also have backup with Bree and with Ben. She hesitates, overwhelmed with conflicting emotions.

We all stand there, none of us moving, and soon the crowd begins to boo. And then, to heckle us. They start throwing down small rocks, and they land all around us, like hail. But the rocks miss, the crowd too far away to do any serious damage.

Just as their booing grows to a pitch, I begin to hear a great rumbling noise. It sounds as if the world is about to explode, and I can't figure out what it is. Until I look up.

I spot a massive boulder being rolled, pushed straight down the cliff. It goes over the edge, rumbling, and comes rolling straight down the walls—right for us.

At once we all run together, trying madly to get out of the way as it comes flying down at us like a missile. I grab Bree's hand as I run, and we all manage to run just hard enough to get out of its way. It misses us by feet. It flies by, stirring up a cloud of dust, and then crashes into the far wall of the canyon like a nuclear bomb. The ground shakes, and it raises an even bigger cloud of dust and debris.

The crowd cheers wildly. The leader steps forward.

"That was only one boulder. We have dozens of others. If you don't fight each other, you will be killed by us within minutes. Now stand and fight!"

The crowd cheers, and Flo slowly turns to me.

"We have to fight," she says. "If we don't, they'll kill us all."

"I don't want to fight you," I say. "There has to be another way."

"There isn't," she says. "If not for our sake, then do it for the sake of the others. You and I have to fight."

I look up and spot another boulder, perched high up, and I realize she's right. If we don't do something soon, those boulders will kill us all.

"No, I don't want you to fight!" Charlie screams.

"Neither do I!" Bree screams.

I turn and look at them, feeling their pain.

"It will be okay," I say. "Don't worry."

Flo turns and walks out slowly into the center of the canyon floor. As she does, the crowd goes wild. As I watch her, I feel I have no choice. I have to do it. If this is what she wants, this is how it will be.

I walk out, too, following her, and the crowd rises to a frenzy. The two of us stand in the center, facing each other.

As I am standing there, wondering if she will really fight, the crowd screaming, suddenly Flo rushes towards me, sneering, raising her sword high. She brings it down, right for my head, and I raise my sword and block her blow at the last second. Her blow is strong, one meant to actually kill. I am shocked. I can hardly believe it. She is not posturing: she really wants to kill me.

The crowd cheers like mad.

As I stand there, blocking her blow with my sword, the strength of her swing is making my hands shake. I'm shocked at the strength in her shoulders. I know that I can't hold her back for long, so at the last second, I step to the side, and her sword goes flying down, to my side. Her momentum carries her flying past me, and as she goes, I wheel around and hit her in the back of the head with the flat of my sword, sending her stumbling forward.

The crowd cheers, and Flo turns and scowls back at me. She charges again, sword high, and slashes down; I stand to the side, and she just misses. I slash back at her, and she blocks my blow. We go blow for blow, swinging and parrying, pushing each other back and forth across the floor.

One of her slashes is slightly quicker than mine and she manages to slice my bicep. I scream out in pain, as blood squirts out. It is my first wound of the day.

The crowd screams like crazy. I reach over and cup my wound and see my hand is red, stained with blood.

She stares back coldly, unapologetic. I can hardly believe it.

She charges again, and we go blow for blow. She is strong, and fast, and I'm getting tired quickly. She is a machine. My shoulders are aching and burning, and I realize I can't sustain this much longer.

For some reason, I think of dad. His words ring through my head, as I think of everything he taught me. All those lessons about fighting. About being tough. About hanging in there. About not fighting on the other guy's terms, and I realize that's what I've been doing: fighting on her terms. I realize I don't need to. I know other ways of fighting. Who said this needs to be a sword fight? I decide instead to make it a hand fight—what I am best at.

As she slashes again, this time I step aside, and instead of slashing, lean back and kick her hard in the ribs.

It works. She wasn't expecting it, and she keels over. The crowd goes wild.

Without giving her a chance to recover, I reach over and grab her by the back of the hair and knee her hard in the face.

She drops her sword as she falls back, landing on her butt, then on her back, her nose broken. She lies there, dazed and confused. She hadn't expected me to turn this into a fist fight.

The crowd screams like crazy, standing on its feet.

I take a step forward, and hold my sword at the tip of her throat. I have her beat. I can kill her easily now if I want to.

"Kill her! Kill her! Kill her!" the crowd chants.

As I stand there, the wound in my arm hurting, a part of me feels betrayed, and wants to kill her. After all, if this were me down there, wouldn't she kill me?

But I see her staring back at me, and I think of Charlie, without a sister, and a part of me just can't bring myself to do it.

"Do it," she smiles. In that moment I realize that she wants me to. She's had enough: she wants to die.

The crowd quiets, and I look up and see the leader step forward.

"If you kill her," he screams down to me, "I will spare you. All of you. All you have to do is kill her. And then you will all be set free."

The crowd cheers. I look down at Flo and see her breathing hard, scowling up at me.

"Please," she says. "Do it."

I see that she is genuine—she really wants to die.

"NO!" Charlie screams. "Please don't kill her!"

I think of the leader's words. If I kill Flo it will spare Bree. And Charlie. And Ben. And Logan. And myself. All for someone who wants to die anyway. For someone who would have gladly killed me.

I know I should do it.

But as I look down at her, a part of me just can't do it. Besides, I want to defy the leader.

So instead, I drop my sword. It lands on the dusty canyon floor with a clang.

The crowd jeers and boos and screams down at me. But I don't care.

Flo slowly shakes her head in disgust. "Stupid," she says.

There is a tremendous rumbling noise, and at first I think it's another boulder; but then I look up and see no rocks coming down, and realize it's something else. The entire ground is shaking beneath me, like an earthquake, and I realize that whatever it is, it's much more ominous.

Suddenly, large steel traps open on the ground and walls all around us, and water comes gushing in. It comes gushing in like a river, like a dam breaking, from every side, a huge tidal wave coming right for us. I look over at Charlie, Ben, Logan and Flo, and see them all looking wide-eyed at the water.

Bree holds out her hands and runs for me. I go to pick her up.

But it is a lost cause.

Suddenly, we're slammed by water from every direction. My world turns upside down as I go head over heels, tumbling beneath the waves. The gushing water picks me up and smashes me down again, and I go tumbling, end over end, water shooting up my nose. I whirl and whirl, trying to make my way to the top of the water, trying to hold my breath.

After about thirty seconds of complete chaos, I manage to surface. The water is swirling all around me, and I can hear the crowd cheering like crazy. I look for signs of the others, and in the distance, I spot Bree and Charlie, their heads bobbing just above water. Further away, I can see Flo, alive, and Ben, flailing. But I look everywhere, and don't see Logan.

Then I spot him: his head bobs up, just feet away from me. He looks in utter agony, and I manage to swim over to him, fighting the current.

"Brooke!" he cries out.

He holds out one hand and I swim for it.

Our hands just touch when I see something in the water beneath us. It is a whirlpool, sucking down everything in its path. Our fingertips graze each other, and then he gets sucked away, the whirlpool pulling him down.

"Brooke!" he screams.

I see the fear in his eyes as he gets pulled away from me, sucked deeper into the whirlpool.

"Logan!" I cry.

He goes down, under water, then disappears.

There is nothing but silence.

The whirlpool disappears—as if someone turned off a switch. I search the calm surface of the water.

"Logan!" I shriek.

But it's too late. He's gone.

I can't believe it. Logan. The backbone of our group. Dead.

My heart breaks. But I can't think about that now. I force it from my mind. The waters are swirling and rising, and I spin around, looking for any sign of the others. I see Bree and Charlie, close to each other, each flailing, struggling, arms up over the water. Luckily, Bree is a strong swimmer—and it looks like Charlie is, too. But I can already tell that Bree is losing strength and won't last long. I have to save her.

I fight the current, swim over to her, the waters rising and frothing all around me; it is like swimming in a giant fishbowl.

Somehow, I manage to reach her; I grab her with one arm, from behind, wrapping my forearm around her chest.

"It's okay, Bree, hang on."

She is gasping for air. The waves have pushed us close to the canyon wall, and I look up and see the rope dangling down the side of the cliff. Just minutes ago, the rope was a hundred feet off the ground—but now, it's right there, in my reach. I can hardly believe it.

I reach out and grab it, it's the knotty rope digging into my palms, then hoist Bree up onto it. Once she's safe, I look over and about fifteen feet away spot Charlie, who's getting swept away in the wrong direction.

"Save him!" Bree cries.

I swim to him, fighting the currents, grab hold of his shirt, and with my last burst of energy, fight my way back, against the current, towards the rope.

I make it, and hoist him, too. Now he and Bree are both on the rope, dangling, and already beginning to climb their way up. I reach up and grab on behind them, and hang onto it, breathing hard, catching my breath. I look around, but see no signs of Ben or Flo. I wonder if they've made it.

But there is no time to search, or to rest on my heels. The water is rising fast all around us.

I look straight up, and see the steep climb ahead of us, two hundred feet to the top of the canyon. We have no choice.

"Climb!" I yell, over the roar of the gushing water.

Bree quickly climbs, as does Charlie, and the three of us ascend, straight up the rope. I use my feet to push off the rock face, as if repelling, and gain momentum.

Soon, the three of us are high up, a good fifty feet above the water. I'm starting to feel optimistic, that we might actually make it out of here.

And then, I hear a cry.

I stop and look down over my shoulder, and can't believe what I see: there, in the center of the gushing waters, swimming for the wall, is Flo. Her face is etched in panic, and she reaches a hand towards me. I've never seen panic on her face before, and I can't understand it: is it because she cannot swim?

But then, I see it, what has her terror-struck—and my heart drops.

A huge tentacle reaches up out of the water, wraps itself around her leg, and drags her down, beneath the water. Flo disappears, bubbling, then moments later surfaces again, gasping for air.

"Please!" she screams.

"Flo!" Charlie screams.

But we are helpless. There's nothing I can do from up here but watch as the sea creature raises its ugly head. It is the most hideous creature I have ever seen: it looks like a giant squid, but with rows and rows of sharp teeth and a single, large eye. Its face is grotesque, some sort of freak animal that probably resulted from the fallout of the nuclear war.

It reaches out with another tentacle, wraps it around Flo, and sucks her down for good.

The crowd roars, as Flo is pulled down underneath the water, and the monster disappears with her.

I look down at the waters beneath me with a new sense of dread. If I slip and fall, I will be finished.

"MOVE!" I scream to Bree and Charlie, who stay there, looking down, terror-struck.

We all climb faster, when I hear a mocking laugh, and look straight up: the leader stands there, less than a hundred feet away, looking down and holding a machete.

"No!" I scream.

But it's too late. He swings it down, chopping our rope.

Instantly, the three of us go hurling through the air, screaming.

EIGHTEEN

I fall faster than I ever have, plunging towards the water. Before I can catch my breath I hit. My world goes dark, as I find myself plunging deep beneath the surface.

For a moment, as I struggle to catch my breath, my world goes black. I see my dad, standing there, looking down at me, hands on his hips.

"On your feet, soldier! What did I teach you? Fight back. *Fight back*!"

I open my eyes, still underwater, and look up towards the surface. It looks to be a good twenty feet away. I kick and swim and fight my way back up.

Moments later, I surface. I immediately look around, and see Bree and Charlie close by. They tread water, and look around, terrified, on guard for the monster.

I look around, too, and now, these gushing waters have a much more sinister feel. I know that the monster is in here with us, somewhere. Flo hasn't surfaced, and I'm sure she's dead, and that Ben must be, too—and that we will be next. I feel helpless. I have no idea what to do now, or where to go.

"Up here!" shouts a voice.

I crane my neck back and see, about fifty feet high up the canyon wall, standing inside a small cave in the side of the cliff, is Ben. He stands there, bow and arrow slung over his shoulder, beside a dangling rope leading up. I am amazed. Somehow he made it to the other rope, managed to climb halfway up the canyon wall, and found a little cave to hide himself in. He is a good twenty feet above the water, and safe.

I spot the rope leading up to the cave, but it is a good fifty feet away. I don't know if we can make it there before the monster finds us.

I swim over to Bree and Charlie.

"We have to make it to that rope," I say. "Can you guys swim?"

They nod yes, their eyes frozen with fear as they scan the water for the monster.

The three of us break into a swim, heading for the far canyon wall, for the rope. I think of Flo's awful death, and I'm half-expecting the monster to drag me down at any moment. I swim faster than I ever have, in terror with each lap. Bree and Charlie swim just as fast beside me.

It feels like a lifetime, as I expect each moment to be my last—but to my amazement, the three of us make it. The monster never surfaces. I wonder if he's disappeared somewhere. Maybe they opened those steel doors underwater and let him back in from wherever he came from?

I reach out and hoist Bree and Charlie up and onto the rope. I then reach for the rope myself, and pull myself halfway out of the water—when suddenly, I feel a thick, muscular tentacle wrap itself around my right leg. My heart stops.

I clutch the rope with all my might, desperate to hang on; but I am losing my grip. The thread cuts into my wet palm, and I am slipping. Finally, I lose my grip.

I go flying through the air, landing in the water on my back. The last thing I see is Bree's terrified face, looking down, watching me. Then my world goes dark.

I am plunged down underneath the water, and as I open my eyes, I see the awful face of the sea monster, all his tentacles flailing in the water, his rows of teeth. I see a piece of a leg stuck between two of his teeth, and realize it is what is left of Flo.

The monster, flailing, temporarily releases my leg, and I waste no time: I race for the surface.

I think that maybe he lost his grip and I can get away. I immediately plunge out of the water, reaching up and grabbing the rope again. But before I can go far, I once again feel his tentacles, wrapping like ice around my calves. It is then that I realize that he never let me go—that this is just the evil nature of this creature. It likes to play with its prey before killing it, like a shark playing with a seal.

As I feel it yanking me, I have a feeling that this time I will go down for good.

Before I go down, I look straight up, and as I do, I see Ben standing there, on the edge of the cave, arrow pointed down, seemingly right at me. Is he going to kill me? Is he going to spare me from a painful death? I almost wish he would. I'd rather die by his arrow than by the creature's awful teeth.

Yes, I will him silently. *Do it. Please.*

He releases, and I watch the arrow sail through the air. I brace myself.

But it doesn't hit me.

Instead, I hear a horrific screech, and turn to see it lodge inside the creature's open mouth.

It is a perfect hit. The creature momentarily lets its tentacles go, and I quickly scurry up the rope, faster than ever; I'm soon dozens of feet high, away from the water.

The monster reaches up again, his tentacles reaching up—but they fall just a few inches short of me. It screeches out in agony and frustration.

I continue to climb, and in moments I reach the cave, Ben and Bree and Charlie standing there, waiting to greet me, to pull me to safety. I am a good fifty feet high, above the water. The creature flails below, but can't get near us. I can't believe it. I made it.

I bend over and breathe hard, my legs burning from where the creature touched them. I feel like I can't catch my breath.

"Are you okay?" Ben asked.

I am. And I've never been so grateful to my life. He saved my life.

I hear the crowd booing, jeering, heckling. I look up and see the disapproval on the leader's face, on all of their faces. We have outwitted them. We have found safe harbor inside an arena where we were not supposed to. This is not how they wanted it to turn out. They are not happy.

We've lost Logan, and Flo, but there are still four of us left. And these sick people are still not satisfied. They want us all dead.

But none of us are stupid enough to climb that rope again. They would only cut it, and send us dropping back into the water. So we stay here, in our little cave, safe, out of harm's way.

The leader suddenly steps forward and the crowd silences.

"Raise the waters!" he screams.

The crowd cheers, and my heart drops as I see the water level begin to rise again. The sea monster surfaces, eager to get its new food, as it rises closer and closer to us.

My heart fills with panic, and I can see the panic on Bree and Charlie's and Ben's faces, too. Soon, the monster will be at our level, and will kill us all. We are out of options.

Then, I get an idea. It is risky, but so is being alive. If I'm going to save the others, and myself, it is now or never.

So without thinking, I step forward, pull out the spear mounted to my back, hold it out in front of me with both hands, and step out onto the edge of the cliff. I look down: the monster rises slowly, getting closer and closer. It shrieks.

"What are you doing?" Ben screams out. Then he must realize. "That's suicide!"

"Brooke," Bree screams. "Don't!"

But it is too late. There's no more time for thinking. Only for action.

I leap off the edge of the cliff, holding the spear out before me, pointed down, with both hands. I hurl through the air, to the wild cheers of the crowd.

I raise my spear high, with both hands, over my head, and aim right for the monster's one eye. As I get closer, the monster rises, right for me, its tentacles squirming, its mouth open, its large one eye looking right at me.

And that is what I aim for. That single eye.

As I go hurling down full speed, I am the spear perfectly. It lodges right in the center and I drive it down, all the way to the hilt, deep into the monster's eye.

It shrieks an unearthly shriek, and the world shakes.

I plunge into the water, and the creature plunges down on top of me, its weight pulling me down. I can't tell if it's alive, or if it's just its weight dragging me down, and as I plunge deeper into the blackness, I still don't know if I am dead or alive.

NINETEEN

I slowly open my eyes, wondering if I'm dead or alive. My head is killing me, feels like it weighs a million pounds, and as I look all around, blinking, I struggle to figure out where I am.

I spot Bree sitting beside me, Charlie by her side, and Ben beside him. We are in some sort of cell, but it is different than the cave. It is a small metal cell, protected by metal bars, leading to an outside tunnel. It is just the four of us in here.

I wonder if I'm awake or dreaming, until Bree suddenly sits up and looks at me.

"Brooke?" she asks.

She leans over and gives me a huge hug. My head is splitting, but I still try to hug her back. Charlie runs over and hugs me, too. Ben kneels down, looks at me, and places a gentle hand on my face.

"You're alive," he says with relief.

He leans in and kisses me on the forehead, and despite everything, I am electrified by the feel of his lips on my skin.

He looks at me with such love, as do the others, and I realize, finally, that I'm alive. We made it.

"What happened?" I ask.

"You killed the monster," Charlie says.

"And then you passed out, under the water, and Ben dove down and saved you."

"When the monster died, they called the game," Ben says. "They ushered us all away, to this new cell. I think no one's ever killed it before. I think they're trying to figure out what to do with us. I don't think they could've killed us right there, in front of everyone. I think the crowd wanted more."

I sit up, rubbing my head, trying to remember. I remember jumping off the cave, stabbing the monster, plunging underwater…but then nothing.

"You're very brave," Ben says.

"How long have I been here?" I ask.

"You've been out for hours. It's nighttime now. They brought us to this new cell. I think something different is happening. I don't know what. But I think we really pissed some people off."

I hear the distant sound of a metal door opening, then slamming. There's the sound of dozens of marching boots, and we all sit up and look.

Several slaverunners appear. They open our cell door, and standing in the center is their leader. He's taller and bigger up close, a shoulder length above all the others, and wears a long green cape. He is holding something, and I am amazed to see what it is.

"Penelope!" Bree screams.

She squirms and barks in his hands, trying to get away; but the leader holds her tight against his chest with an iron grip, practically suffocating her.

"This is your dog," he says to her, in a deep, twisted voice. "Or should I say, *was*. It's our property now."

Penelope whines, and I can see the disappointment on Bree's face.

The leader turns to me, and his smile drops to a frown.

"You have defied me," he says. "I've never seen anyone do what you have done. You have made a fool of me in front of all my people."

I swallow, wondering what's in store for us. I pray there are no more arenas. My body can't take another day.

"But vengeance will be mine," he continues. "Tomorrow, I will have the four of you publicly executed, on top of our highest knoll, for everyone to see. We will send a message to all the others who try to defy our rules."

He takes a step forward, and smiles at me.

"In the meantime, for your final night on earth, I will grant you one last wish. I'm going to allow you to choose one person of the four of you who will live. The choice will be on your head. All the others will die. You can choose yourself if you like."

He looks down at me with an evil smile, and I realize that this is the cruelest of all the things he's done. How can I choose one of the four of us? Of course, I would choose Bree. But that would be so unfair to Charlie, and to Ben. Choosing one would be a death sentence for the others. And Bree would be torn by guilt. I know her. I can't do that to her. I can't have all of our blood on her head.

I think quick, wracking my brain—and I get an idea.

"I choose our dog, Penelope," I say. "Allow her to stay with us for our final night."

The leader looks down at me as if I'm crazy, stares at me wide-eyed, in shock. Then he leans back and breaks into loud, mocking laughter. He reaches back and hurls Penelope, and she goes flying through the air, landing hard on the floor.

"You're stupider than I thought," he says. "I shall enjoy watching you die tomorrow."

He turns and marches out the cell, and his people follow, slamming the metal door behind him and locking it. I listen to their boots march away.

Bree clutches Penelope, kissing her, and Penelope whines back.

Immediately, the others turn and look at me.

"Why did you do that?" Ben asks sharply. "Penelope? Seriously? Of all of us? You could've had one of us live. Bree. Or Charlie. Anyone. Why did you do that?" he asks, his frustration rising.

"I have a plan," I say to him. "See there? On the far wall?"

Everyone turns and looks. There, down the corridor, about fifty feet away, are the keys to all the cells, hanging on hooks.

I turn and look back at Penelope.

"She's the smartest dog I've ever met. She's our ticket out of here."

I look at Charlie.

"Charlie, you said you know the way out."

"I do!" he insists, defensive.

"I believe you," I say. "If we get out of this cell, can you lead us out?"

Charlie nods back vigorously.

"I've seen the tunnels. I know where they go. There's a way out, a back way. To the river. There are boats on the river. We could take one."

Ben shakes his head. "It's risky," he says.

"Got any other ideas?" I ask.

He looks at me, long and hard, then finally shakes his head. "Let's do it."

I turn to Bree.

"Bree. Talk to Penelope. She listens to you. Command her. Tell her what to do. Tell her to get us the keys. The ones that we need."

Bree carries Penelope to the edge of the cell, and we all follow. I look both ways, and see no one.

Bree pulls Penelope close and whispers in her ear.

"Penelope, baby. We need your help. Please. You have to get us those keys."

Bree points to the far wall, and Penelope looks over with her one good eye.

"Do you understand?" Bree asks. "Fetch those keys, and bring them back. Go!"

Bree takes a knee and inserts Penelope's skinny body between the bars, and shoves her into the hall.

Penelope takes three steps, then stops and turns and looks back at Bree.

Bree points to the far wall.

"Go!" she hisses.

Penelope hesitates, then suddenly turns and darts off to the far wall. She runs down the hall, snatches the key ring in her mouth, lifts it off the hook, and races back with it. She runs and runs, slipping between the bars, the keys in her mouth.

Inside our cell, she drops them in Bree's palm.

I can't believe it. It worked. We are all thrilled and delighted. My heart floods with love and appreciation for the dog.

Bree hands me the ring, and it is heavy, filled with keys. I immediately flip through them, reach through the bars, and try each one. On the third one in, it turns with a loud, metallic click, and our cell door opens.

It worked. I can't believe it worked.

We all hurry out the cell, Bree grabbing Penelope and holding her inside her jacket.

"Charlie, it's your turn. Which way?"

Charlie stands there, looking both ways, hesitating. Then, he turns right.

"This way," he says, taking off. We follow him, and soon we are all running down the hallways.

Charlie turns left and right, following the emergency lights, down different tunnels, turning again and again. I can barely keep up with him, and can hardly believe how he's figured all this out.

I am beginning to worry if he knows where he's going when, after several more turns, he comes to a stop before two yellow emergency lights. He goes to a black part of the wall, reaches out, and raps hard with his knuckles. A hollow sound comes back.

"This is the door," he says. "I've seen them use it. It goes outside. You ready?"

The four of us crowd around it, then I yank it open.

I can't believe it. We are outside. He's found it. Charlie was right.

We are outside the prison complex, at some sort of rear entrance. It is amazing to be out in the open sky again, free.

It is night time, and the sky is filled with thousands of stars. It is a cold winter night, the temperature dropping again, and we are out in the freezing elements. I still wear my uniform, as do the others, and it provides some protection, but barely enough to keep me warm.

Charlie points to the river in the distance. It glistens in the moonlight, and I see slaverunner motor boats, bobbing in the water. It is late, and they look unmanned.

We all break into a sprint, racing across the grass for the river, about a hundred yards away. The ground is iced over, and our footsteps crunch as we run. There are watchtowers all around us, but it is a dark, moonless night, and there are no slaverunners standing guard on this side of the complex.

As we reach the river's edge, we head for a motorboat. It is a beautiful, new boat, and it sits there, anchored, no one standing guard. Of course, why would they? We are inside an army complex.

"Let's go," I whisper urgently.

We jump into the boat. As we do, Ben immediately pulls the anchor.

My heart is pounding as I search for the key, then find it in the ignition. I make sure everyone is seated, then turn it, bracing myself.

It turns over. I hit the throttle, slow at first. I don't want to make too much noise until we are beyond the perimeter of the city.

We are moving, and I look all around us as we go, looking for any sign of being followed. But there are none. It must be very late at night, and no one is watching. I look down and see a full tank of gas. I look around and see the tense faces on my fellow passengers.

I want to gun it, but I force myself to go slowly, just a few miles an hour, nearly drifting down the river in the dark night. On my right, in the distance, I can see the outline of the arena, of the stadiums, of all the different competing grounds. In the far distance, I see groups of slaverunners, standing guard. But they are far away, and their backs are to us. No one sees us, here in the river, slipping through. Or if they do, they probably just assume we are one of theirs.

As we get further, the river twists and turns. We are heading north, against the current. As far away from Manhattan as we can get. Towards Canada.

We continue on, twisting and turning, and when we get far enough where I think it's safe, I hit the throttle. The engine roars and we gain real speed. We are now racing up this nameless river, going who knows where. I don't care where. As long as it is far, far from here.

I can't get Logan's and Flo's faces out of my mind. I feel they are looking down, watching us. And that they are smiling.

We have made it. We have survived.

TWENTY

I drive the boat all night long, standing at the wheel, while the others lie down, sleeping, as our boat bobs up and down on the currents. Every so often I can hear Charlie's cries, and I have no doubt that he's thinking of Flo. Bree leans cuddled with her arm around him, his head on her shoulder. The two of them are inseparable, and I think that if it weren't for Bree, Charlie would be devastated right now.

I stare out at the blackness of the water, its foam racing past us as we go upriver—and all I see is Logan's face. I see him in the water, drowning, reaching out for me. I see the whirlpool sucking him down. I see him asking for my help, and my being unable to give it. It tears me apart. Every time I close my eyes, I see his.

I feel that he is with me now, more than ever, that he is a part of me. I feel a burning desire to have him really here, with me, by my side. In some ways, it is the same burning ache I feel when I miss my dad. I want him here, too. To see everything I've accomplished. To be proud of me. To be a part of it all.

Ben, awake, walks up beside me and looks out at the water with me.

"I'm sorry about Logan," he says softly, looking straight ahead.

"I am, too," I answer.

"I can't believe we made it," he says. "I was sure we were dead. That was good thinking back there."

"We haven't made it yet," I caution.

"But we've been driving for hours," he says. "No one's following us. They have no idea. They won't know until morning. And by the time they find out, we'll be at least a day ahead of them."

I shrug, thinking back to all the trials we've been through, and knowing that means nothing.

"I'm not worried about them," I say, thinking about it. "I'm more worried about what lays ahead."

Ben searched the boat earlier, and found nothing—no food, no supplies, no weapons. We are all starving, exhausted, and freezing cold. And the further north we get, the colder it grows. The river is already freezing up in places. I look down at the gauge, and see we're burning fuel fast. We can't keep this up much longer. By sunrise, I estimate, will be completely out of gas, and once again, free-floating, at the mercy of whatever sick predators are out there.

I want to relax, to kick back and think that we found comfort, that everything's going to be okay. But this time, I feel no security. Only a sense of anguish. Of needing to survive.

In some ways, Logan and Flo are the lucky ones. They're out of the game. Now, they have no worries.

"Well, we came this far," Ben says, "and I'm proud of you."

He leans in and kisses me on the cheek. It feels good, and I don't want him to stop, or to go away. But he does. He quickly retreats, and I wonder if we will be close again. Like we were that night.

"Want me to take the wheel?" he asks.

I shake my head no.

He nods, and goes back to his side of the boat.

As I stand there, staring out at the night, I wonder again how all of this will end. I think about that town, that mythical perfect town, somewhere north, in Canada. I guess that's why I'm heading North, unconsciously—to fulfill Logan's dream. To see if it's all true. I know in my mind that it's probably not. But I've finally learned something: we need to have hope. Without hope, we have nothing.

*

The sun rises, and I crack open my eyes. We are bobbing, free-floating in the water, our boat adrift in the middle of the Hudson. We are all huddled together, under a single thin blanket, lying down under the open sky. Penelope lies still in Bree's lap.

The boat ran out of gas hours ago, late in the night. But we all remember, what happened to us back there, the last time we left the boat, none of us want to abandon the boat. So we all instead huddled together, and let the current take us aimlessly down the river.

We traveled for hours last night, and everywhere, there was nothing but a desolate wasteland. No towns, no humanity. In this cold, without warmth or food, we can't survive much longer.

I've been dreaming, peaceful dreams for a change. When I open my eyes, I see the sky flooded with pinks and purples, I'm not sure if I'm awake or asleep.

I'm so weak from hunger, so tired, so cold, I can't even get up. Neither can the others. We are all frozen here, together. I know we will all die here. And finally, I'm ready to accept it. At least we are free. At least we are dying on our own terms.

I open my eyes more, and realize I'm awake. I see a world flooded with soft pinks and purples and muted colors, and it is the most beautiful breaking sky I have ever seen.

As I look up, at the river, I see something, and I am sure I'm hallucinating. I see our boat moving, upriver, against the current. It's impossible.

I see a beautiful, shining white boat in front of us, tugging us, pulling us slowly upriver. We drift gently, being pulled, somewhere north, by this beautiful boat. The wind strokes my hair gently, and as I lean up, I see it pulls us through huge, shining golden gates in the river.

As we go, I see dozens more boats, all shining white, everything perfectly new—and behind them, on either side of the river, I see a beautiful shining city. Everything intact. Stores. Sidewalks. People. Cars. Everything perfect. Immaculate. Clean. Happy. People sitting in cafés, laughing. Mothers strolling with their daughters on cobblestone streets. The mythical city.

I force open my eyes, ask myself if this is perhaps my final dream before I die. I'm not sure, but I can't help feeling that I'm awake. That this is real. That we have found it.

And that everything is going to be okay.

COMING SOON....
ARENA THREE (Book #3 of the Survival Trilogy)

About Morgan Rice

Morgan is author of the #1 Bestselling THE SORCERER'S RING, a new epic fantasy series, currently comprising eleven books and counting, which has been translated into five languages. The newest title, A REIGN OF STEEL (#11) is now available!

Morgan Rice is also author of the #1 Bestselling series THE VAMPIRE JOURNALS, comprising ten books (and counting), which has been translated into six languages. Book #1 in the series, TURNED, is now available as a FREE download!

Morgan is also author of the #1 Bestselling ARENA ONE and ARENA TWO, the first two books in THE SURVIVAL TRILOGY, a post-apocalyptic action thriller set in the future.

Among Morgan's many influences are Suzanne Collins, Anne Rice and Stephenie Meyer, along with classics like Shakespeare and the Bible. Morgan lives in New York City.

Please visit www.morganricebooks.com to get exclusive news, get a free book, contact Morgan, and find links to stay in touch with Morgan via Facebook, Twitter, Goodreads, the blog, and a whole bunch of other places. Morgan loves to hear from you, so don't be shy and check back often!

Books by Morgan Rice

THE SORCERER'S RING

A QUEST OF HEROES (BOOK #1)
A MARCH OF KINGS (BOOK #2)
A FEAST OF DRAGONS (BOOK #3)
A CLASH OF HONOR (BOOK #4)
A VOW OF GLORY (BOOK #5)
A CHARGE OF VALOR (BOOK #6)
A RITE OF SWORDS (BOOK #7)
A GRANT OF ARMS (BOOK #8)
A SKY OF SPELLS (BOOK #9)
A SEA OF SHIELDS (BOOK #10)
A REIGN OF STEEL (BOOK #11)

THE SURVIVAL TRILOGY

ARENA ONE (Book #1)
ARENA TWO (Book #2)

the Vampire Journals

turned (book #1)
loved (book #2)
betrayed (book #3)
destined (book #4)
desired (book #5)
betrothed (book #6)
vowed (book #7)
found (book #8)
resurrected (book #9)
craved (book #10)